Out of Focus

Muriel Bolger is a well-known Irish journalist and award-winning travel writer. In addition to her works of fiction, she has also written four books on her native city, including *Dublin – City of Literature* (O'Brien Press), which won the Travel Extra Travel Guide Book of the Year 2012.

Also by Muriel Bolger

Consequences
Intentions
The Captain's Table
The Pink Pepper Tree

Out of Focus

MURIEL
BOLGER

HACHETTE
BOOKS
IRELAND

First published in 2015 by Hachette Books Ireland
First published in paperback in 2015

A CIP catalogue record for this title is available from the British Library

ISBN 9781473606661

Printed and bound by Clays Ltd, St Ives, Plc

Hachette Books Ireland policy is to use papers that are natural, renewable and
recyclable products and made from wood grown in sustainable forests. The logging and
manufacturing processes are expected to conform to the environmental regulations of
the country of origin.

Hachette Books Ireland
8 Castlecourt Centre
Castleknock
Dublin 15, Ireland

A division of Hachette UK Ltd.
Carmelite House
50 Victoria Embankment
London EC4Y 0DZ

www.hachette.ie

Sandra's story is fictitious, but it's dedicated to those some 52,000 girls and women who went through mother and baby homes in Ireland, and who never got the resolutions or chances that she did.

Part One

Chapter One

2008

Sandra picked up her daughter's wedding photo from the mantelpiece, remembering the day three years earlier and how happy they'd all been. Mal, looking as though he would explode with pride, Leah looking up at Adam, her new husband, and finally her own face, smiling happily under her big picture hat. She was putting it back when the phone rang. As she stretched, she missed the edge of the mantelpiece and the photo toppled off and shattered on the marble hearth.

'Yes, yes, I'll be there for twelve. No. No worries. No, honestly, that's fine.' She slid the phone back into her pocket. 'Damn and blast. I'm not rostered for today,' she said. She liked not to have to go to the courts on Fridays. It made the weekends feel longer.

She turned her attention to the shattered frame. As she was extracting the wedding photo, another, yellowing photograph fell out. *So that's where Mal had hidden it.* She felt a chill as she looked at it, its surface scratched and the edges milky with age. Two girls looked out. They were almost the same height, one with smooth hair hanging to her shoulders, the other with a curly frizz looking like a halo as the sun shone through it. They had their arms around each other and were laughing at whoever was taking the snap. They didn't look remotely like sisters.

Finding that photo always seemed to precede some upheaval or other. She knew it was silly to think like that – how could an old picture have any influence on life? She put it on the nearby table and gingerly picked up the bigger shards of glass.

Mal knew how much the photograph upset her.

'Love, you know you can't turn back the clock,' he'd said when he found her crying over it one day. 'Concentrate on what you have and don't give those dark thoughts any head space.'

Sandra tried to banish her 'dark thoughts' as she got out the hoover to clear the smaller pieces of glass.

She had just finished when she heard the post coming through the letterbox.

Walking into the hall, Sandra picked up the scattered mail. It was the usual mix of household bills, sandwiched between junk mail and charity appeals. Then, she noticed the little sticker on the back of one of the envelopes and curiosity made her look more closely. It just said 'K. Kinsella', followed by an address in 'Stoneybatter, Dublin 7'. She turned it over and realised it was actually addressed to her. She carried it into the kitchen and put it on the drainer. Her hands shook as she filled the kettle. It couldn't be. Could it? She'd waited so long for this but still she wasn't ready. 'I can't go back there,' she said to no one as she made coffee. 'I just can't.'

Years earlier, her therapist had told her to 'take difficult days an hour at a time'. It was the only thing she remembered from those sessions, and it always worked in times of crisis – and today was turning out to be one of those times. They had a fancy name for it now – mindfulness – and every paper and magazine seemed to have an article or opinion on it, as though they had just discovered something new.

Sandra picked up the envelope again – there was nothing distinguishable about it. She read the little rectangular sticker on the back again. 'K. Kinsella'. Kevin? Keith? Killian? Keelan? Kenneth?

Could it be Kyle?

The answer was one quick flick of the letter opener away, but she resisted. She couldn't do it. She pulled out a drawer and slid the letter underneath a pile of tea towels. Mal would never in a million years look in there. She took a sip of her coffee and winced. It was stone cold. She made another cup and took it through to the conservatory. Outside, the dahlias splashed their random colours, but today she couldn't enjoy their beauty.

* * *

Mal Wallace was dictating letters. Even though there were only five weeks until the end of the self-employed tax year, not all of those clients he represented had replied to his earlier letters to return their paperwork as soon as possible. He knew from experience that he was facing a lot of late nights as their accounts dribbled in at the last minute to make the deadline. He smiled as he remembered almost having apoplexy when Leah and Adam announced their wedding date. They planned it to coincide with spring in Tasmania, where they were going for their honeymoon – and that coincided with the end-of-year tax-return mania at Malachy J. Wallace & Company, Chartered Accountants and Tax Consultants. As Mal prided himself on the personal touch, he'd hated having to hand over some of his long-standing clients to others in the firm.

'Still nothing from Billy Byrnes or Amanda Pierce?' he asked his PA as she left his post on his desk. 'They do this every year. My dire warnings of fines and penalties don't seem to bother them at all.'

'I don't see why you should worry about that,' she said. 'You've told them, and reminded them. The responsibility is theirs now.'

'You sound like Sandra. She's always telling me I'll be the one to have high blood pressure worrying, not them.'

'And she's right there.'

But he did worry, just the same.

A glance at the calendar as he reached for his post reminded him to ring his daughter. Although calendars were definitely becoming a thing of the past with laptops, smartphones and tablets nudging people's memories, he liked to keep one on his desk – he liked the page-a-day type, with little mottoes or proverbs at the end of each page. He and Leah each exchanged one every Christmas and she always said, 'Remember, Dad, no peeping at what's on the next page – let each day speak for itself.' And he did. The first thing he did every morning when he got to his office was tear off the previous day's page and digest the newly revealed words of wisdom. Today Aesop informed him: 'Appearances are sometimes deceiving.'

Maybe they could grab an anniversary bite together at lunchtime. He could always make time for that. He picked up the phone and dialled.

'Oh, Dad, I'd love to,' Leah said when he suggested meeting for a sandwich. 'But I'm caught up with something here. Let's leave it until next week.'

'OK. I hope that husband of yours is spoiling you today.'

'Oh, you know Adam. He's always full of surprises,' she said, forcing a laugh.

Leah had been an impish and determined child and after she met Adam, it was obvious to her parents that there was no going back. Mal had misgivings about him being son-in-law, or indeed husband, material before and after it was all official.

'Let's face it, Mal, no one will ever be good enough for your little girl – that's a fact of life,' Sandra had told him one evening before the wedding when he'd voiced his worries to her.

'I know that, and he is considerate, but I feel he's too much of a playboy. He's too flashy. I hope she's not just been dazzled by him and that there's more there for her when the glitz fades.'

'Like there was for us?' she'd said with a grin.

'I think we hit the jackpot. I know I did,' he'd told her, sliding his arm behind her on the couch and drawing her closer.

'Oh, I think I did all right too,' she'd teased. 'Although I still think you were born in the wrong era. You should have been in charge of an estate, a large country pile with farms and tenants, maybe even a ward or two, some tied cottages, and a dower house, with minions and runners to keep everything in perfect order.'

He'd laughed at his wife's suggestion. He had hoped his daughter would be as lucky in her marriage and that Adam wouldn't ever let her down.

Chapter Two

Leah hadn't slept. She had been tempted to ring in sick but she had a deadline. She worked in Concentric Circles and Concepts, a cutting-edge advertising company in Dublin's city centre. A highly successful television and poster ad campaign for a new cereal had catapulted her up the ladder and she was now creative director. Her clients were depending on her to finish an important presentation for a new crafts initiative in one of the high-tech, high-spec buildings along the quays – they wouldn't care that she had married a cheating toerag. She depended a lot on Susie, her zany and colourful assistant, and had more reason than ever today to know she could rely on her.

'Are you OK?' Susie asked. 'You seem distracted.'

'Yeah, I'm fine. Just a touch of migraine.' Leah had never had a migraine in her life, but she couldn't tell anyone the real reason she was so addled.

As she put the finishing touches to her presentation, Leah thought about the previous evening. The champagne she'd bought in anticipation of their anniversary, the sexy new underwear too. It was three eventful, busy and fulfilling years since they had exchanged vows – vows they had written themselves – and Leah had been planning their evening for weeks. She couldn't help but think back to how they met and what an eventful few years it had been.

* * *

She hadn't been long out of college when their paths crossed. Adam was working in one of the four design studios to which she had sent her CV in the hope of joining the 'creative team'. When she went in to 'have a chat', he had been the main interviewer. The other person present, a sleazy-looking man who was introduced as 'the Money Guy', was called Judd something or other, and he spoke with an affected mid-Atlantic accent, and he made her feel uncomfortable by staring at her breasts throughout the interview. When she was asked to display her portfolio on a large table, Judd stood too close to her. She tried hard to concentrate on what she was saying and, turning her back on him, she addressed herself to Adam. That was equally disconcerting. His dark eyes were intense and unreadable and contrasted with the mop of floppy fair hair that fell over his forehead as he perused her work. His aftershave was subtle and expensive.

When she left, she wanted to cry.

'I made a complete botch of the whole thing. They must think I'm an inarticulate idiot,' she told her mother on the phone. 'I know I'm good at what I do – it's just the interviews I hate.'

'You're selling yourself short talking like that. The right one will come along,' Sandra assured her, 'and it will be worth waiting for.'

She was amazed when she got the call to tell her that the job was hers. She settled in easily and, after a while, she and Adam had started dating – although she had a feeling from the very beginning that they would end up together. She confided this gem of information to her only brother, who promptly warned her off getting involved with any work colleague, let alone her boss.

'Oliver, that's so last century. The creative world is very different. Everyone hangs out with everyone and we all celebrate each other's new contracts, and we celebrate when each job is finished. We're much more social than you lot working in finance.'

'With your clients paying though their noses for all that, no doubt.'

'And your clients don't? You're all terrified you'll reveal your leads or your deals.'

He laughed. 'Maybe, but don't say I didn't warn you. I think it's a bad idea to start anything. You should keep work and personal life separate.'

'It worked for Mum and Dad, didn't it?'

Oliver had to agree. He was her junior by fourteen months. She knew he had enjoyed playing the protector when they were at college because she'd heard him boasting to his friends that keeping an eye on his sister meant he could meet her friends.

His warnings turned out to be futile. Leah was smitten and she wasn't about to listen to any brotherly advice. To her surprise, the girls in the office warned her off too.

'He didn't get his reputation for nothing. You know what they say – you can judge a man by the company he keeps.'

If the office gossip was to be believed, Adam did go out on the town a lot with Judd the Stud, as he was called behind his back, notching up conquests as fast as they could. The consensus was that he was definitely easy on the eye, but that was where his appeal stopped. Judd had gone through about four girls in the office before they had all decided to give him a wide berth.

'Judd – who christens their child Judd?' Avril had asked when Leah was trying to find out if Adam was dating. Avril had a disastrous date with Judd and he'd turned quite nasty when she refused to let him see her home. 'I bet he just made it up because it rhymes with "stud".'

'He should have picked Fletcher to rhyme with lecher,' a temp had said.

That got a laugh. Susie had joined in, 'Or Frank to go with wank!'

'Or Merve to go with perve.'

Then Leah had said, 'I bet he's actually a closet Paudie or a Tadhg. Maybe even a Thaddeus.'

His arrival then in the kitchen had stopped that line of conversation.

One Monday, a few weeks later, news spread that Judd was gone – to Melbourne – at a moment's notice. Whisperings around the water cooler revealed an involvement with the wife of one of the company's most important clients. 'I heard the irate husband threatened to destroy the company, and to set the heavies on him, so he ran as far away as he could go – down under.'

Speculation was rife as they gathered later in the kitchen for coffee. 'Where does that leave Adam, with his partner in crime on the other side of the world?' asked Avril.

Leah said nothing in case her feelings showed. She had turned a blind eye to this side of Adam and convinced herself that he was in a completely different league to Judd.

Adam was too clever to say if he missed his clubbing buddy. He was going places, making quite a name for himself in the competitive world of the media. He quite enjoyed his reputation as a bit of a bad boy, leaving a trail of broken hearts and unfulfilled dreams in his wake, but Leah defended him. He wasn't sleazy.

'Maybe not,' conceded Avril, 'or maybe he just chooses his conquests more prudently.'

She didn't reply.

Judd's replacement was a completely different animal. He was a man in his fifties, who along with his former Miss Ireland wife, was often seen in the social pages of the glossies. He played down his successes and wore his family wealth easily and quietly. Rumour had it that he'd been central in the dot.com boom and had brokered deals that sold several start-ups for mega bucks.

Leah continued to watch Adam from afar. Professionally, his character was impeccable and within a matter of months of Judd's departure, he was headhunted. A partnership and a move up, in the pressured world he loved so much, proved to be too good to turn down. It also freed up space on the advancement ladder for those behind him and gave Leah a chance to progress more quickly than she would otherwise have done. She became a creative designer, which meant she now handled specific minor clients of her own.

Adam invited his work colleagues out on the town to help him celebrate, telling them, 'I might as well make use of the expense account while I still can.'

He chose a pricy place to eat and made sure he sat next to Leah.

'I wanted to ask you out from the moment I saw you walk into my office,' he told her, 'but I knew I couldn't. I'd never have been able to work with you if I did. I've done that before, with disastrous results. Now that I'll no longer be there, or your boss for that matter, would you go out to dinner with me?'

That was the start. Adam Boles was seven years older than her and had done quite a bit of living in that time. Everywhere they went, leggy, gorgeous women materialised and flirted with him. Leah found this hard to take in the beginning, feeling she was constantly on display, being vetted and judged by the competition. Within months of starting to date her regularly though, Adam began to change. His friends told her she had finally managed to do what no one had done before – tame the philanderer. Even she had been quite surprised that he was so into the idea of settling down, abandoning his penthouse for a house in suburbia and for marriage, even for kids at some stage in the future.

'Wait until we're three years married, then we'll begin,' he'd said. 'I don't want to be an old dad.'

And she believed him. She never for one moment doubted their future together. Hence the Moët & Chandon in the fridge at home and the flimsy black lingerie that she'd bought a month earlier and concealed upstairs in her wardrobe.

Leah couldn't quite grasp that such a life-changing event could have happened so easily. How had she been so blind? How long had it been going on? While her promotion meant longer hours, she hadn't allowed it to take precedence. She made sure Adam came first. He was her priority, yet earlier in the week, without any warning, apart from the revealing streak of make-up on his shirt, the expected course of her world derailed and she was now headed into a dark, unfamiliar wilderness.

He'd denied it at first.

'What is this then?' she'd asked as she'd picked up his soiled shirt from the bedroom floor. 'Or should I say, whose is it?'

As smoothly as though it were the truth, he'd replied, 'It must be from the samples that came in from that new make-up company we're representing. I should have brought some home for you. The girls were going wild for them.' Feeling guilty that she'd even had a hint of doubt about him, she'd gone to put the shirt in the laundry room. He'd grabbed her as she passed. 'You're too beautiful to need that stuff.'

She'd stiffened – he reeked of some cheap scent, far too much to have been contacted by anyone's casual embrace.

'Do they do perfume too?' she'd asked, knowing full well they didn't.

'You're asking the wrong person. Probably. I'm not sure. I don't think so. They just sent in a big box of stuff, mostly creams and tanning potions, I think. You know me, I couldn't tell one from another. The girls pounced on them like vultures, trying them out. I don't recall any perfume though. I had to remind them we have a campaign to draw up around those things, so they put them back.'

'Then whose perfume are you wearing?' she asked, looking him straight in the eyes.

'What? No one's. What do you mean? What's with the third degree?'

'I think as your wife I'm entitled to wonder why your shirt is covered with cheap slap and why you reek of some awful cloying scent.'

'I told you.'

'I think I might also be forgiven for wondering why you missed dinner without the usual call or text to let me know you'd been delayed. Is that unreasonable?'

For a split second, he looked defensive, guilty almost, then he recovered.

'You know how it is, Leah. That delivery got us buzzing about the new campaign and what direction it should take – I just forgot. I forgot the time too. Sorry, love. I'll make it up to you. It won't happen again.'

'I'm sure it won't,' she'd answered, her voice steady although she was trembling inside. She knew with a wife's instinct that he had been unfaithful. He was reverting to type. Her brother had warned her that it would only be a matter of time – and she hadn't spoken to him for months afterwards. Could he have been right? She couldn't, she wouldn't, allow herself go there.

She tried to act normally at first but she couldn't. Doubts kept haunting her and after a week of tearful conversations and accusations, he'd finally come clean and told her.

'It was just a fumble in the lift when it stalled between two floors. You know the way it does,' he said. She did. It often stalled if two people called it at the exact same moment from different floors.

'She came on to me,' he'd said.

'Is that supposed to make it all right? Am I supposed to say, "Oh, that's OK, darling, so long as it wasn't you who made the first move"? You sicken me, Adam,' she'd said. 'You're telling me this as though I were one of the lads and you're boasting about pulling some chick or other. I'm your wife, for God's sake, but you seem to have forgotten that.'

'I'll make it up to you. It won't happen again. I promise. I have your present ordered.'

'You cheated on me and you think a present will make up for that? You've destroyed everything we had together. You bastard.' She'd started to cry.

He'd tried to pull her towards him but she'd pushed him away. 'Your timing is impeccable,' she'd told him. 'We didn't even make it to our third anniversary.'

He'd tried to placate her. 'We can fix this. Just give me a chance, I promise. It didn't mean anything.'

'If it meant so little, why did you let it happen? And when will it happen again? That's not a chance I'm prepared to take.'

'I'd never hurt you.'

'Listen to yourself, will you? What do you think you've just done? Everyone warned me this would happen and I didn't believe them.'

'That's ridiculous.'

'It's not. What you've broken can't be patched up, no matter how much smooth talk you use. I want time on my own to think. Please just get out of my sight until I decide what I'm going to do.'

She'd known full well what she was saying, but she hadn't thought for a minute that he'd take her at her word and walk out through the hall door. But he had. And he hadn't come home.

She hadn't slept at all and felt dreadful. She couldn't take time off now, no matter what was going on in her personal life. Determined to pretend everything was normal, she did what she could to conceal her puffy eyes and headed to the office. She was checking her mobile for the hundredth time when her mother phoned.

'Happy anniversary. Have you and Adam big plans for tonight? Are you going out, or having a romantic dinner at home?'

'Thanks, Mum. You remembered. You're great.'

'Of course I remembered.'

'Mum, I'm up to my eyes here. I can't really talk.' She knew her mother could read her like a book and would pick up on any upset. 'I'll call you back this evening.'

'No, you don't need to do that. I'll talk to you tomorrow,' Sandra said.

'Are you OK, Mum? You sound a bit stressed.'

'Yes. I'm fine, really – just a few things going on, and I've been called in to cover for someone, so I'm heading in to the courts. I just didn't want to let the occasion pass.'

She wouldn't have to worry about letting any more pass, Leah thought.

As she put her phone down, she got a text from her brother.

I have to hand it to you, sis. I never thought you'd make the first anniversary, never mind the third. Enjoy the day. xx

She knew there would be a few cards waiting at home for her. Her mum would have sent one too.

'It's nice to be remembered and it's very important too,' Sandra had often told Leah and Oliver when they were growing up. 'It costs very little and it can make someone feel special or loved.' Sandra was big into making people feel loved.

Today, however, it was going to take a lot more than a card and her mother's wishes to make Leah feel anything but alone and rejected, despondent and downright miserable. But she wasn't ready to tell anyone what had happened, not yet. Not until it finally sank in and she knew what she was going to do next.

Chapter Three

Sandra made her way to the courts. She'd been a volunteer for several years now as part of the victim support programme. At times, she found it emotionally exhausting, but from personal experience she knew the value of a comforting hand, a willing ear and a non-judgemental opinion. She knew what it felt like to be alone. Now it was her chance to be there for someone else when they needed some support.

Some years ago, when her world had become disconnected and alien, it was one such connection that started to put everything back together for her.

'You're an angel' was a comment frequently uttered after some case or other.

'I'm no angel, believe me,' she'd tell them, and she wasn't. 'But I do have a little idea of what you're going through.'

She'd given up believing in angels long ago, when her beliefs about what was good and what was evil were shattered, and she'd had to figure it out for herself all over again.

Although her work with the courts was now only a small part of her life, it was very important to her. She realised that being there to explain what would happen inside the courtroom, demystifying the rituals or putting nervous witnesses at their ease meant a lot to them. Occasionally, she accompanied French tourists, translating for them.

It had taken Sandra a lot of soul-searching to go into this sort of social work after her own brush with the law. Then, she had been advised by her own medical team to take an extended break from work of any sort.

Mal had added his gentle pressure, and she had acquiesced. She knew how he'd watched his young wife, lost and confused somewhere he couldn't reach her. Later, she'd realised how terrifying that had been for him, wondering if she would ever again be the person he'd married. If she'd had a family to call on, it might have helped, but Sandra had no one apart from him.

She had nothing but a faded, creased photograph, which, instead of bringing back warm, comforting feelings, opened the door to unanswerable questions and heartache in another life.

Most of the time, Mal made her forget. But sometimes, the pressure to escape threatened to engulf her or make her explode. And one day, she did, but that was a long time ago and after that, she had been aware that he was watching her all the time, watching over her too.

Then Leah had arrived and, although she stayed in therapy for a good twelve months after Leah's birth, that had been the turning point. Looking back, Sandra could honestly pinpoint the birth of her daughter as the beginning of her real acceptance of what life's lottery had meted out to her. That was when she began to accept that there were some things she couldn't control and that she had to stop blaming herself for them.

Now that inoffensive-looking letter in the drawer was threatening to blow everything wide open again, overwhelming her. She had known this day might come, and she also knew that as soon as she opened the letter there would be no going back. She'd have to tell Leah and Oliver everything, and she wasn't ready for that yet.

When they had been growing up, she had visualised this moment, composed speeches in her head, to explain what had happened. Speeches that would make them understand. Now they were adults, she hoped it would be easier for them to understand. They would understand – wouldn't they? But would they be able to forgive her?

And there was Mal to consider too. Today was not the day though – she wasn't about to ruin her daughter's anniversary with the dramas from her past life. Any worry Sandra had had that Leah would pick up on her underlying anxiety went when Leah said she'd leave it to the next day to call her back – it became Sandra's turn to worry about Leah, who had sounded distant and subdued.

Sandra straightened her shoulders, took a slow, deep breath and walked into the courthouse.

* * *

Leah got through the day, and her meetings with copy writers and graphics people, grateful that the emails she received didn't require her immediate attention. Still there was no word from Adam.

Back home she ignored the fancy food she had intended to cook and put some bread in the toaster. She was sure he would turn up, contrite and full of promises, but he didn't. Part of her hoped to hear the tyres scrunching on the gravel as he turned into the driveway; but a bigger part of her didn't. She hadn't worked out what she was going to say if he did turn up. Had she been a complete fool to trust him? She couldn't pretend she hadn't been warned. She just hadn't wanted to listen to what people had said.

Leah wandered in and out of the rooms they had so carefully revamped. The lovely master bedroom with its walk-in rain shower and matching sinks – they'd made love on the new bed the day it was delivered; it had still been wrapped in its polythene protection and they'd laughed as their heated skin stuck to it and made ripping noises as they moved about. Now, as she got into that same bed alone, for the second night running, it seemed strangely empty and big. So did the house, with all its promises and hopes. It seemed to mimic exactly how she felt, a discarded shell. In the hall, she closed the door on what would shortly be her home office – the high ceiling and decorative cornices still awaiting freshening; furniture piled beneath dust covers made spooky shadows on the half-stripped walls. They had lived with builders under their feet for months now, and this was the last room to get the renovation treatment. The house wasn't the mock Tudor one with the double garages they'd visualised owning one day – the one they used to see when they went walking some evenings. It was a detached period house in the same neighbourhood though, and it had wisteria climbing over the front, with mature, gnarled branches that twisted and curled promisingly up the front between the sash windows. From early childhood, Leah had loved this plant, calling it 'wistleria' before she could pronounce its name properly. Her father had planted one for them as a moving-in present in their first home, a semi on a noisy road.

He'd told her, 'They used to say you plant that for your grandchildren to enjoy. Happily this is a quick-growing strain, so hopefully you won't have to wait that long to enjoy it.'

'Is that a hint that you want us to hurry up and produce a few heirs?'

'No, I didn't mean it that way.'

She'd laughed, as he appeared embarrassed. 'Don't worry, Dad, I promise we'll give you lots.'

The first year, the wisteria produced a few blue-violet scented blooms, and a lot more the second. They resembled frilly lanterns. She thought they'd be there long enough to see it bloom year after year. Then Uncle Jack died.

They bought the new house with part of the very generous bequest Adam's uncle had left him. Uncle Jack had moved to Tasmania after he'd been widowed. He'd never remarried. Leah knew he'd been something important in an engineering capacity on the Gordon Dam. She knew that because any time his name was mentioned in Adam's home, his mother prefaced it with: 'Uncle Jack, you know he was something important on the Gordon Dam.' As she became aware of this, she was very tempted to join in. 'He tried to make Adam go into engineering too, but he failed,' Adam's mother would add, as though having a creative career was somehow inferior.

What would happen now, to their marriage, their new home, their future – would they even stay together? Could they?

She needed to talk to her brother. She could always confide in him, even though she knew he'd tell her, 'I told you so.' Despite the fact that it was late, much later than she would normally call anyone, she swiped his number on her phone, which is when she remembered he was in the States for a conference. It rang out three or four times before going to voicemail. Maybe it was just as well – by Sunday, she hoped she'd have a better idea about what was happening, and what to say to Adam. She forced her voice to sound light-hearted as she left her message.

Chapter Four

Adam was furious with himself. He'd driven away in anger and gone to a bar. How had he let the stupid flirting game he and Helka had played result in this situation? The bosomy Hungarian part-timer had caught his eye when she'd started taking the coffee and sandwich trolley around a few times a week. They always had a bit of banter that bordered on the risqué. Then, four or five weeks earlier, Helka had just finished for the day and he watched as she went to her desk and started to get her belongings together. He didn't know what made him rush out of his own office to meet her at the lift – maybe it was the fact that it had been a long time since anyone but his wife had smiled at him the way Helka did. He'd only intended to flirt with her a little, but then the lift had got stuck, and they had been trapped there for twenty minutes. He wished then that he hadn't started flirting – Helka was more than willing to flirt back and, with nowhere to go, they had started making out.

After a few whiskies he went to the office and sat behind his desk. He wasn't about to go home.

Surely Leah will forgive me. She knows I love her – and I know she loves me.

Then he wondered what Helka was doing. Maybe he'd give her

a call. Maybe not. He checked the time. He'd Skype Judd. It wasn't too early.

'We just flirted a bit, that's all, and then when we got stuck in the lift, there seemed only one thing to do.'

'That always adds to the excitement – a timer on the frantic fumblings,' Judd replied.

'As you well know. But now I'm up to my neck in it. I never had any intention of letting a bit of playful sex with some temp destroy my marriage.' Adam thought about how good he and Leah were together. 'I can't believe I was so careless.'

'Use that charm offensive of yours to talk her round. Give her time to calm down – and to miss you,' Judd advised, 'and she'll take you back with open arms.'

Adam agreed. He wanted her in his life. It was that simple.

He'd sworn to Leah that his lapse meant nothing – and on one level, it didn't.

'You told Leah it was only a fling, didn't you? So the question is, was it that, just a fling?'

But even as Adam thought about this, he knew Leah was the woman he wanted. Being married meant being faithful, and he didn't like that part of the bargain.

'It can't have gone beyond the fixing everything stage, can it?' Judd said.

'I don't know. I hope not, but I did cheat on her, and then I broke the eleventh commandment.'

'The eleventh commandment?' Judd asked.

'I got caught! You know, Judd, at first I figured that I wouldn't even remember Helka's name in a few weeks' time. Now I have the horrible feeling that I'm never going to forget it.'

'Or be allowed to. You need to do some serious grovelling, dude.'

'I know. Why do women have to be so controlling and demanding?'

'Why do you think I never got caught in that trap, buddy. Hang in there. I have to sign papers for the sale of my apartment so I'll be home for a flying visit in a few days and we'll drown your sorrows together.'

Adam agreed they'd meet up – though he didn't know if that would help his cause at all. Leah had never liked Judd.

'Where are you going to sleep tonight?'

'I don't know. I hadn't thought that far ahead.'

'You're in it up to your neck already, why not pay Helka a booty call and bid her a fond farewell. That's what I'd do. Make the most of your freedom before you go back to Mrs Boles and domesticity.'

Adam laughed. 'You'll never change.'

'Neither will you. Now, I have a day's work ahead of me.'

When Adam had disconnected he sat there, his feet on the desk, in the spookily quiet building. There was something in what Judd said. He had cheated, would one more time make any difference before he had to make amends? Leah need never know.

* * *

Their wedding hadn't been a huge affair, but it did include those who mattered to them – proud parents, well-wishing friends and just a few of those-who-had-to-be-invited guests for the sake of family truces and keeping skeletons under wraps. After months of planning, it had been everything they had hoped for.

'You can do all the wedding-day stuff, but leave the honeymoon to me,' he told her. 'I'm taking you to the other side of the world, to Tasmania. I want to show you where I spent happy times, and I want to introduce you to Jack. You'll fall in love with the place too.'

He'd told her all about Jack, who after retiring from doing 'something important on the Gordon Dam', put his money into farming and began dabbling in cider making, something that surprised everybody.

'He used to come home every other year after the harvests, but had to stop when the journey became too much for him.'

'You'll love him,' Adam's mother had said too. 'Everyone does. He's a really interesting guy. Shame he never had any children of his own, though he looks on Adam as his nearest and dearest – they have a special bond, always have had. Jack never bothers with his other relations. Although come to think of it, I don't think they bother too much with him either.'

'Did you ever go over to visit him?' she asked her future mother-in-law.

'No, never. Adam's dad hates flying and it's so far away. I'm not sure I'd fancy being cooped up all those hours in a plane. It didn't stop that fellow though.' She laughed, looking at her son.

'It's all part of the adventure. I spent three wonderful summers and a gap year with the old fellow and he took me all over the place.'

When Adam took his new bride there on honeymoon, Jack took renewed delight in showing Leah the famous dam.

'You can't believe how hard the conditions were. And the labourers didn't have your new-fangled protective clothing back then. People don't realise it, but up here in the Central Highlands it can be almost unbearable in the mists and the sleet and snow.'

'It's stunningly beautiful,' Leah said, captivated by the towering mountains and the lush valleys below.

'It is that – for trekking and camping trips, but try working up here in the winter months, with the wind whipping around you. It's worse than Connemara.'

She shivered at the thought.

'See those, over there,' he said, pointing to the enormous steel pipes snaking down the mountainside from Tarraleah, 'they've replaced the dreams of the prospectors who came here looking for gold. Now it's computers.'

He had a way of recapturing how it must have been for the early settlers who were banished there. 'They didn't even know it was an island at first. It's fashionable to have a convict in the family tree these days though,' he told them.

'And have you?' she asked.

'Not that I can trace, but I'm sure we all have if we dig deep enough.'

'I love listening to his yarns. I never knew mine, but he fits the image I have of what a benevolent granddad would be like – trying to share all his memories with you, while he can,' she told Adam one night when they were down by the waterfront in Hobart. 'You're so lucky to have him.'

'I know.'

News that he had died peacefully in his sleep, just days before his ninety-third birthday, didn't affect any of his other nephews, nieces, grandnephews and grandnieces to any great degree, but it did affect Adam and Leah. He had often told Adam that he wasn't to go over for his funeral and he didn't want to be brought back to Ireland. He wanted his ashes scattered near his beloved dam. Adam inherited the promised farm and livestock, the cider production plant, some stocks and a very large sum of money.

'Will you go to live out there?' his mother asked.

'Who knows what the future will bring? Not right now though, although I will have to go out to sign papers and things – make it all legal.'

'Don't rush in to anything,' his father advised when the extent of the bequest was revealed.

'We won't, but we are going to move up the property ladder when I get back. We'll take our time and maybe even hold on to our place as an investment. I'll talk to Leah's dad about that and get his professional advice.'

'That's a good idea.'

Adam flew to Tasmania and spent a few weeks sorting Jack's

affairs, leaving instructions and keeping the managers he had had in place. As soon as he returned he and Leah set about finding a house that was big enough for her to work from and where their children – they planned on having three – would have plenty of space to grow up and play, with a choice of good schools close by.

They scanned the property pages and websites and quickly rejected house after house, but when they pulled up outside Orchard Lodge, they had both known that this was a serious contender. It was a Victorian red brick with bay windows on either side of the hall door and corresponding ones above. Inside an elegant stairs curved to the left and right of a half landing and the sun shone through the coloured glass on first return, casting patterns on the stairwell.

'Very Scarlett O'Hara,' Leah laughed. 'But it feels right. I can see myself being happy here, can you?' she asked him, after they had done the tour of inspection with the estate agent. She'd left them alone to have another walk around.

'I know what you mean. It kind of embraces you. It needs lots of work though, but we could stay where we are until it's ready.'

'Do you think its name, Orchard Lodge, is a sign – after Jack's orchards?'

'I don't know,' he laughed, 'maybe he is actually out there somewhere, directing operations.'

They haggled over the price, and brought their folks over for their approval before signing the deeds. Then, they set about getting estimates for the renovation. It needed complete rewiring and a modern heating system. The bathrooms had to be replaced too, but they were determined to keep the period feel.

'You're spending so much time with that contractor, I'm beginning to think you're having an affair with him,' Adam teased.

'He's not exactly my type,' she replied, 'and he's obviously on a one-man mission to save the planet by avoiding deodorants and soap! I have to avoid standing near him.'

When the new kitchen was installed, they moved in, wanting to enjoy it and supervise the rest of the work as it was being done. Adam took a break from emptying the boxes and stood looking out of their bedroom window at the spacious lawn and gardens. A few old trees remained of what had once been a large orchard belonging to the nearby estate that had given its name to the area.

'It's hard to visualise what the future might bring, when we have kids running around, isn't it?' he said, holding his hand out to her as she came over and stood beside him.

'It is, but I'm looking forward to it,' she grinned. 'You, a dad, playing football out there with a brood of mini-Adams running around you.'

'Or you, sitting on a rug, teaching the mini-Leahs to knit?' he teased.

'Knit? What planet did you fall from?' She laughed at him.

'To make sure we get it right, we'd better get practising so,' he said, lifting her off her feet and laying her gently on the bed. He had always said he'd like to wait for three years before starting a family, but what difference did a few months make anyway?

Chapter Five

When Kieron got home, the smell of baking filled the little terraced house, which was stuffed with some large pieces of furniture that Pam had inherited. She'd wanted to sell them, but he kept telling her that one day they'd have a house where they fitted perfectly.

'But I love our little house,' she'd said, 'and we're not mortgaged to the hilt like so many of our friends. People reared five and six children in these houses, so we've a long way to go.'

'That's one of the things I love about you,' he'd replied, 'you're so undemanding.'

As he walked into the kitchen, enjoying the smells of freshly baked cakes, Pam turned round and kissed him.

'That's the passports sorted,' he said, taking them out of his briefcase and putting them on the mantelpiece. 'We'll tell Ryan tonight. He'll love the ferry.' They hadn't said anything to him yet about the proposed holiday in France as they'd been disappointed before.

'I just hope she'll be up to it,' Pam said, nodding in the direction of their little girl who was curled up with her much-loved stuffed rabbit, 'she hasn't been herself all morning.'

'There's still plenty of time for her to get better,' Kieron said. 'You know how she can bounce back.'

'I do, but she's been sitting there like a mouse for a while. I don't like it, she's too quiet.'

'Let's wait and see how she is this afternoon and if she's no different, I'll run her down to the doc. It'll put our minds at ease.'

'Thanks, love.'

'It's one of the perks of being a teacher – freedom to do family things when the kids are off too.'

He had also noticed that Jennifer was off colour, and was keeping a watchful eye on her.

'What about a story, poppet?' he said to her, and she nodded.

'Do you want to sit on my knee?' She nodded again and stood up, settling herself back down on his lap, with her head on his chest. Despite being assured that, thanks to new drugs and treatments, the childhood leukaemia survival rate had increased dramatically in recent decades, there was always a risk. And every time she got a fever or infection, they were worried sick.

'Are you tired, love?' Jennifer nodded, and alarm bells began to ring in Kieron's mind. This morning she had been so eager to go out with him, then she'd changed her mind and wanted to make cakes with Pam. Now she was listless and flushed.

'I think we should ring and make an appointment,' he said to Pam, who took the phone in to the hall, just as Ryan arrived home.

Kieron began to read a story. Usually, Jennifer turned the pages, but today she didn't even attempt to do that. She looked up at him, and he saw the last thing he wanted to see – a garishly red trickle of blood was running down her little face and onto her t-shirt.

Pam came back into the room and noticed it immediately. She grabbed a clean tea towel from a drawer and gave it to Kieron. They both knew the drill. They had been here before. *Hold her nose with a light but firm pressure and keep her leaning slightly forward. This will prevent her swallowing more blood than is necessary.*

'Pam, can you get me some ice, please?' Trying to appear calm and relaxed, he told his children, 'When I was little, some people used to put a door key down your back inside your clothes to stop nosebleeds.'

'Like that would work!' Ryan said.

'Well, apparently, it did. Don't ask me how. We had a master who kept a big old key in his desk drawer specifically for when anyone fell or took a knock when they were playing.' He chatted away as he kept the little girl's nose pinched and an eye on the time. It should stop within ten minutes – mostly they did – but this one didn't.

'Right. Ryan, you're going to need to stay with Mrs Murphy for a while, OK? Don't look so worried – you can bring her some of those cakes and watch a DVD there until we get back. We just need to take your sister to a doctor to stop this nosebleed.'

'OK. I'll go get a DVD.'

While Ryan chose, Pam grabbed the hospital bag from Jennifer's room, where she always kept an emergency one at the ready. Within a few minutes, she took Ryan down the few houses to the widow who minded them when they needed a sitter, and got back to the house as Kieron was putting Jennifer into the car.

'My t-shirt is ruined,' Jennifer said.

'Don't you worry about that.'

The children's hospital was only ten minutes away. They knew exactly where to go. As soon as she'd been triaged and had her nose plugged, Jennifer was admitted and taken to a curtained section off a ward. Despite all the efforts to make the place welcoming and cheerful, Kieron always felt there was something alien about seeing children in hospital.

'Will I have to sleep here?' Jennifer asked him.

'I'm not sure yet, poppet,' Kieron said, 'but don't worry. We won't leave you on your own.'

'No, of course we won't,' Pam reassured her. Jennifer was so listless by this stage that she hardly reacted to the nurse taking blood from her arm.

'Well, missy, you're very brave,' the registrar told her, 'and when your nosebleed stops, we'll get you cleaned up and get you some ice cream. Would you like that?'

Jennifer nodded.

The nurse said, 'I know there's raspberry ripple and chocolate. Chocolate's my favourite. What about you?'

Jennifer didn't answer.

'Or you could have a spoonful of each. Would you like that?'

Jennifer nodded, and the nurse bent down and whispered, 'But don't tell anyone else or they'll all want that too.'

Jennifer nodded and tried to smile.

'I'll be back in a few minutes. I'll just take these to lab,' the nurse said. A doctor arrived, read the notes they'd sent up from casualty and addressed Kieron and Pam. 'It's most likely to be thrombocytopenia, a drop in the platelets, but we have to check to make sure there is no other infection.'

'She has been off colour for a few days now,' Pam said.

'That would be quite normal preceding a long bleed like this, but we'll know more when the lab results come back.'

'It breaks my heart to see her lying there so lethargic, and not being able to do anything to help her,' Pam said to the doctor. 'All those wary eyes and looks of resignation from each bed.'

'Yes, but most of them do well with us. She's in good hands and once those platelets go in, she'll be back to her old self again,' he promised. 'Didn't we look after her well the last time she was with us?'

Kieron thanked him. 'You certainly did.'

That had been at Christmas and they'd brought in her presents and taken photos of her and her brother sitting on the bed, in their new clothes and wearing paper hats from the crackers they had pulled. Ryan the picture of good health; Jennifer looking pale, but excited. Kieron kept one of those snaps in his wallet.

When the lab results came back, they showed that Jennifer had a fever and needed a transfusion. Kieron went back home and collected Ryan from their neighbour, all the time thanking God that his wife was so sensible. Pam loved living in their artisan dwelling, precisely because it was a settled community and had neighbours they could rely on. Mrs Murphy was one of those; her family had grown up and left, but she was only too glad of the extra few bob they paid her for child-minding. She enjoyed the company too and the kids loved her.

'I can hold on to him tonight if you like,' she offered.

'I'll take you up on that another time, if I may. I've already been on to my mam and she's expecting him.'

'I hope the little one gets well soon,' she said.

'Thank you, you're very kind. Now, Ryan, we need to get your things together.'

'Will I have to miss football tomorrow?' he asked.

'I'm not sure. If everything goes well at the hospital this evening, I'll pop down to your gran's and bring you there, I promise.' Kieron felt sorry for his son – when Jennifer was sick that took precedence over everything. 'It's not Jennifer's fault, you know, she didn't ask to be unwell. And besides, you like going to Gran's.'

'I do – she spoils me.' Ryan grinned. 'And I get to play with your old train sets.'

* * *

Kieron sat watching his little girl sleep peacefully, her pink rabbit firmly clutched in her hand, her favourite blanket close by for reassurance.

'You'd think this would get easier, but it doesn't, does it?' he said to Pam as they sat on either side of her bed. The monitors beeped and lights flashed an intermittent coded language, one that the medical staff seemed capable of interpreting fluently. 'You'd think we'd be used to them by now,' he sighed, referring to the frequent blood transfusions that had become part of their five-year-old's life.

In the few years since her diagnosis, Kieron had witnessed Pam reluctantly accepting that Jennifer's condition was no one's fault.

Their little girl moaned and thrust about in the bed. Pam rubbed her daughter's shoulder, shushing softly and she settled again.

'Sitting here like this I can't help asking myself why this had to happen to our little one,' Kieron said. 'I can't help feeling resentful when I see the kids at school and at Ryan's cubs, running around, climbing where they shouldn't, full of life and boundless energy.'

'Life is a bit like Russian roulette – it fires its bullets randomly. Sure, we could have done without this, but we have so much going for us besides this. There's Ryan, he's harum-scarum enough for both of them, and he loves his little sister. You shouldn't resent the healthy ones – that's not fair on them.' Pam paused. 'Do you want to talk to someone about it?'

'I am. I'm talking to you, aren't I?'

'I mean – maybe … maybe a counsellor.'

'That's your answer for everything, isn't it?' Kieron couldn't hide his annoyance.

'I'm trying to help. This isn't easy for me either, you know.'

'And you don't think I can see that, Pam? I see the way you look at her when she's sleeping. I see the way you watch other kids in the park, and it breaks my heart. I wish I could protect you, the two of you, but I can't, and it makes me feel helpless.'

She reached across the bed and touched his hand.

Earlier that afternoon, the oncologist had called them aside to say that they needed to talk about the next step in Jennifer's treatment. As they'd sat in his office, he'd told them that the time had come to seek a donor for a bone marrow transplant.

'I don't want you to be alarmed,' he'd said gently, but they knew enough to realise that this was a serious meeting. 'We can keep her maintained pretty well doing what we're doing for the foreseeable future, but it's a good idea to look further ahead. Have you any relatives you can ask? Siblings? Parents? At this stage, getting new marrow would make a huge difference to Jennifer's quality of life.'

'Of course, but I have no siblings,' Pam had said. 'What about cousins, are they any good? I have a few of those.'

'It's worth tapping every source you can,' he'd replied, turning to Kieron.

'You may remember I told you I had yellow jaundice when I was about ten, and I was told I wouldn't be able to give blood or be an organ donor. That includes bone marrow, doesn't it?'

'I'm afraid so, but perhaps there may be someone among your extended family.'

'I don't know them. I'm adopted.'

'I'm sorry—'

'Don't be. I'm better off without someone who didn't want me.'

Without any visible reaction the oncologist had continued. 'I was about to say I'm sorry you can't look into that side of your family.'

'Can we do anything else for Jennifer?' Pam had said.

'Ask everyone you know. The more people you ask, the better – it helps raise awareness even if they can't donate themselves. Strictly speaking, they don't have to be in the direct bloodline – less than 30 per cent of donors are – although it is often easier and quicker to find a match that way. We'll put her on the registry for a suitable donor and get her into the system. Trust me, she's not in any immediate danger. She can continue to have blood transfusions but, ultimately, fresh bone marrow is what we need to get our hands on. It's easy for me to tell you not to worry, and impossible for you to pay any heed.' He'd smiled at them as he stood up. 'But she is doing well and we really are taking good care of her.'

'Everyone is so nice to her. We do appreciate it, don't we, Kieron?' Pam had said, looking at her husband.

He'd nodded. 'Yes, we do. We really do and thank you. I'm sorry. I don't mean to appear ungrateful.'

The consultant had put his hand on Kieron's arm as they'd left and said, 'Don't worry, it's a difficult situation.' They had left the consulting room and walked back through the corridor to their daughter's cubicle, not touching or talking, each locked in their own thoughts.

Pam continued to stroke Kieron's hand. 'Kieron, I know you're bitter about being given up for adoption, but if there's a thread of hope that there may be a donor in your family – your other family – we should look into it for Jennifer's sake. Why not make contact with your birth mother?'

'No. I want nothing from her.'

'Not even your daughter's life?' she asked quietly.

'That's cruel, Pam. I'd willingly give my own life to make Jennifer better. You know that. I'd do anything for her.'

'Except this.'

'I can't go down that route again, Pam. I just can't. You know what it took out of me when I found out where she lived. I don't think I could bring myself to talk to her …'

He realised as he was saying this just how selfish he was being.

His wife said nothing at first, but then suggested, 'I could see her.'

'No!' His reply was immediate and firm.

They'd sat on in silence until Jennifer stirred, pulling at the cannula that had been inserted in her hand. Kieron gently took her little hand away from it and held it until she relaxed and quietened again, falling back into a deep sleep. He felt a tear escape and run down his cheek.

'I'll get us some coffee,' Pam said, squeezing his shoulder as she'd passed behind his chair.

How could he go through all that again? The pain of searching and then discovery had been bad enough – he hadn't coped very well with finding out where his mother lived. He had walked away without talking to her, which had only heightened his feelings of exclusion and rejection. After that, he had decided to close that door firmly behind him, and had no intentions of ever opening it again. Now it seemed as if he had no choice.

It had been quite a shock when, at seventeen, he'd learned he'd been adopted, although he had always felt a little on the outside, but couldn't have told anyone exactly why. His instincts had told him he was different somehow.

As he sat by his daughter's bed, the sense of rejection he'd felt the one time he'd seen his mother and fled swept over him. He tried to concentrate on other things – on the room, on his daughter's face, restful in sleep, despite the little frown that creased her forehead now and again. But the dam had been opened, and it was too late to stem its flow.

* * *

Jennifer bounced back after the infection cleared. The school holidays ended and when the children had gone to bed one evening Kieron turned to Pam and announced, 'I've decided. I'm going to contact her and explain the situation.'

'That's wonderful, love. I know it's hard for you, but it's the right thing to do.'

'I know that. This time I have no expectations.'

She hugged him. 'That's the right way to look at it. I can go and see her if you like, or we can go together.'

'No, I have to do this myself. I want to look her in the eye and see her squirm. Let her see that her actions didn't only affect me, but are now affecting our family too.'

'I thought you'd let all that go after the counselling.'

'So did I, but it's still there.'

'When will you ring her?'

'I won't. I've been thinking about it and I've decided that I'm going to write to her. That way she'll have to think about her answer instead of giving me a kneejerk reaction.'

He tore up his first letter and his second. After his third attempt, he handed the paper to Pam to read over. She vetoed that one as being too aggressive, so that one was torn up too. Eventually, they had a letter that they hoped said what it should.

'Sleep on it before sealing it,' Pam said. 'You'll see it with fresh eyes in the morning.'

He did, and he posted it on his way to work, feeling relieved and apprehensive.

Chapter Six

Leah woke up to knocking and the insistent ring of her doorbell. Where was Adam and who was calling at half eight on a Saturday morning? Then she remembered, he hadn't come home again. She grabbed her robe and ran downstairs. A deliveryman peered through one of the glass side panels.

'Rise and shine, missus, it's a lovely day,' he said as she unlocked the door. 'I need your autograph on this to show the powers that be that I haven't run off with anything.' He handed her a stylus and a little gadget that recorded his deliveries.

'What am I signing for?' she asked. *Does Adam honestly think a bunch of flowers will fix everything?*

'Those.' He pointed to three small trees, their roots tied in sackcloth and three large pottery containers on the driveway, beside where he'd parked. 'It says here they're ornamental apple trees, miniature, whatever the heck that means. Who'd want miniature apples? They weigh a ton each. You won't be able to shift them yourself.'

'Yes, thank you. They're fine there – my husband will move them later,' she replied. *If he ever comes back.*

'There's a card on one of them,' he said, getting back into his van.

When he'd driven away, she tore the polythene sleeve holding the card and opened it.

To my darling Leah. You've often said you'd like to plant a forest of trees that blossom. These are Sturmer Pippins, miniatures of our ones in Tassie! Happy anniversary.
Love forever, Adam xxx

Love forever! She was beyond anger, beyond tears, beyond feeling. He'd obviously arranged delivery of these before she'd thrown him out. Where had he spent the last few nights? And with whom?

She went back inside and, knowing she wouldn't be able to go back to sleep, started to make some coffee.

Am I being too self-righteous? she wondered. *Anyone can make a mistake, but this is too big to be classed as a mistake. Why didn't he come home? Is he with her now? It really hurts. I want to punish him, make him hurt like this – or maybe it really was a one-off fling.*

Her mind ping-ponged between arguments. *He had changed – I know he had.* Then the doubt came back as she thought about what Oliver had said those years ago. *Was I just seeing what I wanted to see? Is this what for better or for worse means? Maybe I should be the bigger one here and forgive him – it might never happen again. It's worth taking a chance, isn't it? We are good together.*

It was about ten when he phoned. From the background noise, she figured he was in a coffee shop somewhere.

'Well, am I forgiven? Have you missed me?' he asked, as though he had just forgotten to buy milk on the way home.

'What do you think?' she asked, trying to keep control of her voice.

'You know I'm sorry, Leah. Can I come home?'

'I can't stop you doing that, you live here.'

Leah heard a man speak, then laughter, then an accented female voice: 'I got us all almond croissants.' Then, he spoke again, 'Eh, Leah, I have to go. It's too noisy in here. I can't hear you very well. I'll see you later. We'll talk then, OK?' And he hung up.

What kind of fool does he think I am?

She wanted to run away – anywhere – but she knew that wouldn't solve anything. She let her tears fall then, tears of despair and disappointment.

Chapter Seven

Sandra watched through the kitchen window as Mal pulled the cord on the mower a few times. The trusty Atco coughed and belched before it puttered to life. He always cut the grass early on Saturday mornings. The garden was his domain, and he enjoyed looking after it, walking methodically in straight lines, leaving the lawn striped and perfect and looking like the surface of the centre court in Wimbledon. He had kept his lean physique, and had hardly changed during their twenty-eight years of marriage.

This house had been the beginning of a new life for them both. It had pulled the shutters down on her breakdown and the painful past. It was the house their children had been born into and where they'd played and pushed each other on the swing that used to hang from the old tree at the end of the lawn. She studied Mal as she reminisced. His hair had turned silver at the sides, but she thought that made him look distinguished. *Why can't it look so well on women?* She kept her unruly mop a soft ash-brown, but with the help of regular sessions at the local hairdresser. She often told him that he wouldn't recognise a calorie or kilojoule if it jumped off his plate and bit him. She, on the other hand, was on intimate terms with food labels and low-fat products and kept her shape by controlling her addiction to Minstrels, Yorkie bars and Cadbury's Flake.

When she had been recovering, she had munched her way through everything, and between the sweets and the awful medication that made her feel like a zombie, she had put on kilos. Moving about in slow motion, not really connecting to the world about her. Now, Mal always bought her a packet of sweets on Saturdays and Sundays when he went for the newspapers, her little treat.

She could laugh at the idea of addiction now, but then it had been true. She had been so lonely it had hurt physically, and it was a while before she'd realised and accepted that comfort eating provided no comfort at all.

This morning, though, before she settled down with the papers she first took the hidden letter and slid it under the Saturday supplement. She still hadn't decided if she was up to facing its contents.

She fiddled with her engagement ring as she perused the magazine. She stared at the holiday pages that invited her to take a twenty-day cruise from Istanbul to Dubai from €2,229. Patmos in Greece, Haifa in Israel, Aqaba in Jordan, Salalah in Oman. But these exotic destinations quickly vanished from her mind, to be replaced by K. Kinsella's address in Stoneybatter. Was he married now? Did he have a wife and family of his own? Had he found happiness like she had? She was still staring at the magazine, lost in her reverie when Mal came in. She hadn't noticed the mower stopping.

'I was thinking we might pop over to Leah and Adam for a bit, what do you think?'

'What? Sorry, I was miles away.' Sandra quickly checked the letter was still out of sight. 'Mal, I found the photo yesterday,' she blurted out.

'*The* photo?' Mal looked at her quizzically.

'Yes, *the* photo. You'd hidden it well.'

'I'd almost forgotten where I put it. Did it upset you?'

'No, not really. But whenever I find it, it always seems to precede some incident or other.'

'That's just coincidence. It's only a photo. And did it precede some incident or other?'

She felt herself redden. She decided against telling him the truth just then. Instead she told him about knocking the wedding picture off the mantel.

'Don't worry about that – I'll get new glass for it this afternoon. Now, come on, let's head out, we have to give them those new name plates I got for their gates.'

Sandra had welcomed Adam Boles from their first meeting, falling for his charm and his polished manners. Mal had taken longer to come around.

'You know, Sandra, I might have misjudged our son-in-law,' he told her as they drove through suburbia.

'You still have misgivings, I can tell.'

'I'd be lying if I denied that.'

'She asked me once how you know when it's the real thing, something that would last. I told her whoever he is has to complete you, fill the gaps in your soul and be someone who'll always be there for you – someone like you!'

'Did I really do that for you?'

'You know you did – and you still do.'

'That fellow should be thinking of a family now, not cars.'

'Well, at least he's not talking about whisking her off to live at the other side of the world.'

'There is that, I suppose,' he admitted grudgingly, 'but I wouldn't put it past him to move there some day. Being an absentee landlord is not the best way to run a property, or a successful business either.'

Sandra knew Mal tried with Adam, although at times he almost lost it. The Sunday after Leah and Adam had got engaged, she had overheard him saying to Leah, 'I know you think he's the love of your life, but have you looked at him as others see him? Don't you think he might be a little too smooth, a little—'

'Dad, that's rich coming from you. All through art college, you gave me grief about my long-haired, scruffy boyfriends and the way they dressed and looked. Now I have a clean-cut one and you think he's too smooth.'

'I wasn't referring to his appearance – although he does turn himself out well.' Mal stopped short, as though he had been about to say more. Then he added, 'He's very talented, I'll give him that.'

Sandra knew he had been flattered when Adam had consulted him about his legacy, but it hadn't really changed their relationship at all.

'That fellow is too full of his own importance. The money's going to his head and that car – it's so ostentatious.'

'Oh, love, let them enjoy it. If we suddenly became stinking rich, you'd probably do something like that.'

Shortly after they moved in to Orchard Lodge, Adam had imported the classic. It was an impressive-looking, tobacco-coloured Bentley with lots of chrome, cream-leather upholstery, with a burl-wood dash and door trims. He drove it over for them to admire, and he pointed proudly to the winged 'B' logo.

'Monogrammed and all for me,' he remarked smugly. 'Bentley or Boles!'

'For us,' said Leah.

When they had gone, Mal had said to Sandra, 'I don't like the way this is going.'

'Leah seems happy, so let's be happy for them to live their dream.'

As Mal turned his car into Orchard Lodge, Adam was just getting out of the Bentley. He came over and greeted them.

'Hi, Adam,' Sandra said. 'You're out and about early today.' She noted the small bag he had with him.

'Yeah, like yourselves. An early bird, that's me.' He gave Sandra a kiss on her cheek. 'Ah, they've arrived,' he said, indicating the trees and tubs. 'I bought them for Leah for our anniversary. Come on in around the back.'

'Look who I found outside,' he said to Leah.

'I hope it's not a bad time – had you plans?' Sandra asked.

'Of course not, Mum. It's never a bad time for you and Dad to call.'

Mal handed over the parcel. 'They're new names for your gates. I noticed those old ones were a tad past their sell-by date and thought they'd make a good anniversary present.'

Leah unwrapped the paper. 'These are lovely, Dad, thank you so much. They'll look terrific now that the pillars are painted.' Adam agreed.

'You look tired, love,' Sandra said. 'You're working too hard.'

'I keep telling her that, don't I?' Adam said.

Leah didn't reply, but Sandra noticed the hostile look that her daughter gave Adam.

'I'm caught up in a big project at the moment,' Leah said, turning her back to them as she busied herself making coffee. 'We've to present it to the clients next week. And this one is a biggie, so it's been kind of full-on for the past while. What about you, Mum? You can talk, always thinking of others. You sounded hassled yesterday.'

'Oh,' she said, 'that was nothing. I hadn't expected to be called in to work and I had to rearrange a few things. I know your job is important, love, but so are other things – you have to think of yourself too.'

'I will. When this is finished I'll take some time off.'

'That's my cue to tell you all that I was thinking of booking a trip for the four of us to go to Tassie together,' Adam announced. Turning to Sandra, he said. 'You're always saying that you'd love to see the place. I figure there's no time like the present, *carpe diem* and all that. I have some decisions to make about the management of the farm and businesses and where better to make them than in situ?'

'That sounds wonderful, Adam,' Sandra said, hugging her daughter. 'And you never said a word about it.'

'I didn't know a thing about it until now,' Leah replied, a stunned look on her face.

'Very unexpected,' said Mal, 'but you know I can't go anywhere until after the end-of-year tax deadline has passed.'

'Don't worry, Mal, I've taken all that into consideration. I figure you'll have earned a break by then,' Adam said.

'Fine. Great,' he said, smiling at Sandra. 'The farthest I've ever been is Sydney and Sandra's never been to Oz. This'll be a bit of an adventure for us both, won't it, love? And to think all I managed was a few days in Paris for your fiftieth.'

'And they were wonderful too, but I can't believe it. This is so exciting,' Sandra said. 'Thank you so much.'

'It's my pleasure. I just wish I could persuade my folks to come out sometime, but the old man won't fly and Mum wouldn't do it without him.'

'Well, I'm very excited at the prospect. Aren't you, Mal?' she said.

'Definitely. Now, do you want a hand putting those name plates up? I brought my drill just in case,' Mal said to Adam.

'Wise man. You know me and DIY – they'd probably fall down the next day if I were to try to do it.'

As they walked out of the kitchen, Mall was going over the different fixings they could use and Adam, Leah noticed, was giving her dad his full attention.

As Leah was watching her husband, Sandra was watching her daughter. She had been surprised by Leah's reaction to Adam's announcement. Sandra thought her daughter definitely looked under the weather – worried, even – but decided not to press her.

'I'm dying for a cuppa. Would you ever pour that coffee and then you can show me what the decorators have been up to.'

'Sure, my head's all over the place,' Leah said.

'We won't stay too long. Weekends are precious and you don't need your parents hanging around cramping your style.'

'You wouldn't be.'

'I can't believe we'll be going off together – that's amazing. We have so many plans to make.'

'It is amazing, isn't it? But that's Adam for you – full of surprises.'

'You can say that again,' smiled Sandra, but she wasn't fooled by Leah's response. Something wasn't right in her daughter's world. She just sensed it.

In the car, Sandra asked Mal, 'Well, what do you think of that?'

'Unexpected, certainly, A grand gesture. It's a pity we have to share it with him, though.'

'You still don't like him very much, do you?' Sandra remarked.

'Probably not, if I'm honest. I never did really – but, more importantly, I don't really trust him. Neither does Oliver.'

'Oh, you two have been talking about him. Don't ever say anything like that in front of your daughter. He's her husband and she chose him. We have to respect that. Liking it is another matter altogether.'

He agreed.

* * *

When her parents had left, Leah faced Adam in the hallway.

'What the hell do you think you are playing at, pulling a stunt like that? Involving my parents in your stupid games. There is no way I'm ever going to Tasmania with you, or anywhere else for that matter.'

'We'll have patched things by then. I promise. I'll make it up to you. It was just a silly mistake.'

'You talk about it as though it were a paper cut. Stick a plaster on it and, irritating though it might be, it'll mend in the end. Well, this won't. You've destroyed everything we had. Do you honestly think you can come swanning back from your lover's bed and just carry on as if nothing happened?'

'Leah, you're making too much out of this. I truly am sorry and I promise – *I promise* – it will never happen again.'

'Do you expect me to believe that?'

'I'd like you to. And, for the record, I've been planning this trip for ages, it isn't something I thought about since you threw me out. The apple trees being delivered were supposed to be the teaser.'

'As a pre-emptive strike no doubt, in case I found out. Maybe you'd like me to be one of those wives who turns a blind eye to her husband's affairs, just so she can continue to enjoy position and money. Well, I'm not. I didn't marry you for your money or your position, and I can't be bought. You can tell my folks what you did and shatter their hopes for their daughter's marriage – they won't care about the holiday then. I can't even look at you now. I'm going out.'

He said nothing as she grabbed her bag and keys and walked out the door. She didn't know where she was going, she just knew she needed to get away from him for a while.

Chapter Eight

'Hi, how's my favourite sister?' Oliver asked when he phoned the next day.

'I'm your *only* sister!' Leah replied.

'I know – that's why you're my favourite.'

Leah laughed as she always did at her brother's joke. 'I'm fine. When did you get back?'

'At sunrise, jet-lagged as usual and unable to sleep. Bring on teleporting, I say. Can I come around for a coffee? I'll get some Danish.'

'With an offer like that how could I say no?' She was relieved that Adam was out. She had slept in the guest room the previous night, unable to bring herself to share a bed with him.

* * *

'Sis, you look awful.'

'Thanks a million. I know I do.'

'Really, are you OK?'

'You never mince your words, do you? I have to tell you something. If I don't I think my head will explode.' He waited as she put the pastries on a plate and filled the percolator. 'You were right about Adam. He – he ...' She burst into tears.

Oliver came over and put his arms around her and let her cry until she was able to tell him.

'I'll throttle him. I really will. I won't say "I told you so." I don't have to, but you know my views on him. Where is he?'

'He said he was going back to the old house to check it out before the showings begin, but I don't know whether to believe him or not. Is this the way it's going to be from now on? Every time he goes out, or is late, or changes plans will I wonder where he is – and who he's with?'

'Not if I have anything to do with it.'

'I haven't told Mum and Dad. I'm too ashamed.'

'You have nothing to be ashamed about.'

'They called over yesterday when Adam was here and he just announced – out of the blue – that he's taking us all to Tasmania. Not you, just them and me. They were so excited. What the hell am I going to do, Ollie? I keep hoping it will go away, that everything will go back to being normal and that I won't have to tell them.'

'From where I'm looking, telling them is the least of your worries.'

'I know.' She said nothing for a while as she filled their cups, then asked, 'What am I going to do?'

'Nothing for the moment. I'll have a word with him.'

'Do you think you should?'

'I know I should. Don't look so worried. I promise I won't deck him.'

'Thanks. I'm so glad I have you to talk to.'

Over coffee she told him what she knew about Adam's affair and how he'd gone missing for a few days before turning up as their parents arrived.

'It sounds like you've been through the wringer. Call me anytime,' he said as he left.

As she busied herself tidying up, arranging her clothes for the week ahead, she tried not to think.

When Adam came home later that afternoon, he was contrite, telling her that he fully realised the impact of what he had done to her. She knew instantly that her brother had talked to him.

'I'll have Helka replaced immediately. She'll get another job easily enough.'

As if a new job for this floozy is top of my priority list. Leah said nothing.

'Please, Leah. I know I've messed up everything. But we can still make it work. I *know* how special what we have is and I won't risk it – us – ever again.'

'You can't expect this not to have changed things between us,' she said. 'If there's any hope, I'm going to have to learn to trust you again and you're going to have to prove that you're worthy of that trust too.'

'I will. You have my word.'

'I had your word when we made our marriage vows. What makes this any different?' she asked, seeking the reassurance she so badly wanted.

Adam repeated his promises that he wouldn't risk their marriage again. She still didn't know if she believed him, but at least it was a start, and she felt a bit more hopeful than she had earlier.

* * *

Leah went in to work on Monday morning, having spent a sleepless night in the spare room again. She still couldn't face their bedroom – or Adam in it. She needed a clear head to focus on the week ahead and things with Adam would just have to stay as they were for a while. It was an important week not only for her but for her company and clients – things were going to be frantic at Concentric Circles and Concepts. She got through her day, worked late and came home to face Adam across a ready-meal dinner she'd taken from the fridge. 'Are you feeling OK?' he asked.

'Not really. Would you expect me to?'

'I suppose not.'

She picked at her food, which was not very appetising.

'I'm going to have a bath and go to bed – on my own,' she announced, and went upstairs without saying another word.

The following morning she had left before he got out of the shower. At work it was all systems go. The three-dimensional models of the proposed outlets in the docklands development had arrived back from a studio that did this sort of work for them when they needed it. The glossy colour brochures and laminated folders had been delivered from the printer.

'They look terrific. I feel I could recite every header and sentence by heart if asked to,' Leah said as they collated the various pages on the boardroom table.

'I know what you mean,' Susie, her second-in-command, said. 'But there isn't a cliché, piece of jargon or a grocer's apostrophe to be found in any of it – they really benefited from all the—'

Leah looked up when Susie stopped so abruptly. 'What's the matter?'

That was when Susie spotted they were missing a section. 'Where is the celebrity kitchen and cookery school proposal?'

'I haven't seen it, but it must be here. Who signed for the delivery? Wasn't it checked?' Leah felt panic begin to set in. *Keep cool. There's still time. We can handle this.*

They checked the bundles but couldn't find the missing section. Then they called the printer, but they insisted they had delivered the completed order. Phone calls flew back and forth, but the pages seemed to have vanished completely.

Susie went to check the delivery notice while Leah kept looking through boxes in the store room.

'Any luck?' Leah said as Susie came running back into the boardroom.

'Yes, it's on the list as being delivered – so at least we know it's in the building somewhere,' she said, feeling relieved. 'I'll get everyone to stop what they're doing and start looking. Can you imagine what Lars Andersson will say if *his* brochure isn't in the pack?'

Lars Andersson was one of the project's main backers and wasn't the easiest of people to get on with.

'He'll lose the plot!'

It was Susie who traced the missing brochures eventually – hidden under some sample boards on someone's desk.

'Oh, God, I think that was my fault,' Leah confessed, furious with herself for being so careless. 'I remember now I took a call at reception and I must have picked them up without noticing. I'm so sorry for the confusion and the fuss I've caused.'

'You're letting this project stress you out,' Susie told her when they were back in the boardroom. 'It's not like you.'

'I know. I'm sorry, but it'll be over and done with one way or another in a few days,' she said, wishing that the real reason for her stress could have a finite date too.

Sandra phoned her but Leah cut her short. 'Sorry, Mum, can't talk at the moment. I'll ring you later in the week.' When she put the phone down she wondered why she'd said that – 'later in the week'. *I always ring her back later in the day. I can't keep avoiding her forever.*

It was almost midnight when Leah was driving home and, for the first time that day, she had time to think about Adam. She was finding it very hard to imagine how they could regain the intimacy they had so easily shared. She wanted a hug. She needed a hug and to feel the closeness of him, smell his skin and more, much more, but images of him and that girl – whom she'd never met – kept coming between them and she was glad he was in bed when she let herself in and she went straight to the guest room and fell asleep.

She was forced to talk to him the following morning. He was in the kitchen and making scrambled eggs and toast when she came down.

'How long is this cold-shoulder treatment going to go on for?' he asked.

'I don't know. You really hurt me and, for the moment, I just can't get past what you did. I haven't got time to discuss it now.'

'I realise that, but we have to talk soon. I know today is important for you – I hope it goes well. I really do. I'll give you a bell later to find out.'

'Thanks. I have to go.' She was pleased a bit of his nicer side was showing through. She was back at her desk at 8a.m. pleased that the others were all there too. She liked that they all realised how important the presentation was.

'This place smells like an Indian takeaway,' Susie said when she arrived in the office a few minutes later. 'Though that doesn't surprise me given that we've been surviving on takeaways and litres of coffee for days.'

A junior was dispensed to find air freshener and flowers to mask the smell, and others were put on clean-up duties. By the time the dockland delegation arrived, the offices were back to their normal state, and looking fabulous. In the boardroom, the cups and saucers were set out on a side table with an ample supply of foil-wrapped chocolate biscuits and bottles of still and sparkling water.

The suited clients grilled Leah and her team on various aspects of the project, some asking inane questions just to appear to be doing something other than nodding their heads in agreement.

Despite all the trepidation, they got through it. Jason from the media department concluded the presentation by handing out some pages.

'We prepared a press release for you, and after there's a press call and photo shoot, which we'll do on the site.'

There was silence for a few minutes, before murmurs of approval were uttered. The dreaded chairman of the board, sporting his signature bow tie and comb-over hairstyle, stood up, and waited until he had everyone's attention. Leah, who could normally read people pretty well, had no idea how he had received their ideas. She was pretty sure they had a majority of approval, but he was inscrutable. She held her breath.

'Well, I have to congratulate you here at Concentric Circles and Concepts. You obviously listened to our brief and took it all on board. And,' he said, pausing for effect, 'that was a big ask.'

Leah exhaled. There was a round of applause before he continued.

'I appreciate that it's not easy working to a committee, particularly a vocal one like ours,' he laughed, 'but you did and you did it well. That was an impressive presentation. You did what we tasked you to do, now we have to give it our full commitment and get these brochures out to our prospective tenants and persuade them that they can't afford not to be involved.'

Leah was very relieved when the clients suggested that they all go out for something to eat and a drink to celebrate that evening. That meant she could put off her discussion with Adam for another day.

Her phone vibrated a few times but she ignored it. She knew it was Adam. When everyone had finally left, she took it out to check his texts, annoyed that his presence was clouding her mood. She should have been walking on air, but the problems that she and Adam were having were too big to ignore.

She texted him.

Everything went much better than expected. Clients delighted – they want to celebrate so I'll be late tonight. We'll talk tomorrow and tnx.

Glad today went well for you. You deserve that. I may be late myself.

Where is he going? And who is he going to be with? She felt she was on a treadmill. Would she ever learn to trust him again and feel comfortable when he said he had to work late or go out? Or would she turn into a suspicious wife going through his pockets for evidence that might not even exist? She still wasn't sure what she was going to say when they did get around to sitting down and talking things through. She didn't know what she wanted and this was a situation she never had visualised herself having to face, but face it she would.

Chapter Nine

Kieron was getting more and more angry, and finding it hard to concentrate on his classes. He was highly attuned to the troublemakers, the bullies and the disinterested, although the honours Leaving Cert maths class was usually easier to manage. But, from experience, he knew if he didn't keep on top of them, they could spiral downwards very quickly.

His next period was spent trying to engage with a disinterested third-year class.

'Do any of you feel that teachers are becoming redundant?' he asked in the staff room at lunchtime. '3B have absolutely no understanding or curiosity whatsoever about why they would ever need to do theorems or equations when they can Google the answer to everything. And next I've somehow to get 1A interested in chemical compounds when they really only like science because there's a possibility of burning down the school during an experiment.'

'You're in fine form today, Kieron,' one of his colleagues laughed.

'Sorry. There's a lot going on.'

'Your little girl?' Emilie, who taught French, asked.

'Yes, and other things too. Now, I need to make a phone call before facing the next lot.'

Kieron walked outside and took his phone out of his pocket.

'Hey,' he said when Pam answered the phone, 'any post?'

There was a pause. 'I'm sorry, honey ...'

'I swear I'll go around there on the way home and tell that selfish woman what I think of her,' he replied.

'Don't do that. She could be away or she might need time to think about it, and you don't want to alienate her.'

'Alienate her! Don't make me laugh, Pam. I'm the child she didn't want and gave away.'

'You don't know that.'

'Yes, I do. And now when she has a chance to do something right, something good, she's walking away again. What kind of heartless creature can do that?'

'You're making a lot of assumptions when you don't know what's going on. Wait until you talk to her.'

'*If* I ever get to talk to her! Oh, there's the bell. Sorry, Pam, I don't mean to take it out on you. I'll see you later.' He rang off and went to face 1A.

Chapter Ten

It was five days since it had arrived and Sandra still hadn't opened the letter. Several times a day she took it out from the drawer. The urge to open it so strong, but the fear of what it could do to her and her family was even more compelling. Yet she knew she had to face her demons and tell them about Peter and everything else.

She didn't work on Tuesdays or Fridays – they were her 'me' time, the days she bought a new book or two, did the shopping, went to town or met friends for lunch. But today the letter hung over her like a great black cloud, stopping her from doing any of those things. Halfway through the morning, she decided that it was time to get things out in the open. She'd procrastinated for too long. The secrecy was eating away at her. On impulse, she phoned Mal before she could change her mind.

'Can you get away for an hour? We could grab a bite in The Den.' They often went there. It was just around the corner from his office. 'I have something to tell you.'

'You're not ill, are you?' he asked.

'No, nothing like that, I promise.'

* * *

'You're sure you're not sick?' he asked again when they met.

'No, I'm not, but I don't know how you'll take what I'm about to tell you.'

'You don't want to go all the way to Tasmania, is that it?'

'Wrong again. Let's order a sandwich first and I'll tell you.'

She produced the letter – still unopened. 'I got this last week and I haven't been able to bring myself to read it yet.'

'I thought you'd been acting a bit funny,' he said, studying the envelope. 'If this is what I think it is, Sandra, it can't be that bad, can it? It's what you've always wanted. Open it.'

'Would you?'

'Do you want me to read it for you?'

'Would you?' She clasped her hands together to stop them shaking.

He wiped his knife on a paper napkin and slit the top. After he'd scanned it, he looked up at her.

'Well? What does he say?'

'I think you should read it for yourself,' he said gently, and handed the single page to her. 'You've wished for this for so long.'

He sat and watched as her eyes went down through the lines. When she looked up at him, they were brimming over. 'Oh, Mal, how awful. He hates me – I can tell from his tone. It's so impersonal. And his little girl – I have a granddaughter. As if I wouldn't help her – them – if I could.'

'I'm sure he doesn't hate you. Put yourself in his shoes – that can't have been easy for him to write, but whatever he feels, I think it's time you met and faced each other. It's the only way to put things straight between you. You have to tell him your side of the story. You owe yourself – and him – that much.'

'I know I do. Me a grandmother – can you believe that? I want to meet him, but this means that I now have to tell Leah and Oliver about him, about everything. I don't know how to do it. If I'm really honest, I'm scared about what they'll think of me. They'll probably hate me too. You know what, Mal, I'm going to burn that damned photo when I get home. I found it minutes before this letter was delivered. I'm telling you that photo has a sense of its own. Do you think they'll forgive me for not telling them before?

'Don't be so silly, of course they won't hate you. They will certainly be surprised, but you've waited all these years for this letter. You never gave up hope. I'll be there with you – we'll do it together,' he said, stroking her hand. 'You're looking on this as though it was a punishment. Finding the photo is nothing but a pure coincidence. Maybe you should get rid of it if you feel that strongly about it, but not just yet. Your son contacting you could be just the beginning – who knows where it might lead? He might like to see the snap too.'

'That's what scares me. What will I say to them – to him? I can't tell him everything.'

'Don't let it scare you. You'll know what's right when you meet him. We're in this together and I think the sooner we do it, the sooner we'll know what we're dealing with,' he said.

'What would I do without you?'

'You'd manage.' Mal smiled at her. 'Will I call the kids or do you want to?'

'I'll do it when I get home. It's too busy in here. Strike while the iron is hot – or before I get cold feet, or whichever metaphor is the right one. I can't think in straight lines since that letter arrived.'

They sat quietly for a few moments, each contemplating the probabilities, then she said, 'I suppose we should have Adam there too.'

'I was just thinking that. Leah might feel we're excluding him if we don't, and I think she already senses that he's still a bit of an outsider where we're concerned,' Mal said. 'Ring me later and let me know what's happening. I'll come home a bit early if you want me to.'

* * *

'This evening, Mum? On a week night? I'm free, but I'm not sure if Adam will be able to make it,' Leah said, not wanting to go anywhere with Adam, least of all to have to sit through a meal with her family and pretend that everything was normal. 'What's the occasion?'

'It's important. I need to talk to you.'

She was worried by her mother's tone. 'OK, I'll give him a ring and see. Are you sure there's nothing wrong?'

'No, honestly, me and your dad are fine. I'll see you tonight.'

Leah was still holding her phone and thinking back over what her mother had said when it rang again. 'What's the story?' It was her brother. 'A family dinner on a Tuesday? You don't think one of them is sick or anything like that, do you?'

'No. That's the first thing I asked her. But she has been a little off for the past few days, hasn't she? I thought that when they called last Saturday, and then I thought maybe it was because I was trying too hard to pretend that everything was normal.'

'I hadn't noticed. Maybe Dad's going to take early retirement and they're going to sell up and move to France.'

'She wants Adam there too.'

'And are you happy about that?' Oliver asked.

'Not really, but what can I do, short of telling them what's going on, which I'd rather not? If me and Adam get through this, I'd prefer they didn't know anything about it.'

'Your secret's safe with me. I'll be my usual charming self, even to Adam. How are things there anyway?'

'He's been pussyfooting since Saturday and being really nice, but I'm not finding it easy to forgive him – although I do want to. We're going to have a heart-to-heart tomorrow. Thanks for talking to him by the way.'

'Did he tell you that?'

'No, Ollie, but you just have,' she said.

'I fell for that. Anyway, at least we don't have to wait too long until we find out what's going on with Mum and Dad. I'll see you tonight.'

* * *

Kieron dropped his briefcase on the sofa. 'How's my little princess?' he asked, ruffling Jennifer's head. 'I see you've been to the library,' he said, walking in to the kitchen and kissing Pam. 'I was going to take them on Saturday if the weather is bad.'

'Don't worry, at the rate she gets through books, she won't object to going again.'

'I've nearly finished this one already, Dad.'

'Where's Ryan?'

'Upstairs, with a boy from his class. They're building "something technical with Lego",' said Pam.

'He'll be an engineer yet, the hours he spends doing that.' Kieron picked up the post, a few bills, pizza fliers and a misspelled one for asphalt and garden maintenance, even though the houses in their estate had neither. He sifted through them. 'Still nothing?'

'Not since you called me this morning,' Pam said, looking up from setting the table. 'Let's try and get through to the weekend without talking about it, and I promise if we hear nothing by Monday, then you have my blessing to try and contact her again.'

'I just can't fathom how anyone could be so cold-hearted,' he said.

'I'm trying to give her the benefit of the doubt, until I meet her.'

'If you ever do.'

'I'm sure we will. I can't imagine what she must be feeling, getting your letter out of the blue. What if she's never told her husband and family about you? That could cause all sorts of problems for her and her marriage.'

Footsteps trundling down the stairs were followed by Ryan's pleas as the boys burst into the kitchen, 'Mum, we're starving.'

Out of Focus

63

'And hello to you too, Ryan. Aren't you going to introduce me to you friend?' Kieron said.

'He's called Ryan too,' Jennifer volunteered. 'I'm the only Jennifer in my class.'

'And I'm the only Mum around here, so if you all wash your hands and sit down I'll give you your dinner.' The three of them scampered off and Pam looked at her husband. 'Have we a deal until Monday?'

'Yes, we have,' he said, and sat down.

Chapter Eleven

Why should I be so terrified? They're my children, all three of them. I think Leah will understand, but how will Oliver take it? He's always been the only son – it'll be harder for him, I suppose. Sandra argued with herself as she rolled out pastry for a tart, marinated the salmon darnes she'd bought on the way home, chopped vegetables, washed salad, laid the table and changed into a fresh top and trousers. She came down the stairs as soon as she heard his car pull up in the driveway and was in the hall when Mal put his key in the lock.

Without preamble she said, 'Maybe I should I have asked Kieron to come too – I can't even get used to that name – he'll always be Peter to me. I'm going to have to go through all this again with him.'

'Let me get my coat off first, love.' Mal put his briefcase on the ground and shrugged out of his overcoat. 'I don't think that would have been a good idea to have him here. It's going to be a shock for Leah and Ollie, and I think we're better telling them first and giving them a chance for it to sink in. I know this it hard for you, but it has to be done.'

'They'll think I've lied to them all their lives.'

'No, they won't – and you didn't, technically speaking. Did they ever ask us out straight if they had other brothers or sisters? So you simply withheld the information for their own good. The Jesuits taught us all about the justification of withholding information. If I remember rightly, they're called mental reservation, equivocations and amphibolies,' he said, trying to reassure her.

'Oh, Mal, don't ever change.' She smiled at him. 'I'll try and remember that when they challenge me.'

'You'll feel better when it's all out in the open too. No more secrets.' He put his arm around her.

'No more secrets,' she agreed. 'How do you suppose he traced me? He didn't say, but from the tone of his letter, he's absolutely certain I'm his mum.'

'You can ask him that when you meet him.'

* * *

'Relax,' Mal told Sandra as Leah's car pulled into the drive. She was on her own.

'Adam will be here in a bit; he's coming straight from work,' Leah said. 'I'm intrigued, though – what's going on?'

Mal smiled and said, 'You'll have to wait until the others are here.'

'Not even a little clue?' She looked at Sandra.

'Afraid not, love.' Sandra forced a smile even though she was shaking inside, her stomach in knots.

Oliver arrived next, followed closely by Adam.

'I suppose you know what's with all the mystery?' Adam said to him.

'I'm as much in the dark as Leah.'

'Seems like whatever it is it's covered by the official secrets act and still embargoed,' Adam said.

'Don't look at me, I haven't a notion either,' Leah said. 'Can I do anything to help, Mum?'

'Put that on the table for me,' Sandra said, handing Leah a basket of freshly cut bread. 'It's just ready, so you can all go in and sit down.'

Sandra noticed that Adam never kissed his wife when he arrived, as he normally would, and she thought Leah was being very dismissive of him, like she had been the previous Saturday.

Adam whispered to Leah, 'Do they know about – you know – about what happened with me and—?'

'No,' she said, 'and I'd like to keep it like that until we know what this family council is about.' She led the way into the dining room.

They were halfway through their soup when Sandra broke her news. Having worried and agonised, rehearsed and practised, in the end, she just blurted it out.

'I have something to tell you – you have an older brother that I never told you about.'

After a stunned silence, Leah was the first to speak. 'A brother? You can't be serious, Mum.' She looked at Adam, who said nothing, and then at Ollie and then at Mal. 'Dad, did you know? Oh my God, is he yours too?'

'Take it easy, Leah,' he told her. 'He isn't mine, but if he's your flesh and blood, then that's good enough for me.'

'Well, this is the last thing I expected to hear, Dad,' Oliver said. 'I thought you were going to tell us you'd decided to divide the "enormous fortune" with us before you shuffle off this mortal coil.'

They all laughed a little nervously at that. The 'enormous fortune' was a family joke. Mal made them save as youngsters so that they'd have money for a rainy day and they'd ask if he had done the same. He always answered, 'Yes, I've an enormous fortune.'

'How old is he?' Oliver asked. 'What's his name? Is he in Dublin? Don't tell us he lives around the corner and that I went to school with him.'

'He's called Kieron, and he's thirty-seven.'

'Why did you never tell us before?' Leah asked.

'Thirty-seven. That makes him eleven years older than me,' Oliver said.

'Mum, you were just a kid. What happened?'

'I *was* just a kid, Leah, I was thirteen when he was born. I'd rather not talk about the circumstances of that for the moment. I was sent away and he was taken from me, without my knowledge or consent. I haven't seen him since he was eighteen days old. I looked for him, God knows how I looked for him, and now he's found me.'

'So how did he make contact with you?' Adam asked. 'And why now? Are you going to meet up?'

'He wrote to me. I tried every avenue to find him, but never had any luck. And yes, Adam, of course I'm going to meet him, but I wanted to talk to all of you first.'

'How do you know he's genuine? He could be anyone who got hold of information about you – a con man – you hear about people like that, how they prey on others.' Adam looked around the table.

Ollie gave Adam a filthy look. 'Or he could be genuine, a bona fide member of this family.'

'Mum, I don't know how you could have kept this from us. It's not as though it was something unimportant,' Leah said. 'Why didn't you tell us before, and why didn't you keep him?'

'I wanted to, but I was thirteen. Having a baby outside marriage was a sin and an awful social scandal in those days, one that had to be hidden away. I was effectively banished by my family – my parents and my only sister – then he was taken from me to be adopted.'

'You have a sister?' It was Oliver's turn. 'You never mentioned her, and I always thought your parents were dead.'

'They could both be by now – I believe my father died a long time ago – but I was dead to them as soon as they found out I was pregnant. And to my only sister and my grandmother. It wasn't unusual for that to happen then.'

'Where's your sister now and why didn't you go home after you had the baby?'

'Louise, her name's Louise, and she's not quite two years older than me. I believe she went to America, but I don't know for sure. When the parish priest drove me away from my home that was the last time I ever saw any of them. I never saw or heard from anyone in my family again. I wrote lots of letters to them, but they were all returned unread. They had moved away.'

'None of this is making sense.' Leah turned to her father. 'How could they do that? It wasn't the parish priest's business, was it?'

'No, love, it wasn't,' Sandra continued. 'But he made it his business. He told me he was just trying to protect the good girls in his parish and I'd be a bad example to them.'

'Good God! Dad, have you known this all along?'

'Yes, love, of course I have.'

'And do you not think you should have told us?'

'No, I don't. It's your mother's life and it was her wish to say nothing until she was ready, and I've respected that.'

'Were you sent to one of those awful orphanages or put working in a laundry?'

'Initially yes but then I got lucky. I was sent to a nice family, to help them, a French family.'

'So that's where you learned to speak it,' Ollie said. 'Are we going to meet this brother and when?'

'I don't know. I hope so. I haven't spoken to him yet. I wanted to tell you first, to give you time to get used to the idea – but I would like you all to meet eventually.'

'Does he expect to be welcomed with open arms?' Adam asked. 'Like the proverbial prodigal son.' Oliver shot him another filthy look.

'I doubt it. His letter was quite – well – quite cold really.' Sandra hesitated. 'He has a daughter who is ill – she needs a bone marrow donor.'

'So he decided to find you when it suited him?' Adam said.

'You can't know that,' Leah said. 'But maybe you have a point –

why didn't he come looking for you before, and can you be certain he is who he claims to be?'

'Oh, darling, I don't know why. I don't know so many things and I have so many questions to ask and I intend to do that. This isn't easy for me, you know. It wasn't a decision I had any part in making, but it's one that I've regretted every single day of my life. I looked for him, we both did. Meeting your dad was the best thing that ever happened to me, but even that didn't stop me from looking. I was haunted by the thoughts of my baby being brought up by strangers, wondering if he was being well cared for and loved.'

'Oh, Mum, I can't imagine what it must have been like. How could your parents have allowed you to be taken away too? It's inhuman,' Leah said.

'It was nearly forty years ago, and times were very different, especially in a country town where your mother's family were considered to be pillars of society,' Mal said.

'I'm sure if they had wanted to they could have found a way,' Leah said.

Sandra replied, 'I often thought that myself.'

'You and Dad would never have done that to me,' her daughter said.

They sat talking until well after midnight and, eventually, when the others left, Mal and Sandra went to bed.

'I honestly don't know whether I'm relieved or not to have that over.'

'Give them time. They weren't expecting *that* news. You'll feel better too after you've spoken to Kieron.'

'I hope you're right,' Sandra said, moving closer to Mal and putting her head on his chest. She felt safe there, listening to his heartbeat, his arm protecting her from harm.

After a moment she said, 'How do you think they will take the fact that their mother stole a baby?'

'They'll understand what drove you to it.'

'I hope so. Getting that letter from Kieron and telling them about him has brought up an awful lot of things – things I'd put to the back of my mind. It must have done the same for you.'

'It did, but the past can't harm us now. Try to get some sleep. It's late.'

* * *

He couldn't sleep, though. Sandra was right – telling everyone about Kieron had dredged back memories of that bleak time before they had Leah and Ollie, when, with their future together ahead of them, they should have been carefree and happy. He thought they were until he got home from work one evening and instead of the usual six o'clock news, he heard different noises coming from the sitting room. Sandra had a baby on the settee beside her and was cooing at him. The television was on in the corner but the sound was turned down.

'It didn't take that pair long to ask you to babysit,' he laughed, nodding towards the neighbours' house, as he bent down to kiss Sandra on the forehead. 'It suits you, you look very happy there – before you say anything, that's not a hint, I promise you,' he grinned.

'Oh, Mal, I know and I am happy, really happy. I'm beyond happy. Can you believe I found him?' she said. 'And on Baggot Street too. Isn't that a coincidence, what with the cheque and everything? Is that what they call serendipity?'

'Darling, I don't know. Is it? I haven't the foggiest idea what you're talking about. You found who, and what about Baggot Street? What were you doing there anyway? What cheque? Let's start again.'

'Mal, don't be a dork. It's him. I found him – Peter – *my* Peter,' she said, picking up the baby and holding him excitedly out to her husband. 'Say hello to your daddy, Peter.'

Mal was speechless. *What has she done?* But before he could say anything, she was off again.

'We've had such a lovely time together, haven't we?' she said to the little face. 'Yes, we have. We had a ride in a taxi, then our first supermarket expedition but, Mal, I need you to get some things. We've no buggy for starters or a steriliser, like the one they have next door – and a sling. You'll need a car seat too. Oh and more nappies. I only bought a small pack: that was all I could manage. And he'll need clothes, lots of them. Isn't he gorgeous, Mal, isn't he?'

Mal looked at his wife and waited for her to stop. He didn't know what to do or what to say. He'd never seen her so animated. He sat down beside her and she insisted he held the baby.

'It's time you got to know each other. He won't break – here, hold him. Take your jacket off first. He's just been fed so he might burp up on you.'

'Sandra, listen to me. Darling, this gorgeous little boy is not your Peter. Where did you get him? He's not next door's, is he?'

She pushed him away. 'Weren't you listening to me? I just told you, and how would you know anyway? You never saw Peter before. He's mine. I was meant to go there today, to Baggot Street and find him. There he was in his buggy. He was just lying there outside the chemist, waiting for me.'

'You mean you just took him? You do realise that his parents are out there going out of their minds with worry, frantically looking for their baby.'

'You're wrong. I'd know him anywhere.'

'Darling, he's not ours,' Mal said gently. 'This isn't your Peter. Peter isn't a baby any more – he's all grown up now, a boy of nine or ten, going to school, playing football, riding a bike. We have to call the police and tell them this baby is safe and well and give him back to his parents.'

'No-ooo!' she screamed hysterically, frightening the baby, who started wailing too. 'No, no, no – look what you've done. You're not taking him away from me. I thought you were on my side. You promised you'd help me look for him.'

Mal tried to comfort her, to calm her down, but there was no way she would listen. She kept babbling on. 'No one is going to take him away again and that includes you, Mal Wallace. Ever, do you hear me? No one.'

Across the room on the screen he saw a wide-angled shot of Baggot Street Bridge, then a close-up one of a chemist. He walked over and turned up the sound.

The newscaster spoke in a serious tone. 'A three-week-old baby boy was taken from his buggy at lunchtime today on Dublin's busy Baggot Street. His mother had gone into a chemist to collect a prescription for her elderly father. She didn't notice immediately that the buggy was empty. It was only when she got back to her house nearby that she realised her baby was missing and raised the alarm.'

Distressing images followed of a young couple. She was clinging to her husband and sobbing. 'Daniel, he's called Daniel, he has very blond hair, it's almost white. He has blue eyes and he was dressed in a blue and white babygro and he was wrapped up in a blue blanket with embroidery on one corner. He was wearing a knitted hat,' she said. Then the father spoke. 'Whoever took him took his stuffed teddy too. Whoever has him, please don't harm him. Just give him back to us. We're going out of our minds with worry.'

Mal glanced at Sandra. She was clutching the blue teddy, her knuckles white as the realisation of what she had done began to filter through on some level to her muddled brain.

The bulletin continued. 'Gardaí would like to talk to anyone who may have witnessed anything unusual, or seen anyone carrying an infant or behaving suspiciously in the area. They should contact them at Donnybrook, or any garda station. And now for tomorrow's weather – it's over to Met Éireann.'

'Sandra, do you understand, love? That's their son you're holding. And we have to give him back.'

Sandra had calmed down a little, but panicked when he went towards the hall to phone the gardaí.

'Not yet, Mal, wait a while, let me hold him for a bit longer.'

'No, Sandra, we have to do it now. They'll understand. I'll explain. It'll be all right. Really it will,' he said gently. Inside, he was terrified about what the consequences of his wife's actions would be. Would it be splashed all over the newspapers? Would she be prosecuted? Would it affect her job? Or his?

'Please don't tell anyone what I did. Promise me, Mal, no one.'

He put his arm around her. 'I won't.'

He was sure something must have triggered all this, but he didn't know what. She needed help. He wanted to call his mother and get her to come over, but he didn't want to betray Sandra's confidence. He was relieved when the gardaí arrived very shortly in an unmarked car, no flashing lights and no fanfare to draw attention to what had happened.

'Let me do the talking,' Mal said to Sandra before he went out to let the officers in. Sandra couldn't have talked if she'd wanted to. She sat there like a frightened little girl, rocking the baby back and forth. He explained that they had been trying to have a child.

'Will she be prosecuted?' Mal asked.

'We'll have to have the baby checked out before we reunite him with his parents and see what the medical reports say,' the young bangarda said, 'but it's obvious she's very disturbed.'

'I didn't hurt him. I didn't,' Sandra protested. 'I would never hurt Peter. I didn't. I wouldn't.'

'Peter?' the sergeant said.

'My wife lost a baby called Peter some time ago,' Mal told them. 'But I can promise you, she'd never harm a baby. She's fed and changed him. Will you please send my sincere ... *our* sincere apologies to the parents for the horror we've put them through.'

'I will. Could I have a word in private, sir?'

'Certainly, come on out to the kitchen.'

'Pardon me for being so blunt, but had you any idea your wife would do something like this?'

'Absolutely not. I came home from work and there he was. I thought she was minding him for a neighbour.'

'Your wife seems to be in a pretty emotional state. She needs medical attention – tonight if possible. I'm no expert, but it looks to me as if she's had some kind of breakdown. I can't say whether she'll be prosecuted or not, it will depend on her—' he hesitated and looked down '—on her, er, mental state and on whether the parents will want to press charges. Kidnapping is a very serious crime.'

He didn't know whether to be shocked or relieved. 'I don't know what came over her. It's so out of character.'

'That's women for you, those hormones drive them to do strange things sometimes, but she definitely needs help.'

'I appreciate your frankness,' Mal said, realising he didn't know who to call. 'We haven't needed a doctor since we moved into this neighbourhood. Would you—'

'We have a few numbers on file, if they'd be any help. I can contact someone now if you like. We work with Dr Timmins a lot. She's good at what she does.'

Sandra was still rocking the baby when Mal went back in to the living room. The bangarda had her arm around Sandra's shoulder and was talking softly to her.

'It's for the best, love. Trust me,' Mal said.

'It's time to say goodbye to the little lad,' the sergeant said when he came back in. 'I've asked Dr Timmins to come and see you, she's on her way over now. You'll like her and I'm sure she'll give you something to relax you and help you sleep.'

Sandra passed the baby over silently to the younger bangarda, who said, 'His parents will be delighted to have him back safely, and I hope that you'll have one of your own soon. Try to get some rest and we'll be in touch with you in the next few days.'

As they left, Sandra looked at Mal with despair in her eyes. She seemed vacant and forlorn. He sat next to her and enveloped her in his arms, until the doctor arrived.

* * *

Mal was deep in his memories when the cramp in his shoulder got too bad to ignore. He had to shift to get comfortable, and he tried to move Sandra away from him without disturbing her sleep, but when he moved, she sat up.

'I'm sorry, I didn't mean to waken you,' he said.

'I wasn't asleep. I was remembering bits about the time I spent in hospital – or rather the bits I can remember.'

'Forget it, it's all a long time ago.' He stroked her shoulder. But he knew it wasn't that easy. He didn't forget. He'd never forget the look that told him he had betrayed her. He hadn't had any choice – he'd had to tell his parents, but it broke his heart to see his beautiful young wife locked in a different world to his, sitting staring into space, avoiding his eyes when she could.

'I've put you all through the mill, haven't I?' she said, just as he thought she was drifting off.

'You never set out to do that.'

'I know, but I did all the same, making you lie for me to your bosses and our friends.'

The first breakthrough had come when he'd brought Sandra flowers from their garden, ones that he had grown. She'd smiled as she inhaled their fragrance deeply, her first smile in months. After that, he'd made sure her room was never without fresh flowers, and a supply of chocolate.

The psychiatrist had told him she was suffering from a severe sense of inadequacy and separation despair at losing her child and her family too. And that was now coupled with a very real anxiety around the prospects of having another baby and the fear of not being able to take care of it because, in her mind, she failed so badly the first time. He had felt terrible because he'd been urging her to become pregnant.

'Could that have contributed to what happened?' he'd asked the psychiatrist.

'Possibly to some degree, but you weren't to know the extent of her guilt, and her reasons for not wanting that, misplaced as they were. The burden just became too heavy for her to carry.'

'But she has a job with a lot of responsibility, and she's brilliant at it. How could she keep that up?'

'She did it by compartmentalising her life completely until one day those retaining walls weren't strong enough to hold the pressure in any more, and it all came tumbling in on her. She also locked away the hurt of being separated from her parents and sister, and projected those feelings of rejection on to her son, assuming he would feel that way about her. It's as though by locking them away she could avoid facing them.'

'Will she get better?' Mal had asked. 'Would it help if we were able to find her child or her family?'

'To answer the first part first – yes, we have every hope that she will make a full recovery, but it's not a quick-fix situation,' the psychiatrist had said. 'It'll be slow and she may need to keep going to counselling for some time after she leaves us. She'll need lots of care and affection – she's bound to be fragile after this experience, but we'll not let her go until we're confident that she can cope well. And we'll always be here if she needs us.'

The psychiatrist had told Mal that he would advise against trying to find Peter. 'The child was adopted, for the right or for the wrong reasons, and whether he's happy or not, never mind even traceable at this stage, there is nothing to be gained by finding out his whereabouts or his circumstances. What would that do to your wife or to the boy? No court in the land would take him from his adoptive home and give him back, nor would it be the right thing to do. As regards her family, you could by all means try to locate them, although I don't think we should tell her that you're trying to find them. Another knock back might be one too many right now for her to cope with. We're working with Sandra to accept what has happened and to get her to move on with life. I would advise you do the same.'

'Does all this mean she'll never want children?'

'Would that be a deal breaker for the two of you?' the psychiatrist had asked.

'Absolutely not! I've had a lot of time to think about this. I married Sandra, I love her and we're very good together. If there are always only the two of us then that's plenty for me.'

'It's good to hear you say that, but we would be very hopeful that when your wife has dealt with the past, she will be able to face the future, a totally normal future I might add, and that would probably involve having a family of her own too.'

Mal had thanked the psychiatrist and when he'd gone to see Sandra after that, he'd been more hopeful than he'd been in the two months since she'd been confined in the private clinic.

Chapter Twelve

Kieron had gone out early to get the Saturday paper and run the car through the car wash. Pam was drying Jennifer's hair when the little one said, 'Where did you meet Daddy?'

'We met in Australia.'

'That's not what Ryan told me. He fibbed.'

'I didn't,' Ryan said.

'Yes, you did,' she insisted.

'What did he tell you?'

'He said you met down under in a forest. He wouldn't tell me what you were under.'

'Oh, darling, he was telling you the truth. "Down Under" is another name for Australia, where the kangaroos and koala bears live. You know the way on Ryan's globe you can see where all the countries are? Well, Ireland, where we live, is on one side and Australia is on the other side – down underneath us. I'll show you when I've finished drying your hair.'

'Were you in a forest?'

'Actually we were. We were touring around with different groups of friends and we were going to go on a skywalk. That's where you walk on special narrow bridges way up high in the treetops. It's a very special thing to do.'

'Did you get married in a forest?'

'No, poppet. We stayed around a big campfire that night and the next day he went his way and I went mine – in opposite directions.'

'See, I told you I wasn't fibbing.'

* * *

Pam spotted Kieron as they parked the camper van. He was climbing out of an equally battered vehicle with an Irish flag sticker on the back door and another that said 'Up the Dubs'. He was laughing and their eyes met. She knew she wanted to talk to him. Eventually they did speak, as the two groups merged on the walk and they all went to the same campsite that night. She sat beside him as they ate.

* * *

'There's Daddy,' Jennifer said, running to the kitchen as she heard him come back in.

As she filled their bowls with cereal, Pam told Kieron about the conversation she had just had with their daughter.

'We're like homing pigeons, the Irish, we seem to find each other wherever we go,' he said.

'More like travellers of old, tribes constantly on the move, passing news of each other along the way,' she said. 'You told me about being adopted that night, remember?'

'How did we get around to that, I wonder? I seldom ever volunteered that information to anyone.'

'You probably never thought you'd see me again.' She laughed. 'And then I turned up like the proverbial bad penny at that wedding. And saw you there.'

'I'm glad you did.' He put his arms around her and held her close.

'My rabbit doesn't like muesli,' Jennifer said, pushing her bowl away from her, 'and neither do I.'

'You liked it yesterday, and it's good for you,' Pam reasoned, trying not to turn yet another meal into a battle of wills. It was hard enough these days to get through any meal without a rant from Kieron about the blasted letter. In fairness to him though, so far he was keeping to his promise not to mention it until Monday, and she agreed that nine or ten days, allowing for the vagaries of the post, was enough time for anyone to consider a reply. She wished she had gone around to the house herself and appealed, one to one, to the woman's better nature, but he had vetoed that idea every time she'd suggested it. She should never have mentioned it but just gone ahead and done it.

'I didn't like muesli yesterday. I only ate it because you made me, like you make me take my medicine because it's good for me. I don't like that either.'

Pam knew better than to try to reason with her daughter when she was like this. She glanced at her husband.

'Well, I'm going to have some toast with gooey honey all over it,' Kieron said, 'and I'm going to keep it all for myself. None for Mummy, none for Bunny and none for Jennifer and none for Ryan.' He winked at Pam and made a big deal of putting the bread in the toaster, and then opening the honey pot and letting the golden liquid drip from the wooden dipper. Pam smiled. Jennifer could be a stubborn little monkey when she wanted to be. Kieron's phone rang just as he was putting the toast on his plate. Pam heard the one-way dialogue as he walked into the hallway.

'Yes, that's right. This is Kieron.'

'No ... I thought you weren't going to bother making contact.'

'Yes. We should.'

'Wherever you like.'

'OK, tomorrow. What about Clontarf Castle at twelve?'

'Righto. I'll see you then.'

In the kitchen, Jennifer snatched a piece of toast from her dad's plate and smiled conspiratorially at her mum. Pam smiled back, relaxing as she made sense of the phone call. *If there is a God, thank you*, she thought. *And if you're there, God, let it be all right.*

'Was that who I think it was?' She turned to her husband as he came back into the kitchen.

'Yes, it was.'

'Well?'

He grinned. 'I'm not allowed mention it until Monday ...'

'Stop that and put me out of my misery. What did she sound like?'

'Normal really.'

'What were you expecting?'

'I don't know. I'd given up expecting anything at this stage.'

'Give her a chance, love. Hear her out.'

'I will. I'm meeting her tomorrow.'

'Would you like me to come with you? I'm sure your mam would look after this pair for us.'

'Thanks, love, but this is something I have to do on my own.'

She got up from the table and gave him a hug.

'I can't really believe it. I've waited so long,' he said.

'Who are you going to meet, Dad?' Ryan asked.

'Just someone I haven't seen since I was a baby.'

Chapter Thirteen

'Mum, are you there if I pop over for a cuppa?' Leah asked when she rang the next morning.

'Of course, love. I've no plans. And I've just spoken to Kieron.'

'Oh! That's good, isn't it? How did it go?'

'It was strange, awkward really, but we've arranged to meet tomorrow. I hope it will be easier when we're face to face.'

'I'm sure he felt like that too. OK, I'm on my way, put the kettle on.'

It was only then that Sandra wondered if Adam was coming too. She hadn't asked Leah, and she hoped he wasn't. It was all too personal and although he was her son-in-law, she'd feel less intimidated if he weren't there.

'I don't know which way to turn, Mal. My head's in a spin,' she said after she'd finished talking to Leah.

'You're doing fine, and it's much better for everyone that it's all out in the open. I'll drive you there if you like,' he offered.

'I'd like that, but he might feel it's a bit of an ambush if I arrive with back-up; besides, I need it to be a one-to-one. It just feels like the right thing to do. You can meet him next time, if there is one.'

'Of course there will be. You're both bound to be apprehensive, but it'll be fine, I promise you,' he said.

* * *

'I've loads of questions I want to ask you,' Leah said when she arrived, on her own, and carrying an enormous bunch of flowers.

'That doesn't surprise me.' Sandra smiled, hugging her. 'These are lovely, thank you.'

'Go easy on her,' Mal told his daughter. 'I'll have a coffee with you and then get on with cutting the grass – I'll leave you two girls to chat.'

'You don't have to do that,' Sandra said.

'I know I don't, but I will.'

'Mum, there's so much I don't know about your life and I've been thinking about this all night. I know you worked in London and that you shared a flat with Aunty Tanya and Aunty Pearl, but how did you get there – you were only sixteen, by my reckoning. I don't know why, but I always thought you were much older then, yet when I did the adding up last night I realised you weren't. Whenever we asked your age when we were little you always told us you were twenty-five and Dad was ninety-nine.'

They laughed. 'Typical – making me out to be the old crock. We had to stop telling you that when Ollie came home from school really upset one day because somebody's grandfather had died. He *was* ninety-nine and Ollie thought I was going to die next,' Mal said. 'She might have only been thirteen, Leah, but she'd done a lot of growing up by then. She'd had to ... but I'll let your mum fill you in on the rest.'

'What made you go to England?'

'I ran away from the French family I had been working for and I stayed in a hostel in Dublin for a few days. I met some country girls there, who were eighteen, and who had all the contacts for places to stay in London. I told them I was an orphan and I wanted to go with them.'

Leah interrupted. 'Why did you run away and why did you say that?'

'I'll tell you the reason I fled later. As regards claiming to be an orphan, I said that because I felt like one, and I was afraid I'd be found and made go back to the French family. It also stopped the two girls from asking questions. I pretended that I was seventeen. We took the boat to Holyhead from Dún Laoghaire, brought lemonade and a load of tomato sandwiches for the journey, and then took the night train to London. The sandwiches were a big mistake, they were sodden messes when we opened them, but we ate them all the same. Anytime I see a tomato sandwich since I'm reminded of that journey– "the big adventure" the other two kept calling it. I suppose it was, although I was terrified.'

'But did you know anyone over there?'

'Not a soul, but then I knew very few back here either.'

'How did you afford the fare? Had you any money?'

'Funnily enough I had. The Fourniers paid me every week and they put that in the post office. I took it out and put it in the post office in London and I was lucky enough to get a job quickly – in Selfridges on Saturdays. I met your Aunty Tanya and Aunty Pearl, who, as you always remind me, are not your real aunties, at a secretarial college and we decided to share a flat with some others.'

'Miss Fothergill's Academy for Professional Ladies,' Leah said.

'Yes, the redoubtable Miss Fothergill – I've told you about her lots of times.'

'I know, but I never joined all the dots before. I didn't know you had a secret then – a very big secret. There are bits of your life I know absolutely nothing about.'

'I know, and I'm truly sorry about that.'

'Don't be, but tell me what happened when you got there?'

'I knew I needed some formal certification if I was to get a better job, or "position" as Miss Fothergill called it, so I put everything into that course.'

Sandra had figured that it was worth dipping in to her rainy-day money to get those qualifications. As it stood then, her CV would never make it to the top of the pile anywhere.

> Fluent French. Capable of folding napkins into swans and lotus blossom shapes. Plays Chopin tolerably. Good at making choux and puff pastry. Creative at flower arranging. Gets on well with children. No school certificates and no qualifications.

It didn't offer much competition against those with O levels and lightning speeds in shorthand and typing.

'Tanya and Pearl were always in trouble for not taking their lessons seriously enough. When we had our etiquette lessons, they used to say you'd swear we were being primed to work for the Queen.'

'When we had our etiquette lessons ...' Leah laughed. 'It sounds like something from Jane Austen.'

'I'm serious,' Sandra said. 'We had etiquette lessons where we were schooled and groomed in interview techniques. Miss Fothergill sent Tanya outside in the rain to walk around the block ten times because she'd asked how often were we going to be talking to earls and dukes, much less writing to the Right Honourable or the Left Honourable or the Upside-Down Dis-honourables of this world?'

'Miss Fothergill sounds like a right old bat.'

'She was, but her heart was in the right place, and she did have the right connections. She would have been horrified if she'd seen the dingy, damp and dilapidated digs we lived in, but we moved out when we all got jobs – good jobs – because of her. Even though she refused to acknowledge that old-fashioned typewriters would soon be a thing of the past, we all wanted to work where they had electric ones. They were the latest in technology in the seventies!'

Sandra recalled how while she hadn't really known what she'd wanted to do, she'd known she didn't want to spend her life working in financial services.

She told Leah, 'Every morning, Miss Fothergill recited her mantra: "Gels, you must always remember that behind every successful businessman, there's an efficient personal secretary. And, gels, she's as indispensable to him as a good wife." Her other gem of wisdom was: "Gels, you do not go to work – factory gels work – young ladies go to business." It was quite normal to expect your boss to be male then, but, as you know, I ended up working for a woman – two, actually. I was earning a decent salary, for the first time ever, and I was working in the glitzy, glamorous world of publishing. London was a heady place to be.'

'You sound as though you were happy then,' Leah said.

'I was, for the most part, but I was never free of all the lies I had told. No one knew about Peter – sorry, Kieron. It's hard to get used to thinking of him as a Kieron. They knew nothing about me either.'

'Were you never tempted to tell anyone?'

'Never, until I met your dad. I was too ashamed of how I had lost him and the fact that I hadn't a clue where he was. I thought it would get easier, but it didn't. I used to have to stop myself looking at mothers and babies on the Tube, but I always knew I'd have to come back and look for him. Don't get me wrong. The girls and I had good times together. The work was intoxicating.'

'Did you have boyfriends? Was there anyone special?'

'Of course I had, but I never let anyone get close to me. I wasn't very comfortable with male company.'

'Mum, you didn't make it clear last night – and I didn't like to ask – but you were only thirteen when you became pregnant. Were you raped?'

'I was, and I was only twelve when it happened. You don't need to know the details. No one does, and they don't matter now. Whenever the girls teased me about not wanting to get serious with anyone, I pretended I had someone I liked back home. Pearl used to call him the "secret lover back in Ireland", and my attitude was to let them think whatever they liked. I was never going to tell them. Outwardly, I made sure I came across as being carefree and happy-go-lucky. They never saw that inside I was quite broken and terribly lonely.'

'That must have been really hard for you. I can't imagine what I would have done if that happened to me.'

'I'm glad you never had to find out.' She paused. 'I'd hate to give the impression that my life was full of despair. It wasn't all bad. I had some lucky breaks too. The publishing house was in a flux when I began working there. It was in the throes of relocating to larger, swankier premises. Marcie, the boss, was a diminutive five foot two inches, but her presence was enough to scare even the butchest of guys on the staff. But she championed us women, which was unusual enough for the time. It was all first names. Miss Fothergill would have had a stroke at the lack of formality. No 'Mr' and 'Miss', like most other work places, which is just as well considering no one in that country can spell, never mind pronounce, "Mac Giolla Tighearnaigh" anyway.'

'Can you blame them for getting that mouthful wrong?' laughed Leah. 'But it's kind of romantic having an unusual name.'

'Maybe, if it's something like Dominique or Jasmina. I used to say I'd only marry a man with a nice name, one that went with Sandra, and Tanya who was blazing a trail for women's lib used to go mad, telling me it was the seventies. No woman had to take her husband's name any more. That appealed to me as I believed it might make it easier for my son to find me – and for my sister too, if either ever wanted to.'

'But you took Dad's name.'

'I did. I liked the sound of Sandra Wallace! I'd have taken it no matter what he had been called. That's what being in love does!'

Sandra thought about the hectic world she'd lived in. 'It was multi-tasking before anyone ever used that word.'

Initially, she'd filled in where needed and picked up publishing know-how along the way. She'd watched the others in the various offices, the way they wore their hair and their clothes, and she'd started to develop a style of her own.

'Of course, I was flavour of the month with the girls in the digs, sharing some of the perks with them. Samples of cosmetics, hair products, fashions, chocolates and household knick-knacks flooded in and we got to look through the sample box, though only when the senior staff had taken what they wanted. As for the flood of newly published books that arrived weekly, they were relegated to a disused room where they seemed to breed.'

Sandra laughed as she remembered. 'It was because of them that I got my break at work – and Marcie's rarely given approval. I organised a monthly book sale in the company canteen and spent a week of lunchtimes moving and sorting the stacks of new books. I pinned notices all around the offices.

Coffee table and hardbacks – all £1
Paperbacks – 50 pence each

I placed a prominently marked honesty box in the centre of the table and, within a week, the books had been sold and the proceeds lodged to Barnardo's. In the following month's publication, my name appeared in the list of credits as "editorial assistant". I remember going into the local newsagent and opening some of the magazines, just to read it. At times like that, I really wished I had someone back home to send them to, someone who would be proud of me.'

'That's so sad,' Leah said. 'Did you keep any of them?'

'No, when I left London I left them behind too.'

'I don't know how you kept it all together, Mum, pretending everything was normal.'

'I did it by throwing myself into the work and not allowing myself time to wallow in self-pity.' She paused again. 'You know better than anyone, Leah, how the magazine and advertising world works. There are always deadlines to meet and crises to overcome, and they can be a great way to duck out of reality.' She fixed her daughter with a knowing look. 'And if I'm not misreading the signs, you seem to have been doing a bit of that yourself lately. Is everything OK between you and Adam?'

'You know me too well,' Leah said. 'We had a bit of a disagreement over something, but it's OK now. It's nothing for you to worry about.'

'It might not be, but you look worn out, and you've not been yourself since your anniversary. Would you prefer if your dad and I didn't go to Tasmania with you, so you can have some time together? We can go another time.'

'Of course not, Mum,' she replied, a little too quickly, Sandra thought.

Then Leah said, 'Are you trying to change the subject? I'm supposed to be asking the questions here. If you were happy in London, why did you come back?'

'I suppose I felt too far away from where my baby was in all probability growing up. I always felt there was something lacking and that one day he'd come back into my life – I didn't know how or where, but it wasn't going to happen if I lived in London. You've no idea what that was like. Wondering. Was he living in a block of flats somewhere? Or in the country? Or in a nice house near the sea? Was he happy? Did he know he was adopted? Did he know anything about me? Would he ever even know my name?'

'Was there was no way you could find out anything?'

'None whatever back then. It all became much more in the open in the nineties and since all those revelations. I wrote countless letters to the convent, often enclosing a note for him in case he came looking when he grew up, but I never got a reply to any of them. I don't know if they were ever opened or just destroyed.'

'That was cruel.'

'It was worse than that, Leah. It was inhuman and the longer I stayed in London, the more separated I felt. I spent three days enjoying a wonderful family Christmas in the country with Pearl's family surrounded by love and laughter, squabbles and enormous home-cooked meals, and that was when I made up mind that it was time to go back.'

She'd told the girls a few days later, when they were stripping their balding tree of its ornaments. It had been decorated with freebies from work – navy and silver baubles that were 'so last year' that no one else had wanted them. She'd taken a box of orange ones too. She still had one of them. Tanya had called her a deserter and Pearl lamented the fact that they'd get no more freebies and would have to pay for their eyeliner and mascara when Sandra had gone.

Sandra had worked out her notice and contacted a hostel in Dublin to arrange a room. Then, she'd packed her belongings – mostly clothes, some few treasured books and a fistful of snaps of Tanya and Pearl, and the one of her and her sister Louise.

'I remember telling my friends that although I didn't have an awful lot then, one day I'd have my own home – and there'd be no chipped Formica worktops or wobbly chair legs, the dishes would match and all the rings would work on the cooker! I can still see Pearl standing there telling me not to forget the chandeliers and the grand piano, a wealthy hubby and a load of children running around. I nearly broke down and told them about Kieron then. I could never have more children. How could I? No one would ever replace the one I'd lost.'

'But you had us.'

'I know, and I'm so glad I did.'

'So am I,' her daughter said, 'but you had to start all over again. How old were you then?'

'I was just gone twenty when I came back to Ireland. If my life had turned out differently, I'd probably have been finishing a degree in UCD at that stage. I didn't even know if Louise went there. She could still have been there for all I knew. She was very clever. But I realised that although I was going back to Dublin, there was no going back to my past. I dreaded telling Marcie that I was leaving, but she took me completely by surprise by offering to give me a contact of hers in contract publishing back here. When I got back, I got in touch with this woman, Erica Doyle, and we arranged a meeting in the coffee shop in the National Art Gallery in Merrion Square.'

'Are you two still nattering?' Mal asked as he came in from cutting the grass. 'You must know everything there is to know by now.'

'Not nearly. Mum's been filling me in on her life before she came back to Ireland.'

'She hasn't told you how she threw herself at me yet, has she?' he laughed. 'She did, honestly, didn't you?'

Sandra laughed at him. 'Make yourself useful and put the percolator on again. We need more coffee.'

It was true. Sandra had wanted to get to the National Gallery first, to relax and compose herself, but in her haste she tripped ingloriously on the entrance steps and the contents of her handbag spewed around her. A serious-looking man coming out tried to stop her fall, but he was too late. He bent down to help her to her feet.

'She insisted only her pride was hurt and dashed off for her interview. I thought she looked great, despite the laddered stockings and bloodied hand,' he told Leah with a grin.

'Apparently, Marcie had given me a glowing recommendation. She'd told Erica that I was someone who could think on my feet. God knows I'd had plenty of practice doing that. I couldn't take my eyes off Erica as she filled me in on what they did. Everything about her exuded an energy and confidence that showed she was in control. Her eyes were a lovely pale grey and her hair was beautifully cut, her nails buffed and her accessories matched. I'd never have put her in a job writing about banal subjects like what was hot in screwdrivers and jackhammers and the like.'

'She was a foxy lady all right,' Mal said, bringing fresh coffee over to the table.

'All the men fancied her.'

'I never fancied her. I only had eyes for you,' he said, touching her shoulder affectionately.

'Contract publishing wasn't as sexy or glamorous as fashion and gossip, but it had its moments and the salary was really good. That's how I found myself working after only being back a week and then your dad walked into my life, or rather I walked in to his office – he only came in every second Friday to do the books.'

'She didn't even recognise me!'

'That's true, but you've heard all this before,' Sandra said. 'How he swept me off my feet in a whirlwind courtship.' She laughed at him.

'Yeah, but not in sequence. And I wouldn't have put you down as being the impetuous sort, Dad.'

'I was afraid someone else would get there before me.'

'But you were happy then?'

'Of course I was happy. I had it all, your dad, our own little house, a challenging job, but that wasn't to last. I had a nervous breakdown a year after we married. I just snapped one day when it all got too much for me.' Sandra's voice cracked. 'And I did something terrible, something that hurt a lot of people.'

Leah stood up and went over to Sandra. 'Mum, I can't imagine you doing anything deliberately to hurt anyone. And I'm sorry – I didn't mean to upset you.'

'You didn't. It's not you, love. It's just that – I haven't talked about this for a long time and ...'

'Well, let's leave it there. You can tell me another time, if you want to. No pressure, Mum, I promise.'

Mal intervened. 'I think that's a good idea, what with your mum meeting Kieron tomorrow and the stress of that. Maybe we should go down to the pub for a bit of lunch. Ollie phoned me while I was in the garden. He's going to pop over, I'll text him and tell him to meet us there.'

'I'll put these things away. Mum, you go and put your face on.'

Sandra gave Leah a long hug and went upstairs to get ready.

'What did I do to deserve such a caring daughter?' Sandra asked herself as she changed for their impromptu pub lunch. She looked again at the photograph hanging on her bedroom wall. It had been taken shortly after she'd met Mal, and she smiled as she remembered how quickly her life had changed.

Chapter Fourteen

1980, Dublin

Sandra was rushing to get her work finished one Friday afternoon, when Erica asked her to bring the sales figures through to the accounts department. 'Who gets these?' she asked, holding up the folders as she walked into the accounts office.

'They're for Mal over there,' a bubbly brunette said, nodding in his direction. 'And, Sandra, we usually go into Keoghegan's for a drink to start the weekend off on the right note, do you want to join us?'

'I'd love to,' she said. Flat-hunting could wait until the next day.

She handed the files to Mal. He seemed vaguely familiar, but she didn't know how she'd know him. She hadn't met anyone apart from her new colleagues. He obviously reminded her of someone she'd known in London.

'I'll wait for you in reception at half five,' Grace said as she left.

Sandra didn't enjoy going back to her hostel every night, either stopping for a sandwich on the way or buying one to eat in her room. Apart from the odd pleasantry, the other residents didn't really engage with her at all, and that suited her. She wouldn't have to answer awkward questions and, anyway, she'd be out of there as soon as she could.

Keoghegan's was packed and smoky when Grace and Sandra

walked in. Some of their colleagues had got there beforehand and had bagged two tables beside each other.

'Do you know everyone yet?' asked Grace.

'She doesn't know me,' a voice behind her said.

Sandra turned. 'I do, I saw you today – in accounts – Mal, isn't it?'

'That's right, but we weren't introduced properly. I don't know who you are, except you're the new girl. Although we have met before, but you didn't give me your name then either.'

'Have we? I don't recall. I'm Sandra Mac Giolla Tighearnaigh and you're …?'

'Malachy Wallace – Mal to my friends.'

'Did we meet in London?'

'No, but let me just say I don't expect the same greeting as the last time – when you threw yourself at my feet.'

She felt her cheeks redden as she remembered. 'The National Gallery – on my way to the interview. You were the man who helped me up.'

He smiled. 'I see you got the job. Congratulations.'

'I didn't know you worked there.'

'I don't and I do,' he told her. 'I work for their accountants. I only come in every two weeks to keep the books in order, but they let me join them for the Friday-night drinks when I do. So this must be destiny or fate or whatever they call it, bumping in to you twice.'

They joined the others and they filled her in on the office gossip. The pub quietened a bit as the after-work crowd thinned out.

'I'm starving. Can we go somewhere to eat?' he asked.

Sandra agreed, already trusting this tall, quiet guy with soft eyes and an easy smile.

'I have to be in by eleven,' she told him, after they'd eaten and talked a whole lot more.

He looked surprised. 'A very strict papa?'

'No, nothing like that. Just hostel rules. I need to find a flat and I need to find it soon. I have a few to look at tomorrow.'

He suggested she ask in the office, telling her these things are often found by word of mouth – it was something she hadn't thought about.

He saw her to her lodgings. 'Well, I got you back before the clock strikes, so you won't turn into a pumpkin or anything like that!'

She laughed and told him she'd really enjoyed the evening. He said he had too, but she was disappointed when he made no suggestion about seeing her again.

She found it difficult to sleep that night. She couldn't get his voice out of her head – or his face or his pale-grey eyes or his hands or what he'd said or even the fact that she could talk for so long to anyone. She realised he was the first man for years who she felt totally at ease with.

She viewed some flats the next day, but they were all dingy, rundown and dilapidated, and reminded her of her first digs in London. She knew she could never live in any of them. With mouldy grouting and stained shower curtains, they made the chipped Formica in London seem classy. Disheartened, she marvelled at how landlords could get away with putting such places on the market. They weren't suitable for anyone to live in.

* * *

'You were getting on very well with a certain Mr Wallace on Friday,' Val, the receptionist said as she came in on Monday morning. Sandra laughed. 'What time did you go home at?'

'Early, and I wouldn't call it home exactly. I'm in a hostel that I thought was pretty basic until I saw what was on offer under the guise of flats at the weekend. I had hoped to get a place of my own, but I'm beginning to think that's a bit ambitious. The modern ones are out of my price range, so I'll probably have to share.'

'Why don't you stick a notice up on the board in the kitchen – someone's bound to know of someone or somewhere decent. Maybe even both,' Val laughed, giving Sandra a wink.

By Wednesday, she had found a flat to share with a girl from sales that was within walking distance of the office. 'Ironically,' Jo had said as she showed Sandra around the flat, 'my previous flatmate is moving to London to seek her fortune and you've come back to find yours.'

'I hope it's as easy as that,' Sandra laughed.

'I'm out on the road a fair bit, so you'll have the place to yourself a lot. No wild parties mind, not without me being there. The neighbours are OK and they like to be invited. They have lots of dishy friends and they know how to throw a party too. So what do you think? Could you see yourself sharing here with me?'

Sandra had already visualised herself living there, and had worked out the sums in her head. The rent was more than she had expected but with no bus fares and her raise in salary, she'd be able to afford it. A holiday might become a reality too. Yes, she'd decided, she could well afford it. Jo had shaken Sandra's hand to seal the deal, and she'd agreed to move in the following weekend.

As the week went on, Sandra was surprised that she hadn't heard from Mal. She had felt sure he would call. She stopped herself from mentioning his name and from asking questions about him. On Friday, she looked into accounts in the hope he'd be there, but his desk was empty. She didn't go to Keoghegan's with the others, using her house move the next day as an excuse. Instead, she packed up her things and wrote to her friends in London.

I have my own room. There's a huge built-in wardrobe just waiting to be filled, I have my own shower but there's a bathroom too and I can use

that if I want to have a soak. And there's plenty of
space for visitors. And the cooker works. And I met
a dishy fellow – but that didn't work!

She sealed the envelope, realising that this was the first personal
letter she had written in years. She stuck the stamp on it. It felt good.
Her next letter gave the girls more details.

Of course I miss you both, but life is good here and
I'm glad I came back. The flat is super – I luv it. Jo
is a hoot – you'll like her and she's tidy (not that
I'm comparing her to anyone in particular, Tanya!).
I treated myself to new bed linen and lamps at the
weekend.

The job, or 'being in business' as Miss Fothergill
would call it, is working out well too. I'm really
enjoying it AND I can stay in bed an hour longer
each day because it's only a ten-minute walk to the
office. They are nice people to work with and they
didn't make me feel like the new girl at all. A few of
us went to the cinema on Tuesday, some subtitled
French film which was very, very dark and not really
enjoyable at all.

Oh, and I have a date on Saturday night … with the
fellow who I thought wasn't interested in me. Yes,
he's the one I mentioned before – the one I did my
dying swan act in front of on the way to my interview.
Apparently, he went to the pub the previous Friday
to find me, but I hadn't gone that night. Anyway, he
asked me out!! Will keep you posted … then again,
I might not!

Sandra did keep Pearl and Tanya up to speed with her romance, her first really serious one. She always felt in her heart that what had happened to her when she was much younger had nothing to do with love and that if, and when, she met the right person, it would feel right. She fervently hoped it would.

And with Mal, it did feel right. It felt *so* right, the closeness, the bond, the way she smiled when she thought about him, and the loving. It all fitted perfectly. But she never felt comfortable talking casually about sex, the way the girls in London had. She and Jo were discussing this one night after watching an old black-and-white film on their little television.

'After all that passion and raw desire, and all he did was kiss her chastely on the lips – her closed lips – before he left,' Jo said.

'I saw a programme once about the studios and they had codes of conduct or ethics or something like that, that forbade them from showing lustful embraces. One of the couple had to have one foot on the floor at all times in bedroom scenes to prevent horizontal positions.'

'You can't be serious,' said Jo.

'Absolutely. There was a mermaid scene in one which had to be cut for screening in the States, back in the early days, because her tail was on the bed and not touching the floor,' Sandra said.

'I find that hard to believe, I mean a mermaid ...'

'I know. They weren't allowed show toilets either. I think it was the French who broke all those taboos. Who were they protecting? I mean, we all have to use them.'

'People really did have skewed ideas of morality then. Sure weren't half those stars sleeping around despite their virginal reputations?' said Jo. 'My mother, whom I never saw in her bra and panties, incidentally, was always on at us about modesty, even between us sisters.'

'That sounds familiar,' laughed Sandra. 'When I went to London first and began sharing, I was mortified when the girls in the flat stripped off and changed in front of each other. They used to tease me about that too, about my prudish Catholic attitude to nudity. Living with an ultra-conservative grandmother didn't help my inhibitions. She used to tell us that our bodies were "the temples of the Holy Ghost", and we had to keep them "pure and undefiled". Sure we hadn't a clue what that meant.'

They laughed, and Jo said, 'Thank God those dark ages are gone. Could you imagine marrying someone you had never slept with?'

'No,' said Sandra. She had often thought about this when she listened to the talk in the office between the girls who had 'done it' and those who hadn't, mainly because of the fear of getting pregnant.

'It's about time they allowed condoms go on sale here without prescriptions and all the cloak and dagger stuff about bona fide family planning. I wouldn't fancy taking the pill long term, would you?' Jo said. 'You wouldn't know what it would do to you. And I don't want to have a gaggle of kids.'

Sandra agreed, but if the pill were the price to pay for prevention, then she'd be willing to take her chances. She'd do whatever it took to ensure she would never be pregnant again. She was sure Tanya or Pearl would help her there.

* * *

Mal was the first man she felt she could go all the way with, given what had happened to her when she was twelve, although deciding to do it was a bit like standing on a springboard, looking down at the water below, not knowing if she had the courage to jump, and, if she did, would she surface again safely? The thought of it terrified her. She had held off a few times, but her instincts told her that he understood and he hadn't pressured her until she told him she was ready.

Mal still lived at home and, when it happened, Jo was away

on one of her sales trips, so they had the place to themselves. She hadn't felt the panic she had feared she would, but she had felt other emotions – good emotions that made her soul feel as if it were flying, soaring and gliding with pleasure and desire and then there was the wonderful feeling of release and of having shared something tender and beautiful. She had never felt like this before. She told Mal as they lay, limbs still entwined, that she felt she had come home.

After that, they both looked forward to their special intimate time together.

On one such night, they had just enjoyed an hour of passion when he turned on his back and said, 'Sandra, I love you and I want to marry you, more than anything in the world.'

'I want that too, but you don't really know me. We've only been going out for eight months.'

'I know all I need to know. You'll be twenty-one in a few weeks' time, and I'd love to put a ring on your finger that day, if you'll let me. What do you think?'

'I'm astonished and flattered. Are we not rushing things a bit, are we not too young?'

'I don't think so. I'm twenty-five and I'm ready to settle down. My parents married when they were twenty and twenty-three.'

'Mine were not much older,' she said, catching herself off-guard. She normally never mentioned them to anyone. 'And I'd love to marry you, but—'

'Is that a big "but" telling me I have no hope, or a little "but" that'll allow me some?'

'Only you can decide on that. I'm not playing hard to get. I would love to marry you, Mal, more than anything else in the world.'

'Then let's announce our engagement at your party. We'll be saving for a while before we tie the knot anyway, even with my promotion. What do you think?' He ran the back of his fingers gently down from her neck to her breast and finally to her flat stomach. She felt herself responding instantly, arching to his touch. She sighed and moved closer, her hands exploring his body. She loved the smell of him, clean, fresh and masculine, and how soft his hair felt at the back of his neck and on his chest.

'You're very persuasive,' she murmured.

'And has it worked?'

'In lots of ways yes, but – and this is a really big but – there is something I have to tell you and I'll understand if, after that, you want to change your mind and never see me again.'

'That sounds drastic but it's not going to happen. Nothing will change my mind – unless there's a husband hidden away somewhere, who'll come back to steal you from me.'

'It's not a husband – it's a son, Peter.' She watched Mal intently as she divulged her secret to someone else for the first time. She scrutinised his expression forensically, testing him. If he could accept her past, she'd accept a future with him. If he couldn't, then this was the time to walk away, no matter how hard it would be. It was a lot to ask but no one was going to make her deny him again.

'A son! Where is he? Why have you never mentioned him before?'

'I don't know where he is, but I'd give anything to find him – or just to know he is all right. I didn't mention him because I never tell anyone.'

'I'm not just anyone.'

'I know – that's why I've just told you.'

Mal stayed over that night and they talked until the dawn began stretching luminous fingers across the dark sky. She told him what had happened, dredging up all the details, some that she had locked away and hadn't allowed in her headspace in the intervening years. He held her and let her talk.

'I promise you, Sandra, this doesn't make the slightest difference to how I feel about you. I love you with my whole being and can't imagine life without you in it. Knowing what you just told me only makes me want to look after you all the more. You've had to do so much growing up so quickly – and by yourself – I just want to protect you and mind you. I promise you, you'll always have my total love and support. We'll try to find out where Peter is too, if that's possible.'

'When you put it like that, how could I refuse? I love you too, Mal, with my whole heart and soul. What did I do to deserve you?' she asked.

'I hope you'll always feel like that.' He kissed her. 'Now I really do have to go home and change for the office. I'll see you this evening. You've missed out on too much fun. We have a party to plan and you have to meet my parents before I tell them you'll be joining the family.'

'Do we have to tell them about Peter? I'd rather not,' Sandra said. 'Maybe in the future.'

'Then, we won't. You needn't worry about that. Your secret's safe with me.'

* * *

Jo went into overdrive organising Sandra's twenty-first. Pearl and Tanya came over from London – Sandra hadn't an inkling that Mal had invited them. Mal's parents were the only guests who knew about his plan to propose. When the cake had been produced and the candles blown out, Sandra closed her eyes and made a wish. When she opened them, she saw Mal watching her. He was the only one who could guess what she wanted more than anything, and it felt good knowing that he'd be with her no matter what life threw at them.

'This looks so gorgeous I hate cutting it,' she said as she poised the knife.

Mal smiled at her and announced, 'Hopefully the next time we are all together we'll be cutting our wedding cake.' He went down

on one knee and slipped the ring on her finger. It was beautiful and
fitted perfectly.

'I love it. I love it. I love it.' She laughed, extending her hand to
view it better, admiring the way it caught the light and seemed to
twinkle. It was a three-stone setting – two matched diamonds with a
larger deep blue sapphire in the centre. Later when they were alone
he told her, 'The sapphire is for your little boy, wherever he is.'

She burst into tears.

'I didn't mean that to upset you.'

'It hasn't. It's just such an unexpected and thoughtful gesture and
it means more than I could ever tell you.' She rubbed the precious
stone pensively.

'We better not have too many kids of our own, or it could turn
out to be an expensive tradition I've just started,' he laughed.

She didn't look up at him. She hadn't told him that there weren't
going to be any more children. Mal's mother was as excited as she
was about the wedding. 'I'm tired of listening to my friends making
arrangements with and for their daughters' big days so it's great to be
allowed help out with yours,' she said.

'It's great for me to have you as well,' Sandra replied, genuinely
fond of this motherly woman who should have had a dozen kids, but
who had been denied the chance by a series of miscarriages.

'Well, you'll soon be my daughter and the mother of my
grandchildren – that makes you very special.'

Sandra felt panic rising, but said nothing.

'Don't look so scared,' she laughed. 'I promise I won't be one of
those interfering mothers-in-law, who'll smother you both. Between
you and me, I had one of those and it used to drive me mad. Actually,
it drove the two of us mad. What Mrs Wallace said, Mrs Wallace
got.'

'She sounds like a real control freak,' Sandra said.

'She was, but she wouldn't admit it. She said she just wanted the best for her son – and that wasn't me. In fairness, it wouldn't have been any woman. So, believe me, I know how to keep my distance, but I want you to know that I'm always here if you ever need me.' She squeezed Sandra's arm. 'For what it's worth, I think he made a very good choice too.'

Sandra longed to be able to talk to someone about her real feelings, about how she really wanted her sister to be her bridesmaid, like they had planned when they saw weddings in their local church, and how she would have liked to have her father walk her down the aisle, and not Mal's dad. But she couldn't, because it would mean having to explain why they weren't around and she wasn't prepared to do that.

These tinges of regret vanished when she started to walk up the aisle and saw Mal standing waiting for her, his face breaking into a broad grin as their eyes connected and he reached a hand to her.

The photographs showed how happy they were that day, and she often laughed through the years at how it was the hairstyles that dated them, not the clothes so much. They moved in with Mal's parents and she found it strangely familiar yet bittersweet to be part of a family setup again. Mealtimes reminded her of sitting around the big kitchen table in Mayo, with her and Louise pushing and shoving and laughing at things their gran said, while her father regaled them with the latest news from the school and her mother served up mouth-watering meals. It also reminded her of happy meals later on in the Fourniers' kitchen, learning the French terms for all the ingredients from her young charges and teaching them the English words.

They had already put a deposit down on a house, thanks to help from Mal's parents, and were waiting for it to be finished. 'It's like a toy town,' Mal had commented as he and Sandra studied the model of a completed development of new houses. It was of an estate of identical rows of identical three-bedroomed houses in identical closes, crescents and cul-de-sacs, which the blurb described as in a semi-rural setting of south county Dublin. It was in Ballinteer

and they were as excited as though they were buying into a stately
mansion.

The model showed landscaped front gardens and there were Lego-
like ornamental trees in the verges and two miniature cars parked in
each driveway. 'Two cars. We should be so lucky,' Sandra said.

'They kind of stretched the meaning of landscaping in those
models,' Mal said to his dad as they studied their sparsely seeded
patchy front lawns and un-dug back gardens, the odd token tree
struggling to gain purchase in the baldy verges on the roads. 'On
the plus side, it's a great way to become friends with the neighbours.
We're all out there sweating like pit ponies discussing the best thing
to do, while our wives are inside drinking coffee and getting to know
each other. The country lads are all for sowing potatoes the first year
to purify the soil or something like that. Can you imagine me with
a crop of roosters or Kerr's Pinks?'

'We never saw you as being a bit of a farmer, and in Dublin 16!'
They laughed.

'Is this what maturity is, Da? A few months ago, I didn't even
know what renovators did. Now I even know where to go to hire
them.'

'There's a bit more to it than that.'

The first weekend's digging produced a crop of granite boulders, a
boot and a blue-and-white-striped mug, fully intact, a lace-less shoe,
bits of metal and no less than three horseshoes.

'That's for luck,' said Mal, when he unearthed the first one.

'You have to turn it the other way up,' Sandra said, 'or the luck
runs out.'

'I never heard that,' Mal said. 'Why are they supposed to be lucky
anyway?'

'I haven't a clue, but we'll keep it just in case. No need to tempt
fate.'

'You know, I quite like this physical work – I never thought I would. I even have blisters. It's made me realise just how much part of a cycle we all are. We start as a seed, then we grow, live out our given life span and then we wither, if we're not eaten, that is.'

'That's very deep for a Sunday afternoon – and not very optimistic,' Sandra said. 'But I think I can promise you that's not how you'll meet your end. No one's going to eat you, but I'm looking forward to being able to pick fresh peas and lettuces from the vegetable patch.'

'Don't get carried away, Miss Mac Giolla Tighearnaigh, or should I say Mrs Wallace. You said you wanted flowers and that's what you'll get, if they'll grow for me, and a lawn for our kids to play on.'

'Of course they'll grow.' She smiled confidently at her husband, hiding yet again that she never intended to bring another child into this world. She had forfeited the right to consider herself worthy of that task.

When the in-laws came by, Sandra could see them eyeing her waistline, as her mother-in-law enquired not so discreetly, 'Any news?' Sandra ignored the question and always told them about her latest project or crisis at work, tickets they had got for some gig or other, and Mal downplayed his work as he always did. 'You know accountancy – it's not like the publishing world, so it's not exactly filled with gossip.'

One day, though, he did have something to tell them. 'I have applied for another job – it's more money, more responsibility and I had the first interview today.'

'That's great news. Moving up the ladder and all that. I'm proud of you. When will you know?' his father asked.

'Sometime next week, but I think it went well.'

Mal made no secret of the fact that he was looking forward to being a father. He didn't see the point in waiting, and most of his friends had already embarked on and embraced parenthood. When he got the new job, he rushed to tell Sandra, 'It's almost twice what I'm earning now. That will make it much easier when we start a family and have to think about education costs and all the rest of it.'

She laughed, before saying, 'Don't get carried away.'

How could she ever bring another child into the world, when she had failed as a mother to the baby she'd already had?

* * *

'We'll be able to put some money by to change the car,' Mal said as he sorted the household bills at the end of his first month in his new job.

'I'm really proud of you,' Sandra told him, admiring his thoroughness. 'We're not even a year married, and you're talking about changing the car. And I think you're great, the way you slotted in so easily at Cradock's. That was a big promotion.'

'It wasn't that difficult really. It might be a much larger operation, but it's well organised, and there's quite a buzz about being given sole responsibility for my own clients.'

That night though, they had another row, about the only issue that ever caused tension between them – starting a family. They had made love and were lying together afterwards. Their neighbours three doors up had just announced their good news and Sandra felt that there was pressure coming at her from all angles. Would Mal feel totally rejected if she told him how she really felt?

* * *

In Sandra's office, they had just put the hardware trade magazine to bed and were focused on trying to meet a deadline for a glossy publication for a group of estate agents, when she noticed that some photos had been duplicated. The correct ones were missing from one of the full-page colour adverts. Sandra volunteered to go to their head office in Baggot Street at lunchtime and pick up the replacement artwork. She wanted to get out for a while. She needed to think, which was next to impossible in the oversized storage room that they all referred to as the canteen. She and Mal had had yet another of *those* conversations the night before. She would admit to herself that she was feeling broody – but she wasn't going to get pregnant.

Their argument went round and round in her head as she walked towards Baggot Street. Whenever she heard that street name mentioned she was transported back to that fateful day when they handed Peter over to complete strangers. She could still vividly see the little hand and perfect fingers opening and closing randomly. How could she not have known …?

'Do you think it's too early to be checked out to see if there's a problem?' Mal had asked.

'Probably. Let's wait a few more months and see what happens,' she'd replied. She hadn't told him she was on the pill. She'd asked Tanya to post them to her in her workplace.

'I don't mind being tested if that's what it takes,' he'd volunteered.

'I know, but let's give it a bit more time.' She wasn't happy about deceiving him. She had promised they'd have no secrets and she'd meant it, but this was different.

Their next-door neighbours had become new parents in the past few weeks, a honeymoon baby, they boasted, and, of course, they had invited them in to inspect their little marvel. They were just two of several neighbours who had all moved in to this enclave of suburbia around the same time and who were already starting families.

Over the garden wall on the clothesline, pastel-coloured babygros and tiny vests danced to the whims of the breeze in un-choreographed moves. Sandra found herself looking at them with envy; she'd almost broken down when she went shopping for a gift for the little one. She hadn't expected it to be so hard to keep her promise to herself.

She woke in the middle of the night and could hear the new-born's cries through the adjoining wall. It wasn't the first time that had happened. She found herself waiting and listening. Her reaction was visceral. She was back in nursery in the convent, and she felt lonely and lost again, the way she had for a very long time after losing Peter. What was happening to her? She loved Mal above everything else, but sometimes as she lay beside him listening, she wondered if it was enough.

When Peter had cried in the middle of the night, who had been there to pick him up and snuggle him?

* * *

Sandra hadn't returned to the office by two or three or four. Phone calls to the company verified that she had indeed collected the relevant material and signed for it, at one twenty-five, but she hadn't come back.

When Jo returned from her meeting, Erica was like a person possessed. 'If we miss this deadline, we can kiss goodbye to the rest of their business, and that means we'll lose serious money. We have a lot lined up with them, but nothing on paper, so they can still back out. What is Sandra thinking about?'

'This isn't like Sandra,' Jo said. 'She'd never let us down intentionally.'

'But she's done it royally this time, hasn't she?' Erica said.

As the afternoon wore on, everyone became more concerned.

'Something must have happened. Perhaps she's had an accident. Should we ring the hospitals?' Jo asked.

'They don't give information like that out to anyone.'

'Should I try Mal?'

'And worry him over something that might be nothing?' one of the others said.

'But if she has been knocked down or anything like that, he'd want to know,' Jo argued.

'Oh, do what you like, I have to try to sort this mess out,' Erica said as the production manager came rushing in to her office with an envelope – the missing envelope.

'Apparently it was delivered a few hours ago, but it has "to be collected by Sandra Mac Giolla Tighearnaigh" written on it. Jean was holding it at reception to give it to her when she came back in. It was delivered by some taxi man.'

'I don't know what the hell is going on, but if and when Sandra decides to show her face again, tell her I want to see her. Now get out, all of you – and get on with your work. We've wasted half the afternoon already.'

Jo decided against calling Mal. There had to be a perfectly good reason why Sandra had done a vanishing act that afternoon, and she had saved her hide, and probably her job too, by getting the artwork in. Grateful and all as she was for that, she'd have questions to ask her friend the next day.

But Sandra didn't show up at work the next morning, or the one after that either.

* * *

The sun was shining as Sandra walked along Baggot Street that lunchtime, making her way through the office workers. There was very little of that country girl still in Sandra; Dublin was her home now and would continue to be.

A young woman was cleaning the array of brass plaques beside one of the iconic panelled doors. The brickwork around the edges was stained from years of buffing. She let one of her polishing cloths drop and bent over to retrieve it. This gesture and her provocatively skin-tight jeans elicited a wolf whistle from a passing cycle courier and the girl looked up and blew him a kiss. Sandra found herself smiling. All these houses had been private homes, with loves and losses, dramas and heartache, and she remembered what Mal had said about being part of a cycle of life. *In another hundred years, less even, all these people will be gone too*, she thought.

She thought of their three-bed semi, lovingly decorated with flowers and shrubs in the garden to soften the bareness and hard lines of the sterile streetscape. *In a hundred years, would our cherry blossom still be blooming for future generations to enjoy?* She wondered what it would have been like to have lived in one of those Georgian piles, before there were cars and motor bikes constantly whizzing by and when maids in frilly aprons and caps polished the door brasses. She smiled. It was a good image. She continued on her way to the bridge over the canal.

She didn't often come to this part of town, she had no real reason to. As she waited for the lights to change, she noticed the street name plaque on the building facing her and she remembered something, a flashback that came out of nowhere. The words 'Baggot Street' had released it from some deep recess in her mind. The cheque – that cheque that she had pushed to the back of her memory – it had been drawn on a bank with an address in Baggot Street.

She was shaking, even her voice trembled as she said to the bored receptionist who was preoccupied with filing her nails, 'I'm here to collect an envelope for—'

'You must be Sandra Mac Giolla Tighearnaigh,' she drawled, putting the emery board down. Before Sandra could reply the receptionist continued, 'I have it here. You'll have to sign for it.'

Sandra took the pen, scribbled her name in a book and retreated hastily. She needed a coffee before she headed back.

She looked into the nearest café and spotted an empty table. Squashing past the others in the cramped space, she managed to shoehorn herself in to a seat in the window. She ordered a coffee and a scone and put the envelope down beside her bag.

From her vantage point, she could see no less than three banks. They couldn't help her, could they? Could they provide the missing link? 'Don't be fanciful,' she told herself, as she remembered shoving the cheque back into the envelope and returning to her hiding place behind the chapel plinth. She hadn't a name, only the amount and the date, give or take a day or two, and she didn't even know which bank it had been drawn on. If only she had realised the significance of it then. It hadn't seemed important; but that was before she discovered Peter was gone. She hadn't known the little bundle leaving the chapel with that couple had been her baby boy.

Her heart was pounding, the way it used to. She could feel it thumping in her chest and hear the blood pumping in her ears. She had to get some fresh air. Her palms were sweating, her breathing irregular. She thought she was going to faint. She had to find him. As she passed a chemist, she noticed a woman parking a pushchair outside and going inside.

Sandra peeped under the hood. It was Peter – she was sure of it. He was wearing a little blue hat and his frizzy blond hair was escaping at the front, a little teddy tucked in beside him. But she had to get the envelope back to the office – they were waiting for it. She walked to the kerb and hailed the first taxi that came along. She handed the driver the envelope and more money than was necessary, stressing the urgency of an immediate delivery, then she turned around.

She had to have another look.

Yes, it was definitely Peter.

She had found her baby boy.

Chapter Fifteen

Sandra changed her clothes three times before finally deciding on a red jacket, slacks and a blouse with a small poppy print.

'I don't want to look too formal or too business-like,' she told Mal as she got ready to keep the one appointment she had given up thinking would ever happen, 'but I don't want to look like I didn't care either or be too casual, like one of those women you see in the shopping centre in their logoed golf gear.'

'But you don't play golf,' he laughed.

'That's not the point, Mal. It's ... oh look, forget it. Do I look all right?'

'Perfect,' he said. 'He probably won't even notice what you're wearing. Besides, it's not an examination.'

'It feels like one, and I honestly don't know what sort of image I want to project.' She turned to her husband. 'Do you think he's doing the same – wondering about me? Has he an image in his mind of what I'm like? It's a peculiar thing, but for all the years of longing, I can't imagine him as a man. I still see the little mop of frizzy blond hair peeping out from a blue blanket. I hope he won't be disappointed.'

Mal saw her out to the car. 'I can still come with you if you want.'

'No, I have to do this on my own, but I'll tell him you wanted to come and meet him.'

The roads were relatively quiet as she drove along by Sandymount Strand, dog walkers and knots of people out enjoying their Sunday morning, some strolling, others jogging, all oblivious to her dilemma. The tide was out, leaving damp sand and puddles in its wake. There was an autumnal haze across Dublin Bay, almost obscuring Howth. She drove to the toll bridge, checking for the umpteenth time that she had the correct change. On the far side of the Liffey a cruise ship, glistening white, dwarfed everything around it. She and Mal often talked about doing a cruise, but that could wait for another while. They had their trip to Tasmania to look forward to first. With everything that was going on, she realised they hadn't discussed that at all.

She headed for Fairview and out the road to Clontarf Castle, becoming more and more nervous as she approached. Would she see anything of herself in him? How much could she tell him? Did he look like his father? She hoped not. Mal had told her to answer his questions truthfully and she fully intended to, but she was still terrified. She read that psychologists had proved that it only takes one tenth of a second to make a first impression, and she wanted so badly to get it right.

She recognised him instantly, as she got out of her car. He had a look of Leah. He was walking in her direction and she, instinctively, went forward to embrace him. She sensed his body tightening as she put her arms around him, and her tears started flowing freely. He stood there rigidly until she released him.

'I never thought this day would come,' she said as soon as she could talk.

'Neither did I, but it has, so I'll get to the point.'

She wanted to tell him to slow down. They had so much to say, that she didn't know where to begin, but she didn't get a chance. He started talking again as though he was a little boy who had rehearsed what he wanted to say and needed to get it all out in one go in case he forgot anything.

'My daughter Jennifer needs a bone marrow transplant and we need to find a match for her as soon as we can. I know it's a big ask, but would you be willing to be tested?'

'Of course I would.'

He stood looking at her.

'You look surprised. Did you think I'd say no?'

'I wasn't sure. Frankly, I didn't know what to expect.'

'Look at us – still standing in the car park. Let's go inside, where we can talk properly. There's so much I don't know about you.'

'Well, that's hardly my fault, is it?' His bitterness was tangible.

'I can explain, if you'll let me.'

'I doubt you can, but you don't have to. I was obviously an inconvenience in your life that you had to get rid of. It was a long time ago, a lifetime in fact, and now here I am, turning up like a proverbial bad penny.'

'It wasn't like that, I promise you, and I'm so glad you found me.'

'From my viewpoint, it was.'

He stood back to let her walk into the foyer in front of him. They found a quiet corner in the lounge and he asked her if she'd like a coffee. He ordered before giving her his full attention.

'Well, shoot. What's my story? Who am I? Where am I from? Was, or is, my father a pauper or a politician? Did you marry him? And who are you?'

'That's a lot of questions.'

'I've had a lot of time to think about what I wanted to ask.'

She was thrown by this approach. She expected and understood that he might be resentful, but she wasn't expecting him to be quite so hostile. She drew in her breath and exhaled slowly. He certainly wasn't going to make it any easier for her.

'Before I start, could you tell me have you had a good life? Tell me you're happy, apart from your little girl's illness, Kieron. Kieron's not the name I gave you, so forgive me, it feels strange saying it – all these years I've imagined you as Peter.'

'That's my middle name.'

'I'm glad you still have that.'

'I never knew it had any significance. You didn't exactly leave me any clues.'

'I couldn't, I wasn't given any options, but I hope they gave you to a caring family and that you had a good life. That's all I wished for all these years.'

He didn't say anything to that, but she had things that had to be said and she had no intention of letting the opportunity pass without doing so. He might not give her another one.

'I'm from Mayo, although I haven't been back there for a very long time. Your father was from Kerry.'

'*Was* – is he dead?'

'I honestly don't know.' This was painful, but at least he was talking. 'And your parents, are they still alive? I saw them when they took you away, though I didn't realise at the time that that was what was happening.'

'My da isn't. He died three years ago.'

'I'm sorry to hear that. And your mother?'

'Ma's fine. She's half-German, but you probably knew that.'

She shook her head. 'I didn't know anything about them.'

'She's a music teacher. He was only a few years older than her, but he always seemed much more. He drove a lorry, but he had a bad back that often meant long stretches when he couldn't work. She supplemented the family coffers by giving music lessons. They both grew up in Fairview, two streets away from each other, and didn't go very far when they married. She still lives in the terraced house that they moved into then.'

'Do you play anything?'

'Music wasn't my thing. I was useless at it. I preferred train sets and model railways, but I always felt I played second fiddle to my two brothers.'

She didn't know how to answer that. 'I learned the piano and play sometimes for my own amusement, but I do love music.'

'You'd have fitted in at ours so – better than I did probably. I always felt different – there was always someone preparing for their grade exams, so scales, lessons, rehearsals and recitals took up huge chunks of their lives. I hated sitting in halls at feiseanna and competitions, and I hated having to be quiet when they practised. It paid off for them – my brothers are both musicians now, totally unscarred by all the teasing they got and happy in a world of quavers and master classes.'

'Are they adopted too?'

'No, they're not. I'm the odd one out in more ways than one. I was probably as geeky as they were. Most of the boys in my class went into trades and apprenticeships when they left school. I wanted to become a secondary-school teacher. They used to call me "the professor" to annoy me, but it didn't really. Now I spend my life covered in chalk dust and surrounded by disinterested teenage boys.'

'Oh,' she muttered, taken aback by that revelation. 'My father was a school teacher.' She didn't tell him his father had been the school principal. 'What are your subjects?'

'Maths, science and civics – although that's a bit of an afterthought.'

'The difficult ones – not the civics, the other two. I don't even know where you went to school, or where you grew up.'

'Well, that's hardly my fault.'

'I know that, and you have every right to be angry, but I want you to know that I didn't give you up. I wasn't even consulted about it. They told me afterwards that because I was underage, I had no rights. You were taken from me and I never got over it. I've tried to find you, but I had nothing to go on, not even your right name, it seems. I spent years looking in to prams, hoping to find you.' She paused and her voice broke as she remembered how manic she had become. She swallowed hard and continued. 'As time went on, I began to realise that perhaps you were better off in your new life. I couldn't have given you the things you needed.'

'You couldn't have known that.'

'I didn't then, but I was too young to work and had hardly any schooling.'

'You don't seem to have done too badly.'

'I was given a second chance and I never stopped looking for you.'

He didn't say anything to that.

'I used to imagine you having holidays abroad with your family and running around with a dog, I don't know why. Did you have a dog?'

'We did have one once. Our holidays were to Clogher Head. Friends of my da had a mobile home there and they used to let us use it. It wasn't very big, but we had good fun there and it was a piano-free zone.'

She smiled at that. 'I know what you mean. My children – my other children – learned piano, though only one of them plays now. I had two others besides you, later on, when I married. So you have a half-brother and a half-sister – Oliver is twenty-six and Leah is twenty-seven. She's married to Adam. I'd like you to meet them and my husband, Mal. He wanted to come to meet you today, but I wouldn't let him. I thought it should be just us.' Stop babbling, she told herself.

'Did they know about me or was I just a guilty secret?'

'I've always felt guilty – guilty that I was helpless to keep you, but not because I had you. And, no, I didn't tell Ollie or Leah, the time never seemed right, but they do know now. I didn't open your letter until last Tuesday, and I told them that night. Mal has always known, since before we married.' She paused to give him a chance to say something, but he didn't. 'Tell me about your life and your family. Have you other children? Are you and Jennifer's mother married?'

'We are, her name is Pam. We met backpacking in Australia and then again, not quite accidentally, when we were back in Dublin. We have a boy too. He's called Ryan. He's almost ten now and perfectly healthy. It's been hard on her and him, with Jenny's illness.'

'I can't believe I have grandchildren. Did you bring any photos?'

'Not specially, no. I wasn't sure if you'd be interested. But I do have one.' He leaned over and took his wallet out from his back pocket. 'There you are – that's my family,' he said with attitude. 'This was taken last Christmas, in the hospital.'

Sandra was stunned when she saw the little girl who was propped up on the pillows, fairy lights twinkling along the bed head. She was the image of Louise. The boy on the bed beside her looked more like the woman who had her arms around the two of them.

'They are gorgeous, all three of them,' she said, regaining her composure. The family likeness had thrown her. She hadn't been expecting that.

'You're very like Leah,' she told him. He had the same eyes and intent expression and she suspected if he smiled, he'd be even more like her, but he didn't.

'You still have your curly hair. You were born with a mop of it: it was so blond it was almost white.'

'It's a long time since it was that colour.'

'Tell me about your little girl. Is she very ill?'

'She has leukaemia. It's under control with transfusions and she's being constantly monitored. We've been told it's time to consider a bone marrow transplant, but there's no way of knowing how long it will take to find a match.'

There was an awkward silence before she asked, 'Can we help

out in any way, apart from being tested – maybe with the medical expenses? They can be very costly.'

She saw his face darken. 'I don't want your money. That's not why I contacted you. I did it because of Jennifer – and that's the only reason.' He went to stand up and she put her hand on his arm to stop him.

'I'm sorry. Don't leave. I didn't mean that to sound patronising or to offend you.'

He relaxed. 'She needs a donor and we were told a brother or sister or parents are usually the best bet – it's because of the similarity in the genes or something like that – it makes matching easier and speeds things up. Failing that, she's already on the national register but that could take forever. Pam's an only child and I'm – well, you know what I am.'

'Tell me what I need to do, and I'll do it.'

He gave her a printout of phone numbers and times. 'You'll have to make an appointment.'

'I will. I promise. I'll do that tomorrow.'

He stood up, indicating he was finished, and they walked back to their cars without saying anything to each other.

She turned to him and said, 'Can we meet again? I'd really like to …'

'Probably, let's get this out of the way first.' Then he climbed into his car and drove away.

She took her phone out of her bag and rang Mal.

'It was awful. He was so resentful. I didn't know what to say to him. He kept taking control of the conversation. And turning it around.'

'I'm sure you were fine. Is he coming to see us?'

'I did ask him, but he was non-committal. I think he's afraid if he introduces us to his family that I'll disappear again. For all his bluster, I think he's very vulnerable, so it's understandable that he probably fears another rejection.'

'Are you going to be a donor?'

'If I can, but it's not that simple. I just can't walk in and donate. There are blood tests to be done first to see if I'm a suitable type. If I'm not, perhaps Leah or Ollie might be, but that's down the line. The actual transplant op is not too bad at all, apparently, and it could change her life.'

'Let's have the bloods done first and see where that takes us,' Mal said.

'What do you mean *us*? Would you be willing to be tested too?'

'Of course I would. They're your flesh and blood. I know it's a long shot but I might just turn out to be suitable. We'll never know if I don't get tested.'

'Thank you, Mal, you're amazing. I really hope I can do it. It would make me feel much better about what happened to us all those years ago. The battery's dying on this thing. I'm on my way home now. And Mal Wallace – I love you.'

'I love you too, Sandra Mac Giolla Tighearnaigh. Drive safely.'

As she drove home she tried to reconcile this tall man with the unruly curly hair with the tiny baby boy she had fed and cuddled in the convent nursery. He had grown up. He wasn't the little baby she had imprinted in her mind, his white-blond hair peeping out from beneath his little knitted hat, the tiny, perfect hand making exploratory shapes above his blanket. That image was so deeply engraved on her consciousness that it had been the one which kept her searching, looking in to prams and buggies. It was the one that had driven her to stoop down and lift a stranger's baby from his buggy, careful not to disturb or waken him. It was that memory that forced her to nuzzle her nose against him, inhaling that evocative baby smell she had never forgotten. It was that primeval instinct that had driven her to step into a shop doorway with him in her arms and watch until the woman came out and put her purchases in the basket strung between the handles of the pushchair and wheel it off in front of her.

As she drove home, she was oblivious to the familiar landmarks on the way – she was right back there remembering how she had needed to get something essential for him before he woke up and she hailed a taxi and got in the back, telling the driver to drop her off at her local shopping centre. On the way, she thought up her list – bottles, teats, formula, nappies and powder. She had Peter back and she couldn't wait to introduce him to Mal. When he came home, she'd get him to pick up anything she'd forgotten, or hadn't been able to carry. He would help her.

She shivered, despite the heat in the car. *He didn't look remotely like Dominic O'Sullivan.*

She was no sooner in the hall door than Leah phoned. Sandra glanced at the ID and handed the phone over to her husband.

'Tell her I'll call her in a while. I'm drained. I just want to think things out for a bit before I talk to anyone.' When he'd finished talking to their daughter, Mal sat down next to Sandra and held her. 'She's fine. She understands,' he told her, and he let Sandra cry for the years of denial and loss. She eventually stopped from exhaustion and fell asleep. He managed to extricate his arm, and got a rug to cover her. He then went into the kitchen to prepare something for them to eat.

If the kids were shocked now, he wondered how they'd react when they heard the rest of the saga.

Chapter Sixteen

Adam had been reading the Sunday papers but was actually keeping an eye on Leah. She was sitting in the kitchen looking lost. He wanted to go and put his arms around her, but he held back. Sandra's revelation had brought about an uneasy truce between them, and although she was still in a different bed, he felt he had made some progress – at least they were talking again. He saw her pick up her phone and punch in a number.

'Hi, Dad, I wasn't expecting you to answer Mum's phone. What's the latest? Is she back yet? I'm dying to hear all about it … Oh, OK … Are you sure? I can come over … OK, if you're sure … Give her my love.'

'How did their meeting go?' he asked.

'I'm not sure. Apparently Mum isn't ready to talk about it yet. She got Dad to tell me she'll be in touch later.'

Adam wondered about this fellow who had suddenly come out from the undergrowth. He could be anyone preying on a gullible woman, and his story about needing a donor – wasn't that a perfect heart-tugger? Was that really his motivation or was he after money? Nowadays anyone could find out anything about anyone if they delved deeply enough. Just because Sandra hadn't told her children she'd given a child up for adoption didn't mean she hadn't told her friends or her colleagues along the way. Lots of people probably knew. Maybe he knew about Uncle Jack's legacy – hadn't news of that made it on to the financial pages when it happened? But Adam was in no position to say these things to Leah. Even a hint of doubt had pushed her brother into overdrive and Adam knew Ollie hadn't had much time for him, even before he was caught out about the Helka business. He had to admit, though, the timing was good as it took the focus off him.

'How do you feel about the revelation now you've had time to digest it?' he asked Leah.

'A bit weird and, if I'm honest, a bit hurt too. I'm mad with her for never telling us, and I keep wondering if it could have been me she'd have given away if I'd come along first.'

'She didn't, and that's all that matters. You don't know all the circumstances. Maybe she really had no choice.'

'I know that's what she's said – and I keep telling myself that – but she should have told us we had a brother. We should have known about him. Why did she keep it a secret? And her sister – I never knew she had a sister. That's my aunt we're talking about. Where is she? Why didn't Mum mention her either? And her parents – we thought they had died years ago. Do you think something awful might have happened to them all – something that's too painful for her to talk about?'

'That could be one reason,' he answered. 'Maybe you should go easy on her, Leah. I'm sure now that she's opened up it'll all come out in time.'

She didn't say anything.

'Do you want to meet him?' Adam asked.

'What sort of question is that? Of course I do.'

'I just thought – well, you might have nothing in common.'

'Maybe not, but I'd like the chance to find out.'

'I know things are not right between us right now, but I'm here for you, Leah. I want you to feel you can depend on me.'

'Thanks for that, Adam,' Leah replied, and he sighed with relief. She hadn't shut him out altogether. 'But I don't want to talk about us today. We can talk tomorrow, after work.'

Chapter Seventeen

Oliver arrived a while later.

'I hope I'm not intruding.'

'You never intrude,' Leah told him. Even though Adam had been civil to Ollie when he'd opened the door, she could feel the tension between the two men.

When Adam went out of the room Ollie asked, 'So, Sis, what's the story? Are you going to kick him out or what?'

'I don't know what's going on any more. I don't want to discuss Adam. I'm in no state to make decisions about my marriage, and I don't want to make the wrong one and regret it later.'

'OK. No need to bite my head off. I come in peace. I'm only looking out for you.'

'I know you are, sorry. But are you not mad with Mum and Dad for not saying anything to us for all these years?'

'I'm more puzzled than anything. Mum with a secret past, who'd have thought that? She always seemed so open. And I have to admit I'm curious to meet this guy. Look on the bright side, we might even like each other and you could find that you have another ally to keep Adam in line.' He grinned. 'Sis, was that the hint of a smile?'

'Maybe, but Ollie, I'm so confused. Two weeks ago life was normal, whatever that is, and look what's happened in that short space of time. And look at me, criticising her and keeping what's going on in my own life a secret from her – but I really can't tell her right now, can I? If she knew, she'd be so unhappy for me.'

'I wonder if she would ever have told us if Kieron hadn't tracked her down,' he said.

'And her sister – Louise. We don't even know if she's alive, where she lives, anything.'

'Do you think there are any more revelations?'

'Yes, but don't let her know I said anything. On Saturday when we were having our heart-to-heart, before we met you in the pub, and before she got too upset to tell me what it was, she told me that she'd done something terrible that hurt a lot of people. She had a breakdown too – when she was only twenty-two.'

'God, it's no wonder she didn't want to go back into her past. It sounds horrific.'

'I didn't tell Adam,' she whispered, as she heard her husband coming back down the hall.

Ollie nodded and winked at her. 'I'll phone her later.'

At that point, Leah's phone buzzed. It was Sandra. Leah put her finger up to silence her brother.

Chapter Eighteen

Driving home after meeting Sandra, Kieron thought about their conversation. When he pulled up outside his house, he saw the curtains twitch before Pam opened the door, and he realised he had no recollection of the drive home – he'd been on auto pilot, replaying everything Sandra had told him.

'Well? How did it go? What was she like? Will she help?' Pam gushed.

'It's like being on *Quick Fire Questions* around here,' he said, pecking her on the cheek.

'I'm sorry, love, but I've chewed my fingernails off with worry, wondering how it was going.'

'Mam won't let me bite my fingernails,' Jennifer said, coming up at the rear.

'And she's right too, poppet,' he said, scooping up his daughter. 'It's not a nice habit. Let's see if there's a cartoon on that you can watch while your mum and I have some grown-up talk.' He settled her down on a beanbag. 'Where's Ryan?'

'In next door, watching a soccer DVD. Now start at the beginning,' Pam said. 'What was she like?'

'Fine. She was fine, very pleasant and very nice, actually. She's much younger than I expected. I thought she'd be more Ma's vintage.

I wanted to hate her, but I couldn't. She was very nervous and she cried a bit. She kept asking me if I'd been happy, if I'd had a good life.'

'Will she help us if she's suitable?'

'She said she would. Oh, and I was right – I do have siblings – real-blood siblings, a half-brother and a half-sister.'

'That's terrific, isn't it?'

'I'm not sure. I suppose it is. It's a very strange feeling. They didn't know about me either – she never told them until the other night. It seems like I was the invisible man in their lives, but she said they might be willing to be tested too, although she hadn't asked them yet.'

'Do you look like her?'

'I don't know, but she says I'm the spit of my half-sister – Leah is her name. Her other son is called Oliver.'

'You'll have to tell your mam you've met her. She'll probably be upset at first.'

'I suppose we could drive over there now and tell her. If the old man were still alive, I think he'd take it harder. The only time I mentioned trying to trace my roots, he told me to forget it, that it would break Mam's heart. He said they were my family and I was theirs. Mam will be more understanding when she gets used to the idea and realises that I won't be forgetting her. I'll always be her eldest son and she will always be my mother. No one will change that.'

'Be sure you let her know that's how you feel. A bit of reassurance will go a long way.'

'I will. Anyway, she'll be delighted there might be a better chance of a genetically related donor for Jennifer.'

'Did you find out anything about your father? Are they together, or in touch, or anything like that?'

'She said very little, just that he's not around anymore – not that he ever was. I don't know if that means he's dead or just not on the scene. Funnily enough, when I found out I was adopted I wanted to find my mother, but I never had the same urge to find my father. Her father was a teacher too. Isn't that strange? Anyway, she didn't give much away about him – and I didn't ask. There's a lot I didn't ask.' Kieron stopped there and thought for a bit. 'I'm going to have to stop being so bitter, aren't I?'

'That would be nice,' she said, putting her hand over his on the table. 'Let's take it a step at a time. You didn't expect instant solutions, neither did I, but you have to start somewhere.'

'I suppose I've waited half my life to ask these questions and now that I can, there's a part of me doesn't know if I want the answers.'

'I think it's perfectly natural to have conflicting emotions. It's like a huge jigsaw with lots of missing pieces. Now you've the opportunity to find them and slot them into place. Better to take things slowly and get to know each other.'

'That's a nice way of putting it,' he said, 'and if it's anything like Jennifer's puzzles, there are bound to be a few bits missing.'

'We'll face those gaps when we have to.'

'Would you believe my grandfather was a teacher too?'

'That's amazing. See, you've already found another piece.'

'I'm glad you're such an optimist,' he said. 'You're the yin to my yang, or should that be the yang to my yin? Whatever, I'm glad that ordeal is out of the way. I'll go get Ryan and we'll go and tell Mam.'

Chapter Nineteen

1983

When Sandra was well again and Leah had had her first birthday, she told Mal she felt strong enough to go back to her home town in Mayo and to confront her demons.

Sandra remembered it all as being much bigger, both the house and the few scrappy, hilly fields where she and her sister had played. It had been in her family for generations – her father and grandfather had both been born and had grown up here. She and Louise had been born in the same bedroom, the third generation, the one that broke the tradition.

She hadn't been back in twelve years. She'd been a child when she left. Now she was a married woman with a family of her own.

At first glance, it all looked the same, then she noticed the pale cream wash that now coloured the walls of the house, softening the greyness. The blue hydrangea shrubs still bloomed in the garden but there was a neatly trimmed hedge that hadn't been there when she'd lived there.

Mal knocked on the door and Sandra's heart pounded as they waited, holding her daughter in her arms. She remembered tracing her finger around the lead beading that held the rose and lily patterns in place in the two stained-glass panels, and how the morning sun elongated them in the reflections on the lino in the hall. No one answered. He knocked again and they waited.

In the top field, where the donkey used to graze, one of those pick and mix catalogue bungalows that occupied open spaces around the country had been built, and there were no cows or sheep to be seen. Croagh Patrick still stood out like a beacon, a view that had been so familiar but which somehow felt alien to her now. She used to be able to see its stony peak from her bedroom window, though it was often hidden by the low clouds that frequently hung in the west for days at a time. On cloudless nights, she and her sister used to try to count the stars and guess which constellation Mr Sandman lived in.

Sandra clung on to Mal's hand as she surveyed the territory, the sweep down to the sea, the scattered islands catching the sun, where the ocean quietened as it surrendered to their jagged edges, and the narrow road that led up the hill to *that* place.

'Do you see that spot over there?' she said, pointing to an inlet below. 'That's where the picture was taken.'

She didn't have to explain, he knew which picture she was talking about – the only one she possessed of her childhood and of her sister.

'You don't have to do this,' Mal said gently. 'We can go back to Westport now, to the hotel.'

'But I do – and I'm here now. I have to find out what happened to them. Let's put Leah in her pushchair and try the new house first. If they know nothing, then we'll go to the post office.'

They walked towards the new house, noticing a child's plastic car parked drunkenly beside a Volvo, probably abandoned when something more interesting had captured its owner's attention.

A woman came to the door. 'I really wouldn't know, I'm afraid, I'm a blow-in – I've only been here for five years. The Nolans live there now,' she said, nodding towards Sandra's old home. 'But it was empty before that, for quite a while I believe. I think they emigrated.'

They thanked her and left to walk back into the town. The

newsagent where she and Louise had bought sweets and their weekly comics still had the same sign in Irish over the door. The butcher's had changed. It now had a swanky red-and-white-striped awning with 'victuallers' written on it in fancy script. The 'shop' where they had bought pencil sharpeners, rubbers, hair slides, light bulbs and pretty much everything else had been replaced by a Spar that seemed to take up the length of three of the original buildings.

There was a billboard on the pavement outside the barber's on the opposite side of the street with 'Uni-Sex' written on it. This was propped up against the green letterbox, which, for no explicable reason, was four doors away from the post office itself. Buckets of colourful cut flowers took up half the pavement outside An Siopa Bláthanna, where the wool shop used to be. Next there was a gaudy video rental outlet, the same as dozens of others all over the country. Its two-toned plastic franchised front contrasted unpleasantly with the other traders who had obviously made a huge effort to brighten up their town. Then there was the post office.

'Let me do the talking,' Mal whispered before they went in.

It smelled exactly the same, as she looked around. It hadn't changed all that much either. The brass grilles to prevent a stick-'em-up-type raid had been augmented by toughened glass, and it wasn't Mr O'Kelly who sat behind the counter, but a young woman with chunky earrings and pink lipstick that clashed with her orange sweater.

'Isn't it a grand day altogether?' she said as Mal approached. 'What can I do for ye?'

'I'm visiting and I used to have distant relatives living around here when I was young. I was hoping to say hello, if they or any of my cousins are still alive.'

'I don't know everyone, but I might be able to help ye, or tell ye who might. We're always getting folk coming in looking for long-lost family, probably hoping someone left them a fortune,' she laughed.

'I doubt that in my case,' he replied. 'It was the Mac Giolla

Tighearnaighs. He used to teach in the local school.'

'I remember them – Con Mac Giolla Tighearnaigh – he taught all my brothers. There were two girls and an old woman.'

Sandra nearly choked. Leah chose that moment to make her presence felt and let out a demanding cry. Sandra bent over her and turned her back on the counter, keeping out of the teller's line of vision. She didn't want questions for which she had no answers.

'She was a snobby old biddy if ever there was one. I probably shouldn't say things like that. Me da would kill me for it. He used to run this place—' Sandra felt a wave of panic crawl over her body, the woman had to be Detta O'Kelly who had sat beside her in school '—and he tried to drum it into my head that although the postmaster knows everyone's business, he should never pass it on to anyone, a bit like the seal of confession, I suppose.'

Mal smiled. 'Probably. Would you know if any of the family still live around here?'

'No, they've been gone years. When the old bid— I mean when the old woman died, the place was sold. There was no one in it for a while. There was some scandal if I recall correctly, I don't know what it was, but he went off – the da. It was the talk of the place at the time, but I don't remember all the details. They had seemed to be such a tight couple, everyone was shocked. I was still in national school. Did he die? I can't remember. I think the others went to America or maybe it was England. I couldn't be sure though. Ye know what young ones are like, not interested in grown-ups' gossip.'

'That's true. Oh, well, I suppose it was a long shot expecting that they'd still be here.'

'No. I'm quite sure there isn't anyone left. If there is they're not living around here, but I could try to find out for ye, if ye're staying locally.'

'No, we're headed south this afternoon, but thank you for your time.'

'Ye could always ask Fr O'Flaherty. He might know more,' she shouted as Mal opened the door for Sandra.

'Whew. I'm glad she didn't recognise me,' she whispered when they got outside. 'And that's what they thought of my gran – an old biddy. She was too, now that I think about it!'

The church stood at the fork in the road, in front of the graveyard, where Sandra's granddad was buried. And her grandmother now, she supposed. The parish priest's house stood a bit to one side, its granite façade softened by tubs of summer bedding.

'Like I said, love, you don't have to do this,' Mal said, looking at Sandra with concern.

'But I do. I need to see for myself when she died. That might explain her silence. You know, she never spoke to me after she found out I was pregnant, but I always thought she might come around and be my ally after … well, you know, when I came back here. I've often wondered if my parents would have found it easier to forgive me if we hadn't all lived together. And my dad dead? Surely I'd know if he'd died, wouldn't I?'

'I wouldn't put too much store in what she said. She was a bit scattered and vague.'

'She was, wasn't she? But she seemed to be implying that my parents split up. People didn't do that back then, did they?'

'Some did, of course they did. But with no divorce in Ireland the majority just gritted their teeth and soldiered on, didn't they?'

The parish priest was walking up and down, breviary in hand, reading his daily office. He nodded as they passed by. She didn't recognise him, but she remembered exactly where her grandfather's grave was. It was a large plot on the path to the stream and was marked with a tall Celtic cross. She found it easily. 'Tomás Paul Mac Giolla Tighearnaigh, 19 September–' tentacles of ivy obliterated the date, but she knew it was the year before her parents had married. She remembered her mother telling her that was why they ended up living with her grandmother. That had never been their intention. Beneath his name, 'Doreen Mac Giolla Tighearnaigh, nee Cummins' had been added. The date of her death was clearly visible: '20 February 1971'.

'Mal, she died only weeks before Peter was born. That's why I never heard from her. And they never let me know. She didn't live long enough to know she had a great-grandson.'

'This is very hard for you.'

'No, I'm glad I came back here, I needed to do it, but I don't care if I never do it again.'

He held her close, looking over her head past the stream to a less populated part of the graveyard. 'Do you want to ask that priest if he can tell us anything else?'

'No. I'd just love to know if they left here because of me. He wouldn't have been here then so he wouldn't have any of the answers I want. Anyway, I've had enough emotion to last a lifetime. I just want to get back to normality.'

'It really makes no difference now, Sandra. It's all in the past. Let's leave it here where it belongs and look to whatever the future holds for us.'

'You're right, Mal. Let's go.'

He pushed their daughter back out to the street to where they'd left the car.

'You know, Mal, I still have so many questions I need answers to, but I don't know if I'm ready to cope with what the answers might be.'

'You've been very brave coming back here. I can only imagine how hard it must be. I'm so proud of you.'

'I don't know about being brave, but I had to do it sometime.'

* * *

When they had Leah tucked up in her cot that night, Mal sat next to Sandra and put his arms around her. 'We've done all we can. Leah and I are your family and you're stuck with us, forever.'

'I don't think that will be too much of a burden, Mal. Thank you for everything – I couldn't have got through all that has happened without you.'

'That's my job. I'll always look after you. I promise.'

'I know you will,' she said, snuggling closer to him. 'I feel so safe with you.'

He kissed her gently, then more intensely, as though sealing a bond. She responded with fervour, their desire mutual, urgent, demanding and passionate.

That was the night Ollie was conceived.

Despite having learned to accept that there were some things she could never change, since Leah had been born she found it impossible not to wonder what Peter had done at each stage of his development. When and where had he taken his first steps? What were his first words? Every year, she made a cake on his birthday. No one but Mal knew its significance.

As they drove back to Dublin, some ghosts laid to rest, others refused to disappear. Sandra was still dwelling on Detta O'Kelly's revelations in the post office the previous afternoon. Leah had dropped off to sleep almost the minute the car had started.

'I still find it hard to credit that my parents could have gone their separate ways. They always seemed happy. Mam used to tell Louise and me how Dad had surprised her with his proposal after a walk on the beach, when the full moon was shining. She told us he'd been carrying the ring around in his pocket for weeks, trying to pluck up the courage to ask her. He still lived at home with his parents but the cottage, beside the one we called to yesterday, at the top field, had just gone on the market and he was hoping to get a loan to buy it for them to start out on their own.'

'You know, Sandra, you've told me more about your family on

this trip than ever before,' Mal said. 'You've always been so secretive about your past. I don't mean about Peter, about the rest of it.'

'I know. It's dredging up memories I thought I'd forgotten. They never intended living with my gran, the old biddy.' She smiled. 'She didn't approve of Mam anyway because she wasn't a local girl. She thought she had airs and graces – when it was my gran who had those. She always referred to my granddad as "my husband, the headmaster". But he died suddenly just after Mam and Dad got engaged. He was found in the barn behind the farmhouse where he'd lived all his life. They felt they just couldn't abandon Gran, so they compromised and moved in with her. Bit by bit they modernised the house. Whenever we asked if we could have a brother, Dad used to tell us he couldn't afford it – when Louise arrived, it was just after the new Aga had been installed and when I came along it coincided with the new windows and doors, and we believed him!'

'God, Sandra, it's great to see you laughing about all this. You've kept it all bottled inside for too long.'

'I know.'

'Did your mother get on with your gran? It's never an ideal situation, two women in one kitchen, but it happened a lot in the country back then.'

'Most of the time it worked, but it was always Gran's house and what Gran wanted she got. Mam wasn't a pushover though, they were both strong women. There were many clashes of wills. Mam used to take us for long walks to keep out of Gran's way, till they both cooled down. Dinah, the housekeeper, was often called on to mediate or referee! When they weren't speaking, they'd talk through her.

'Louise and I used to help Dinah with little jobs. Gran loved flowers about the place so we'd collect wild flowers and greenery of some sort, even if it only came from the hedgerows and fuchsia bushes on the road outside our gate. When the hydrangeas in the garden were in bloom we were allowed cut some of them. They lasted much longer than the bluebells and honeysuckle.'

'Well, there's something you've inherited from her – your love of flowers,' he said.

'I never thought of that – you're probably right.'

'What was she like? Did you like her, as a person?'

'I loved her. She was my gran, always there in my life. You don't think about those things when you're a kid. She was very demanding and thought Louise and I were given too much freedom, allowed to get up on the donkey like tinkers. It wasn't politically incorrect to say that back then.' She grinned as she remembered. 'We went to a circus and came away both fancying ourselves in pink tutus, standing up, balancing on the horses' backs as they galloped around the ring. That didn't go down well at all. We had to set a good example, that was always being drummed into us, so you can see how I was such a disappointment to them.'

'That's their loss and my gain,' he said.

In the back of the car, Leah woke and demanded attention.

'I'll pull over.'

'I realise I haven't stopped talking since we left Westport. I'm sorry for going on, Mal. You must be bored stiff.'

'I'm anything but bored,' he said, stopping the car in the gateway to a field. 'I'm fascinated. You don't often talk about these things. I'm finally being allowed in to the private world of Miss Mac Giolla Tighearnaigh. Thank you.' He leaned over and gave her a kiss on the cheek.

Chapter Twenty

Leah tried to put the events of the previous week out of her mind. She was in the office, and trying to concentrate on her work and pretend that everything was normal. With the docklands project safely delivered, it was time to move on to the next one.

If only life could work like business, or like men, she thought as she backed up the last files and drew a line under Project Dockland Regeneration. Perhaps that was the difference between the sexes – men could switch affections on or off, or move on without a backward glance. Women, it seemed to her, usually let their affections become bound up with other complicating factors, like love, loyalty, memories, hopes and dreams – tangible things that were not so easy to detach from their souls. Men simply changed the programme or opened anther file – a fresh sheet. She smiled at the irony she had not intended, but yes, in some cases yes, it was to fresh sheets they went.

Susie interrupted her thoughts.

'Can I come in?' she asked, and without waiting for an answer, she deposited two coffees and a bag of pastries on Leah's desk. 'What's next now that Operation Swedish Chef is done and dusted?'

'I hope that's not going to turn up on any of the paperwork,' Leah laughed.

'So do I!'

'The feedback has been very positive and we've already had some enquiries from two potential clients – who could have quite substantial projects.'

'That sounds positive, and I haven't seen you crack a smile for a while, hence the pastries and cappuccinos. Let's start the new week off on a bright note.'

'That's really thoughtful. You'd cheer anyone up,' Leah said, taking in Susie's colourful clothes. She was dressed like a children's television show presenter this morning – red denim dungarees, a yellow shirt; her hair tied in a blue bandana. Leah was wearing charcoal-grey slacks and a silver-grey sweater with a chunky aquamarine pendant. She felt colourless beside her colleague, but maybe that was because of her mood.

'Yes, Leah, I do my best, and as the song goes, it's a new dawn and a new day and I'm feelin' good. Who knows what this week will bring. But seriously, are you OK? You seem a bit out of sorts.'

'There's a lot going on at the moment, family stuff. I'll tell you another time, but I'm fine really. That, and the painters are in finishing off the house, so everything is in disarray. I need a week off just to get it sorted – and I might just take one – but, for now, I need to get started on preparations for the meeting with the new nursing home people on Friday. It could be a good one to get and there's plenty of money behind them.'

'Right. I can take a hint,' Susie said, gathering up the paper napkins and cups. 'I hear Judd the Stud's back in town for a week.'

'What? Where did you hear that?'

'When I was out clubbing on Saturday. I suppose Adam will be meeting up with him.'

'I don't know. He never said anything. Mind you, I don't think they're in touch very often. He never mentions him. Now scoot, I have work to do.'

But Leah couldn't work. She was looking at her computer, but thinking about Adam. He'd wanted them to go out for a meal that evening, but she said she'd prefer it if they talked at home. It was time to decide what to do, to sit down and have it out with him. It was their marriage they had to fix. She didn't doubt that she loved him, and she wanted to make it good again, but it wasn't that simple any more. She had to decide if she could regain her trust in him and every time she thought about it, she ended up being more confused.

* * *

He was home and had a pasta dish ready to cook when she got in. Their conversation was stilted at first, keeping to safe topics, testing each other's mood.

She went to have a look at what was going to be her home office. All her books were still in packing boxes in the centre of the floor.

'Can you believe they've finally finished?' he said, following as she inspected the decorators' progress. 'This is a fabulous room, with great light.'

'It's really lovely and the colour turned out just as I'd hoped,' she replied, thinking if things didn't go well that evening, she might never get to use it. She realised that wasn't the right frame of mind to be in approaching such a serious discussion. Had she really given up so easily?

'Will we ever get rid of the smell of paint?' she said, opening the windows before heading back for the kitchen.

'How's work?' he asked as he stirred the pasta sauce.

'It was a bit of an anti-climax today after the mayhem of the past few weeks, but a very welcome let-up really.' She couldn't bring herself to ask him how his work was going without images of him with his conquest in the lift. Instead, she tasted the carbonara. 'This is really tasty, thank you. I didn't feel like cooking. To be honest, with everything that's been going on, I feel wrecked.'

After an awkward pause, they both started talking at the same time and stopped, then he began again.

'Look, Leah, let me have my say first. I'm sorry. Seeing you so fired up about this long-lost brother has been a wake-up call for me too. I never really thought about how important family is. I just took it for granted, but I now realise that's what I want, more than anything. I was an idiotic fool to jeopardise what we have. I'm begging you to give me another chance. And if you'll let me, I'll make it up to you, I promise. I know I've told you all this already but you have to believe me. I don't know what I'd do without you.'

'And I feel the same way, but—'

'I want to sort things out, but I don't know what you want me to do to make it up to you.'

'Neither do I, Adam. I wish it was as simple as pressing a delete button, but it doesn't work like that. You cheated on me, and that really hurts. It also makes me wonder if I was wrong about you all along. Do I really know who you are at all?'

'I realise that and, yes, you know me better than anyone, Leah. Please give me another chance to prove how much I love you and how much I regret the way I've behaved.'

'I'll try, but I'm not ready for intimacy yet. That's going to take longer, so don't rush me.'

'Take as much time as you need. We have our trip to Tassie to look forward to with your folks. It'll give us some quality time away from demanding clients and deadlines for a bit. Has your dad mentioned when they'd like to go?'

'It hasn't been discussed, what with everything that's going on in their lives at the moment.'

'I can appreciate that. That's not a problem, but I can't put off going there indefinitely. There are decisions to be made and I have to find a new manager for the place. The old boy is determined to retire, but he promised he won't leave me in the lurch. Whoever gets the job will need six months with Harvey to see how it all works through the seasons. I've been thinking – lying in bed on my own has given me a lot of extra time to do that,' he said, looking at her like a lost puppy, a look that usually melted her heart. 'I'm seriously thinking that maybe we should both take a year out and live down there to see if we'd like to stay and make our home there. It's a great lifestyle. It's something I've always imagined I would like to do, even before Uncle Jack died, and lately talking to Judd has made me realise maybe it's time to give it a go.'

'I didn't realise he'd been in touch,' she said, wondering if he knew or would say anything about him being back.

'We send emails from time to time,' he replied.

She knew he was being evasive. 'Has he settled down there for good?'

'I think so. It's a different way of life.'

'You say that as if you envy him.'

'He's in the city. I prefer Tassie, the open countryside and the pace of life. Maybe when we go, you might be persuaded to give it a try – the two of us – a new beginning together. It would be a great place to bring up kids, and your folks could come over any time they liked, and Ollie too – and your new family.'

'Let's not get carried away here. Let's take one thing at a time,' she said. 'Let's try to get our marriage back on track first before we do anything else.'

'Righto. It makes me very happy to hear you say that – and you can call the shots.'

'Marriage is supposed to be an equal partnership, with neither one "calling the shots", as you put it.'

'It is.'

'Good. So don't go hitting me with surprises like notions of emigrating. I'm not even sure that I'd want my children growing up so far away from their grandparents. This is all very sudden. Have you been thinking like this for a while?'

'Jack's dying and then buying this house and thinking about starting a family have all made me realise that I'm – that we – are planting our roots here, and maybe – just maybe – we should be doing that over there. I'd hate to wake up one day and regret not giving it a shot.'

She sat digesting where this conversation was going.

'Well? Say something,' he urged.

'I don't know what to say. You seem to have been making plans and decisions for both of us.'

'Will you think about them? That's all I ask.'

'I'll certainly do that,' she replied, 'though they've taken me by surprise.'

'Thank you.'

'I haven't agreed to anything. I only said I'd think about it but, Adam, this is all getting away from the core of this discussion. I want you to know that if you ever hurt me again, we're finished – and that's non-negotiable, whatever part of the world we live in.'

'I won't,' he replied, 'and I mean it.'

She wanted so much to believe him.

* * *

Leah met Oliver for a quick coffee the next day.

'Have you heard any more about the prodigal son?' she asked.

'No, but I'm sure we will very soon. Mum's going to invite him to the house, with his wife.'

'What about the children?'

'I never asked about them!' he said.

'I know what you mean. After that long session on Saturday, I'm giving Mum some space. She can make the next move.'

'You're not very happy about all this, are you?'

'I don't know. Everything is up in the air and I don't know

where I'm going to land. I don't want them to know that things are so off-kilter between Adam and me. They have their own issues just now, and they'd be devastated if they found out about us.'

'What are you going to do?' he asked.

She told him about Adam's plans to head off halfway around the world in the next few weeks.

'He wants me to go with him then, whether it suits Mum and Dad or not.'

'I wondered why he was bringing them out, coming out of the blue like that. I reckoned he had to have an ulterior motive.'

'You would, but Ollie, if I don't go, he's going anyway to sort a load of things out down there, both with the farm and the distillery. They're legitimate reasons and he'll be gone for a while. Maybe he felt if they saw the place they'd understand why he'd want us to settle there.'

'He might have a point, but it might also do you good to have some time apart. To get a proper perspective on your relationship.'

'That's what I think – or rather what I thought. The more I mulled it over, the more I realised that I wouldn't have a minute's peace wondering if he was being faithful to me or not. And I wouldn't want Mum to think I was abandoning her right now or was upset by her revelations.'

'She'd never think that. Forget what I just said. From where I'm sitting, you seem to have a damned good perspective of your marriage, and of your husband. If you feel that insecure about him do you really want to give him another chance?'

'Everyone deserves a second chance. I can't back out that easily. It was supposed to be for life,' she said sadly.

Ollie backed off. 'It's your decision, Sis. But you only get one life, don't let anyone destroy yours. You have to do what's right for you, but remember I'm at the end of the phone if you need me. Now, I have to get back to the office.'

Chapter Twenty-one

After Kieron's call to say he would bring Pam and their children to see her, Kieron's mother put a fresh cloth on the table and set it with matching embroidered napkins and her best china cups. She always had a fire lit in the compact dining room, winter and summer, and the brass fire irons gleamed from years of polishing. She took great pride in her little kingdom, and liked nice things around her. The sitting room housed her treasured piano and an assortment of cased violins. The collection of eclectic sheet music was methodically filed. There were trophies and framed certificates arranged in groups everywhere.

When they arrived, she hugged and kissed her only grandchildren. When Pam saw the table she teased, 'I see we're getting the royal treatment today, Marie.'

'I've decided there's no point in keeping things locked away in the china cabinet for show – they survived the war in my grandmother's time, they survived me and my three rowdy sons and their horseplay – so I think it's their time now and I'm going to enjoy them,' she said.

'They are very pretty,' Pam said.

'My mother used to tell us about having high teas in my grandmother's house when they still lived in Munich, and about her warm *apfelstrudel* and fingers of iced cinnamon cake she'd serve them on these very plates. She never took to Irish apple tarts. She always spoke in German when she talked about the old times, but we weren't allowed speak it outside the house.'

'Why not, Gran?' Ryan asked.

'Oh, because they were living here then and had to learn to speak English properly,' she answered quickly. He was satisfied with that, and asked if she had made cinnamon cake for them.

'No, not this time, but I do have some gingerbread for you two,' she said, smiling at them, 'and some of your favourite tea brack, Pam.'

'You spoil us, Mam,' Kieron said.

'I figured you might drop over today, so I made them yesterday. And if you didn't, they wouldn't go to waste – they'd go down well with my pupils during the week.'

She showed them the postcards she had just got from her other two boys, both working abroad now with renowned orchestras; Liam was a concert pianist and Derek a violinist.

'We're going to have to get you into using modern technology – then you could email and Skype them whenever you felt like it, instead of having to wait for the postman to come.'

'No, thank you. If I did that I'd have nothing to look at only an impersonal bit of typing on a screen that I probably wouldn't be able to find in the first place. With these, I can visualise them in places I never got to see and am unlikely to at this stage.' She spoke without rancour. 'Your father was a good man, but an adventurer he was not! He was a man of habit and he liked his Clogher Head breaks, but I couldn't get him near an airport.' She laughed.

'When Jennifer is well again, I promise we'll take you abroad on a real holiday, won't we, Pam?'

'Definitely. That's a date and you can choose where we go.'

'I'd love that. I can pay my way,' she said.

'Don't be ridiculous,' he laughed. 'Practical as ever.'

'Now, you wanted to tell me something?'

'Will I take the children out for a walk? We need some milk at home and I could get it now, it would save us having to stop on the way back,' Pam said.

When they had the house to themselves, Kieron came straight to the point. 'Mam, I don't want you to get upset—'

'Have you had bad news about Jennifer?'

'No, but—'

'Oh, why do I get the feeling that I'm not going to like what you're about to say?'

'Maybe you will, maybe you won't. I've been curious about my natural parents for years. When I brought it up with Da once, he begged me not to go searching. He said it would only upset you and, as you know, we never talked about the subject much at all after I discovered I was adopted.'

'I would have understood. It's only natural you'd be curious.'

'I was, and I decided some time ago to try to make contact. I didn't want to say anything before in case it was a fruitless search and I'd be upsetting you for nothing. But I found my birth mother, or rather I found out where she was, and I met her this morning.' He studied his mother's face, trying to read her reaction.

She put her hands up to her cheeks and uttered, 'Well, that's a relief. I'm so glad for you. When Pam took the children out, I thought you were going to tell me something awful – I was afraid that you'd had bad news about Jennifer.'

'Mam, you're great. I was petrified at how you'd react, but I never expected this.'

'Of course I'm happy for you. It's your right to know, but how did you find her?'

'That's a long story. Believe it or not, it was through a Christmas card, a concert programme and a bit of luck, but first I have to tell you you're my mam and you always will be, no matter what. I accept I haven't always been the ideal son and I was angry for a long time, too long when I look back, but I appreciate everything you did for me. And Da too. I just hope he realised that.'

'He did, and we were lucky to get you,' she said, reaching out to take his hand. 'And we should have told you the truth when you were younger. It was wrong not to. When we didn't, it just became harder and harder to find the right time,' his mother tried to explain. 'But to us you always were our son, just as the other two are. We loved you all the same.'

'I know that, Mam, and I suppose now that I'm a parent myself, I can be a bit more objective. I can see that I was angry at being given away and at not knowing who I was. It wasn't your fault that I didn't fit in. I hadn't inherited your talent or an interest in classical music like Derek and Liam.'

'No, but you got those brains from somewhere. You were always the smartest academically. Your da and I tried to ignore the differences, but they were very obvious with each passing year. We agonised so much over how and when to tell you, all of you, and we just kept putting it off. Then your hormones started hopping and we were worried that you'd feel even more ostracised.'

'There probably isn't a right time,' he said.

'We should have made one. Believe me, I did try, we both did, several times, but we always chickened out, I'm afraid. I know that was the wrong thing to do.'

'I could have got a worse family,' he grinned again. 'It's not every child whose mother played him to sleep to the strains of Debussy and Brahms.'

'I did my best,' she laughed. 'But tell me about your birth mother. I'd love to meet her and thank her for you.'

'Maybe you will at some stage, but the good news is she's willing to be tested as a possible donor for Jennifer, and if she's not a match, she has two other children – I have another brother and a sister.'

But Kieron realised his mother was still in the past. 'I'll never forget your reaction when we finally told you. Do you remember what you said to us?' she asked. 'You asked if the boys knew and when we said they didn't, you told us your whole life had been a lie. They didn't know who you were, we didn't and neither did you. I cried that night for you. I didn't have the answers you needed and I knew I never would have them. I felt we'd let you down.'

'Oh, Mam, I was such a brat. I'm so sorry.'

'I couldn't be more pleased for you, Kieron. I've seen the hurt and the pain you've gone through. And I didn't know how to go about fixing that. When you met and married Pam, I hoped you'd feel more secure. I was so happy when your children came along, a family of your own, but it never quite filled the gap, did it?' she asked.

'If I'm honest, no, it didn't.'

'Well, I hope now it can, and, Kieron, I'm so glad that we're having this conversation now. I just wish that we had had it a long time ago.'

'It doesn't matter now.' He walked over and gave her a long hug, neither saying anything. 'Thank you,' she said when he let go of her, 'you always gave the best hugs.' They laughed.

'I want to know everything. What's she like? What did she say? Do you look like her?'

'You're as bad as Pam.' He laughed and told her everything he could remember, feeling lighter in spirit than he ever had before.

'Kieron, I feel this is the start of something precious and I am genuinely pleased for you. To me you're my son, just as though we had conceived you, but to that woman you'll always be hers too. That's a bond that is seldom ever broken.'

'I think I'm beginning to realise that too.'

He filled her in on how he had found Sandra three years previously, but hadn't followed through at that time.

Pam arrived back, and when Marie opened the door she asked, 'Is it safe to come in?' holding out a big bunch of flowers.

'It is,' she laughed, 'but don't tell me these people live in a swanky house in Dalkey or Howth, and that we're not good enough for you now.'

'With that china set, they'll have a bit of competition, even if they do,' Pam said.

'I'll make more tea.'

* * *

Later, back home when the kids were safely upstairs in bed, Kieron and Pam were tidying the kitchen. 'I can't believe how fantastic she was about it,' he said.

'She's such a strong woman. I really admire her. The way she looked after your da too. She could have wallowed in self-pity after he died, being on her own for the first time in her life, but she didn't, she kept up her teaching and her concert hall trips.'

'I know, and I didn't give her an easy time. The night I found my birth cert in a drawer in the dresser and discovered the surname on it was different to my brothers, I went mad. They told me I was theirs, just like the other two were, but I shouted, "I'm not. I'm a stranger no one wanted." I didn't think I'd ever be anybody's.'

'I would think that was a pretty normal reaction to finding that out.'

'My brothers came down to find out what all the noise was about. When I realised they hadn't been adopted, I freaked. I didn't even belong to them. I stormed out of the house and slept in a friend's garden shed, under some old carpet. I was terrified lying there, visualising rats chewing my toes. Histrionic or what? I wanted to get away, but didn't know where to go. I never felt so lost or alone in my whole life – and do you know something, Pam? I never really shook that off. Since then, I've always felt there was something missing. I never wanted to go home again. I only did because my mate's parents got suspicious after he went in and out a few times during breakfast to sneak me some food.'

'You never told me that before. Your folks must have been frantic with worry,' Pam said. 'I bet they were relieved to see you.'

'I wouldn't be too sure about that. I was a monster. I wouldn't talk to my brothers for weeks. Everyone got the silent treatment while I tried to work things out.' He laughed. 'Remind me why I went in to teaching angst-ridden teenage boys – I must be mad.'

'You're not. All that probably made you perfectly qualified to deal with their insecurities. I love you, and I love your mothers, yes, both of them, for today and for making you look this happy.'

'I'm emotionally drained, but there is something that might even make me happier,' he said, reaching for his wife, 'and I think I might just be able to summon up energy for that. What do you think?'

'Turn out the lights on the way up,' she laughed, making for the stairs.

Chapter Twenty-two

Sandra kept her word and she and Mal had their bloods taken. Over dinner that night, she told Mal about her day.

'Three rental cars had been broken into and the visitors from France found themselves without clothes, camera, passports and their airline tickets. They'd gone off to get a meal and had parked beside each other. The thugs must have been watching them. A passer-by managed to trip one of them up as they were running away and that's how they tracked his accomplices down.'

'What a great impression those visitors will have of Ireland.'

'It's good to feel you're doing a little something to counteract that.' Sandra then asked Mal what was really on her mind. 'Should I phone Kieron or wait until we get the results of the blood tests? I don't want him to think I'm holding back on letting him meet the family.'

'I think I'd take the lead from him,' he advised.

'I could ring and tell him we've done it,' she suggested, and Mal smiled at her.

'Nothing I say will make any difference, will it?'

'Probably not! Would a text be too impersonal?'

'Go with your gut instinct.'

She texted him.

Within minutes there was a reply.

'He wants to meet up again,' she said, reading it, 'and he says thanks for doing the tests.'

'That's all good, isn't it?'

'He seems hostile still.'

'You can't tell that from a text,' Mal said. 'They always sound hostile.'

'I know, but I sense that and it makes me defensive and then I come across as being stilted and distant.'

'Maybe he's as awkward with you as you are with him. It's not exactly a regular situation.'

'I was going to suggest lunch on Saturday – here – but I don't know if that's the right thing to do. It could be a disaster.'

'Maybe make it more casual,' Mal said.

* * *

In Stoneybatter Kieron immediately reacted to the beep that indicated she had replied.

'She's asked us to drop over for a cup of tea on Saturday afternoon, all of us, if we'd like,' he told Pam.

'That's really nice of her,' she said. 'But is it wise to involve the kids just yet?'

'Probably not. I'll ask Mam to take them for us.'

The phone beeped again.

'She's probably had second thoughts,' he laughed, picking it up again. 'She wants to know if I'd like to have my half-siblings there too.'

'She's giving it a lot of thought. What do you think? Are you ready for this?'

He grinned. 'What do you think? Of course I am.'

'Why not ring her and tell her that – I'm sure she'd appreciate it.'

'Cosy chats? I don't think I'm that ready,' he said, starting a reply.

'Tell her I'm looking forward to meeting her.'

Chapter Twenty-three

'Do you need a hand?' Leah asked when Sandra rang to tell her about Kieron's visit.

'No thanks, love, maybe a bit of moral support. Come over early, will you?'

'Of course, can I bring anything?'

'No, but could I ask you something, and please don't take this the wrong way, but would you come in your car and not in Adam's? I don't know their circumstances and I don't want to come across as being ostentatious and showy. Not that I think you are. Oh God, I'm really making a mess of this, aren't I? Forget I said anything.'

Leah laughed. 'Mum, relax. It'll be all right and we'll leave the blingy Bentley at home. You know I feel exactly the same way about it as you do, but don't tell Adam – he thinks I love it like he does.'

She was relieved to see Leah and Adam arrive in her Auris. She brought an apple tart and a big bag of cookers. 'They're from the old trees at Orchard Lodge, all six of them,' she announced proudly.

In the light of what Leah had told her about having a few problems, Sandra was on the lookout for any signs of tension between the pair of them and was happy to see none.

'If his wife likes to bake, she can have them.'

'That's a nice thought,' Mal said. Leah put the tart out on the table in the conservatory. 'It's like a cake shop in here.'

'Is it too much, do you think?'

'No, it's fabulous, Mum, you can never have too much cake. And I just wanted to tell you I'm happy for you. I may have reacted badly when you told us, but it was the last thing I ever expected to hear. After what you told me since, I can't even begin to understand how you must feel, or have felt, all these years.'

Ollie pulled up outside at exactly the same moment as Kieron and Pam. He hopped out of his car and waited for the others to open their doors.

'You must be the big brother. I'm Oliver,' he said, holding out his hand. 'Ollie to the family. God, you look like my sister. And this is …?'

'Pamela, my wife. Pam to the family,' Kieron said as he took some flowers off the back seat.

'Well then, hello, Pam, welcome to the clan, both of you. This is so weird, isn't it, or is it just me?' Ollie said as they walked towards the house.

Pam replied, 'It is a bit, but it's bound to be awkward, I suppose.'

'Let's go in and you can meet the rest of us,' Oliver said, leading the way. 'Look who I found outside,' he announced when he opened the hall door. 'Pam, this is Mam, Sandra, and Mal, my dad, Adam Boles is Leah's other half and this is Leah, my favourite sister.'

'His only sister,' she laughed.

Sandra came forward and hugged them both. Kieron was more responsive than the first time they met.

Pam thanked her for having them over. 'It means so much to us.'

'And to me too,' she said. 'You can't imagine how I've dreamed about this day and I just hope it all goes well.'

'It will,' she said, squeezing her arm.

'I'm dying to meet the children too. Is that too presumptuous of me? I often wondered if I had grandchildren.'

'Not in the slightest. We'd like that too,' Pam said, 'but we haven't told them anything about the whole situation yet.'

'That's understandable,' Sandra replied.

'We'll bring them next time, I promise, if that's not presumptuous of me,' Pam smiled. Sandra sensed an ally in this young woman and liked her instinctively.

'Of course it isn't,' she replied. 'Look at us still standing here in the hall. Come through and sit down. I still find it hard to think of you as Kieron,' she said to her son. 'You've always been Peter in my mind and when Mal and I talked about you.'

'Ryan's second name is Peter too,' he said.

'I think you look very like me! That's a shock,' Leah said.

'I spent a lot of time looking in mirrors, wondering if I looked like anyone, and to find I do was a bit of a shock for me too.'

Sandra found that conversation was much easier with the others there and Ollie chatted easily with Kieron. Adam took a back seat for a while before asking Kieron where he went to school and if he was into rugby. Then he asked, 'How did you trace Sandra?'

'Yes, we're all dying to find that out,' Mal said. 'We've tried for nearly thirty years to find you and we never got anywhere.'

'It was pure serendipity, karma, fate, destiny, call it what you like, and it helped that the name on my birth and baptismal certs wasn't a common one like Walsh or Murphy. A combination of a lot of detective work and a concert programme led me to your door three years ago.'

'But why did you wait until now to contact us?' Sandra asked. She saw Kieron look at his wife, who was about to speak and he went to stop her, but Pam overruled him.

'No, Kieron, it has to be said if we're to move forward. He didn't contact you until now because he was feeling hard done by. I know that sounds cruel, but it's a fact. He was mad at all of you, but mostly he was angry at not being a part of your life. It brought up all the feelings of rejection he'd been dealing with since he found he'd been adopted.' She looked at Leah and Oliver. 'He didn't discover that until he was seventeen. It might have been easier if he'd always known.'

'I don't know what to say,' said Sandra. 'I'm sorry, and saddened, to hear this. That doesn't come anywhere near to what I feel. I know it's a cliché, but I wish I could turn the clock back.'

'It wouldn't change anything. You did what had to be done in the times we lived in,' Mal said, 'and you'd do exactly the same again if you could go back.'

'And it's not exactly their fault you felt like that, now is it?' Adam said, addressing Kieron. Sandra saw both Leah and Ollie shoot him glances that silenced him.

'I'm sorry, Sandra, we didn't mean to come to your home and offend or upset you. I'm just trying to put things into context and I think to do that we have to be honest with each other,' Pam said.

'It's OK, we understand,' Mal said. 'There's no blueprint for a situation like this and we're all a bit out of our depth.' Sandra was sitting beside him, fiddling with her rings as she looked from one of her children to another wondering if any of them would ever forgive her. He took her hand. 'And as we're being honest here, I think you all need to know the facts, all of them. Your mother always wanted to find you, Peter … Kieron. She didn't put you out of her mind when you were taken from her and given away without her consent, which is what happened. When I asked her to marry me, she wouldn't accept me until she had told me the whole story. She made it clear in no uncertain terms that if I couldn't accept what had happened, there'd be no wedding.'

'I still don't know the whole story,' Kieron said. 'I know very little.'

'We don't know either,' Ollie said, and Leah nodded her agreement.

'Your mother was the victim of rape, and I'm sorry if this is hard for you to take, but we're dealing with the facts here. It was a different Ireland thirty-odd years ago – she was twelve when it happened and thirteen when you were born.'

'I was very naïve – I was sent to a convent, but I honestly believed that when you were born I'd come back home again, with you,' Sandra told Kieron. 'I didn't know that had never been an option. We lived in a "what will the neighbours say?" culture and preserving your good name was more important than anything else, it seems.'

'Unmarried mothers were the pariahs of society. There was no such thing as an unmarried father,' Mal said. 'They got to walk away. The powers at the time considered the solution for everybody was adoption. Remember, there were no fertility clinics or IVF or whatever methods are used to help couples who were not able to start families of their own – so babies were in great demand. With the collusion of the local priest, these "fallen women" had to be hidden away for fear of the scandal they would cause. Your mother was one of these victims, and I don't use that word to shock you. She was a victim. No one considered her feelings or the consequences of what was happening to her. All they thought about was the damage that her family would suffer if people knew what had happened. Her parents were both teachers, her grandmother the local midwife. Her grandfather had been the head in primary school for years before he died, so they were a "respectable family".'

He paused and looked in turn at Pam and Kieron, and at Ollie, Leah and Adam.

'There's no easy way to fill you in on your family history, skeletons and all. It is what it is. After Sandra was taken away, she never saw her family, including her only sister, again.'

'That's inhuman,' said Pam.

'It was inhuman. Her grandmother, who lived with them all her life, died before you were born, Kieron, and Sandra never knew that either until she saw her gravestone years later. She never saw you, Kieron, after you were a few weeks old. She wasn't even allowed say goodbye to you. She was underage; even if she had given her permission for you to be adopted, it would have been invalid. Her education stopped then too, so if you think you had a hard life, son,' he said, directing his comment to Kieron, 'you didn't.'

Sandra was so proud of the way he told them what had happened, and loved him more than ever right then. She had tears in her eyes after his speech, so too had Pam. Leah went over and sat on the arm of the sofa beside her mother and hugged her.

'I didn't have a bad life at all,' said Kieron, clearing his throat. 'I didn't mean to give that impression. I had a very loving home, I just never fitted in there, and I never knew why I always felt the odd one out. When I learned the truth, it made sense in a weird kind of way, but I went through some very angry years before I finally made peace with the fact that I was different. My father was still alive then, and it would have killed him if he thought I was looking for you, so I didn't. He'd have regarded it as a criticism of his parenting skills.'

'I'm so glad you did look for me. I wrote to you every year on your birthday and sent letters to the convent in case you ever came looking for me,' Sandra told him. 'Did you get them?'

'No. When I enquired, several times too, all I ever got was a curt dismissal telling me that their files were confidential and I had no right to them. I wrote to you too. I don't suppose—'

'No, I never heard anything either.'

'Those people have a lot to answer for,' said Mal.

'Mum, we thought your parents were dead, and that it upset you too much to talk about them, so we never did. Isn't that right, Ollie?

'Did your parents know who was responsible?'

'No one did. I was too scared to tell them.'

'Not even your sister?' said Pam.

'No, not even Louise – she had just gone away to boarding school that September. I was supposed to go the following year, but that never happened.'

'Have you ever gone back?' Kieron asked.

'Only once, a long time ago. Mal took me when you were a tot, Leah, and that was when we found my gran's grave. She died when I was in the convent. We talked to the woman in the post office, I'd been in school with her but she didn't recognise me. She told Mal she'd heard that my parents had split up and gone abroad. I couldn't believe that, but then I wouldn't exactly describe her as a reliable witness. She wasn't sure about that or whether they'd gone to England or America. It made little difference to me then, as I was clearly dead to them at that stage anyway.'

'That's shocking,' Ollie said.

'It may be, but it's still the truth. I said goodbye to them one morning and was driven away by the parish priest. I remember his name was Fr O'Looney, and that was the end of my childhood and everyone in it. None of them ever got in touch with me again.'

'Have you photos of any of them?' Leah asked.

'Just one, of Louise and me together. Mal, will you get it for me? It was taken when she came home for her first half-term from boarding school.'

Mal left the room and came back a few moments later with the old photo. 'It's a bit out of focus, but your mam hasn't changed much,' he said, smiling at Sandra and passing it around for them to inspect.

'My God, she looks just like Jennifer, doesn't she, Kieron?' Pam said as she studied the faces.

'Sandra said that when I showed her the photo of our two. She could be her sister,' he agreed.

That was the first time he'd used her name, which made her happy, and she felt everything would work out.

'You're not a bit like one another,' Leah said, studying the snap.

'No, we weren't. She always looked perfect. I had wild hair. We had a housekeeper called Dinah, who used to tell me I looked as though I'd been dragged through a hedge backwards. That was the last time we ever spent together. She went back to school the next day and I never saw or heard from her again.'

'This is all so weird,' Ollie said. 'I'm not often stuck for words but I really don't know what to say, Mum. We never knew you'd gone through any of this.'

'After I said I'd marry Mal and told him everything – he had already bought the ring – he brought it back and had the centre replaced with a sapphire, blue for a boy, for the little boy I'd lost, and I've never taken it off since. This was all I had as proof that you ever existed, Kieron.'

'Dad, you old romantic!' Ollie said.

'I've never told anyone that until now,' she said.

'Are there any more relatives or secrets anyone would like to share?' Adam asked. 'I'm beginning to feel left out of this charmed circle.'

'That's a bit insensitive, don't you think?' Ollie retorted.

Ignoring this exchange, Mal asked Sandra, 'May I tell them the rest?'

She nodded and replied quietly, 'I suppose we have to.'

'Your mother had a breakdown not long after we married. Our friends and neighbours were all starting families and showing off their precious little bundles and it was more than she could handle. She always felt guilty about letting you be given away, though in time she learned to accept that she couldn't have stopped it happening even if she'd known.' He explained about what triggered her impulse to take someone else's baby, believing he was her Peter, and outlined how difficult she'd found coming to terms with life again as she'd recovered.

'I'm not proud of what I did, or what I put the poor couple through,' she said.

'I can understand why you did, though,' said Pam. 'How dreadful for you. If anyone tried to take my babies, I'd have killed to get them back.'

'I was like something possessed when I thought I'd found you, Kieron. You'd have been about eight or nine by then, but to me you were my little bundle in blue, as you were when last I saw you in the chapel.' She told them how she had seen a baby leaving with its new family, unaware that it was him and that they were ripping part of her soul away.

'I don't know what to say, Sandra.' He'd done it again, used her name as naturally as if he'd always known her. 'Thank you for telling us all that. I came here feeling the aggrieved one, hard done by because I felt you'd just decided that I was an inconvenience to be given away. Now, I'm beginning to see the other side and I'm sorry for my attitude.'

'There's no need to apologise, I can understand why you would feel like that too,' she replied. 'I'm just glad we've been given this chance to say these things to each other.'

'Mum, I'm really shocked. I never knew you'd suffered so much. You always seem so happy and caring,' Leah said.

'That's because she is. She's an extraordinary woman and I'm very proud of her.' Mal put his arm around Sandra's shoulder and pulled her close. 'Now if you have any more questions this is the time to ask them, because I know how hard these revelations have been on her, and I don't want us, any of us, to have to go through all of it again.'

'I'm going to make more tea,' said Leah. 'This could be a long afternoon.'

'I'm going to ring Mam and tell her we'll be a while yet.'

'Go into the hall, you'll have some privacy there,' Mal said. There were so many issues and questions to be addressed that they talked for another two hours. Sandra felt a peace she had never felt before as they chipped away at barriers, some self-erected and imagined, others very real and still very raw.

When he came back in, Adam said, 'Now it's your turn, Kieron. How did you solve the puzzle of who and where your mother was?'

'Sandra, when we met in Clontarf Castle, you told me you played the piano and I told you my mother is a music teacher and both my brothers are professional musicians. What I didn't tell you was that Liam – he's the one who plays piano, Derek is the violinist – Liam played in the last Dublin International Competition three years ago and was at a barbecue here in this very house!'

'I don't believe it. Did he know?' asked Mal.

'No, none of us did. You were hosting a Russian competitor, Ivan or Viktor?'

'It was Viktor,' Sandra said.

'Hold on a minute,' said Ollie, 'I remember him being here – he has dark floppy hair, taller than me by a good few centimetres.'

'That's him – he makes me look small.'

'But we all went clubbing afterwards, remember? Leah, you and Adam came too.'

'That's incredible, your brother being here. I can't credit that,' said Sandra. 'It's too much to take in, and I still don't understand how you found out.'

'It gets even better. I think you and my mother, my adoptive mother, actually met each other briefly the night of the finals in the National Concert Hall.'

'No … I can't take this all in. Were you there too?' she asked.

'I was, but I met so many of Liam's friends as well as Mam's past pupils over the two weeks that I honestly can't recall.'

'I always take those weeks off from court duties to devote the time wholly to the competition,' Sandra said. 'I love it and there's a great social element to it. Last time Viktor was allocated to us. He's terrifically talented and is already making a name for himself on the concert circuit.'

'This is the third time we've been hosts,' Mal said. 'We wanted him to enjoy his time with us and we told him to feel free to invite anyone he wanted to the house – it was to be his home for his stay.'

'On the first day, sponsors, competitors, volunteers, judges, the whole shebang, gather in the National Concert Hall and it's like the Tower of Babel in there, with all those languages. I don't recognise half of them,' Sandra continued. 'We spotted some familiar faces while Viktor joined the contestants for their introductions and instructions.'

Then Kieron spoke. 'And that night, I drove my mam and brothers to the gathering and Liam joined the contestants waiting to be given details and schedules. She was so proud that Liam had got in, never mind how he'd get on. I remember her saying how sorry she was that Dad wasn't around to see it. He'd only been dead six months at that stage.'

'When Viktor was knocked out, Mum decided we should have a barbecue to cheer him up,' Leah said.

'Liam was knocked out in the same round, and that's how he came to be invited to your barbecue. But let me backtrack a little,' Kieron said. 'On that first meet-and-greet night, I drove them home before going back to my own place. When I got back to the car, I noticed that Liam had forgotten to take his folder and competition schedule. I went back to the house to give them to him. I flicked through the pages of the programme, thinking of the mammoth amount of organisation involved. A name in one of the lists jumped out – 'S. Mac Giolla Tighearnaigh', the name of my mother on my birth cert.

'You don't usually use your maiden name, Mum,' Leah said.

'No, but there's a whole clatter of Wallaces, including the publicans, who are patrons too, and the first year we were involved it caused all sorts of confusion – everyone thought I was one of them – so the next time I decided to revert to my own name.'

'Did you say anything to your brother?' Ollie asked.

'No, which is just as well, because he hadn't met you all at that stage and I mightn't have delved any further.'

'That wasn't much to go on,' Adam remarked.

'That's what I told him,' Pam said. 'There must be lots of people called that, and I asked him, assuming he could discover who she was and where she lived, what he would do – he couldn't just walk up to this woman and say, "Hi, I wonder if we're related?"'

'But the name is not exactly mainstream, is it? It was the first time I'd ever come across it – even among all the kids in the two schools I've taught in, or in college. Anyway, I felt it was worth trying,' said Kieron.

Kieron told them that they followed Liam's progress, going to some of his rehearsals for support and they celebrated as he was included in the twenty-four who made in to the second round, and then into the twelve finalists. His opposition included the twenty-six-year-old Viktor, whom he had met the previous year at master classes in Berlin. But by the end of the afternoon, they had both been eliminated.

'They're all winners in my book,' Mal said. 'I never really appreciated orchestral music, symphonies and all this before I met Sandra. I wasn't destined to be a Richard Clayderman. The calculator is my keyboard.'

'Neither was I,' said Kieron, 'but the years of practice paid off for them, and I'll be able to spend my old age boasting about my two famous brothers, citizens of the world with a violin and piano for passports.'

'But I don't understand – you never called, or made any contact …' Sandra said.

'That's not technically true. I did find out where you lived and I did turn up outside your house one day. I actually saw you leave and drive away and then I did too.'

'But you never came back after that …'

'I didn't know what to expect from making that visit, but I know that instead of getting any satisfaction or sense of closure that day, I felt more invisible and more excluded than ever after it,' Kieron said, 'and I suppose I just pulled the shutters down on the whole situation, until this business with Jennifer cropped up and Pam persuaded me to contact you.'

'I'm so glad you did,' said Sandra

They chatted back and forth, the siblings wanting to find out more about each other's lives. Much later Sandra and Mal watched them get ready to leave, with promises from Ollie, Leah and Adam to have blood tests done, if she and Mal weren't suitable matches for Jennifer. No matter what the outcome might be, they all promised not to lose touch ever again.

'I'm delighted to have met you, Pam, and Kieron. Please bring the children with you next time. Oh, and tell your mam she did a good job on you and I'm very grateful to her.'

The embraces and goodbyes were genuinely warm and much less guarded than previously. Sandra and Mal watched from the porch as Leah and Oliver walked to their cars with Kieron and Pam, who was clutching the bag of cooking apples Leah had brought, laughing at some exchange, Adam a few paces behind.

'I think our family has just grown considerably, Sandra. What do you think?'

'You know what I think, Mal? I think I need a stiff drink!'

Back inside, she crashed into an armchair and said, 'I feel as though I've been flattened by a steamroller, but you know, Mal, I feel two stone lighter.'

'So do I, and I really like him, and his wife too.'

Chapter Twenty-four

'How do you feel after that?' Pam said to Kieron on the drive home. 'I thought it went really well – and I like them. They're all really warm, aren't they?'

When Pam had phoned earlier, Kieron's mother had offered to hold on to the kids until the next day. 'Would you like to go somewhere for a drink?' he asked.

'No, let's go home and have one there,' she said. 'We have to celebrate now that your search is over.'

He nodded. 'Good idea.'

They drank a bottle of Burgundy and went to bed exhausted and elated, taking advantage of having an empty house. But Kieron couldn't sleep, his mind was overactive, thinking about what Sandra had told him, so he slipped out of bed and went downstairs. He opened the box file where he kept any documents of significance. It was time to start joining the dots. His tenacity had paid off before and he was determined it would again. He had to find out what happened to Sandra's family – after all, if it hadn't been for him, she'd never have lost them.

He took out his birth and baptismal certs and looked at them. Mother: S. Mac Giolla Tighearnaigh, father's name unknown. Her occupation was listed as student.

He also looked at his adoption papers; his mam had given them to him years earlier. He'd write again to the religious institution that sent a card to his mother each Christmas. He'd change his tack too. This time, he was in control. He was in possession of real facts and he'd use them to find out what had happened to all the letters that he'd written to Sandra – and the ones she'd written to him. Her parents and sister probably did write, but why had they never gone to see her or taken her home afterwards, especially as he was adopted?

I just got lucky the last time, finding Sandra, he thought, and he wondered if it would be as easy to trace the rest of her family. Back then, he had looked up phone directories in the library for the various counties, but managed to get only a handful of entries under that surname, and none with the initial 'S', and none in Dublin. He'd go back and check for 'Ls' this time. He'd steered away from using Facebook last time, rejecting it as not being the forum to declare why he was looking for Sandra. This was different – he was just trying to track down a relative, it would be OK if he were careful how he worded his posts.

He heard Pam's steps on the stairs.

She shielded her eyes against the light. 'Kieron, it's half three, what on earth are you doing?'

'You don't really want to know,' he said, standing up and closing his laptop. 'Let's go back to bed.' He turned the lights out and followed her. He'd made a decision and was going to enlist Leah and Ollie's help.

On Monday, he phoned Leah. 'I have something I want to run by you, if you're willing. Could we meet for half an hour or so?'

* * *

'I'm intrigued,' she told him when they met in a pub close to her offices. 'If you have more questions, I'm afraid I don't have any more answers. As we said, we were hearing everything for the first time too.'

'It's not that, but I have an idea. I've asked Ollie to join us – he texted to say he's running a bit late.'

'Now I'm even more intrigued. But I want to ask you something – we started so many conversations on Saturday, and half of them went off at a tangent, but you said you traced Mum over three years ago. Why didn't you tell her who you were then?'

'Put it down to bloody bad timing! I rocked up at your house, just as you were coming out the door on Mal's arm, on the day of your wedding!'

'My God, I don't believe it.'

'It's true. I stood outside the gates, at the back of the gawkers, neighbours I assume, and watched who I now know to be Ollie escort two very glamorous older ladies out to the car.'

'They were my aunties, Tanya and Pearl – they're not my real aunties at all, Mum worked with them in London. They joke about how they were penniless together. They've been friends forever.'

'Then came the bridesmaids with Sandra. That was my first glimpse of her. I don't know what I was expecting, but it wasn't a vision straight from a fashion catalogue. I could hardly see her under her hat! When I told Pam, she wanted me to describe what she was wearing and I told her I hadn't a clue but that she'd been wearing a hat – a very large hat.'

'Typical man,' Leah laughed. 'You can tell her she wore a smoky-grey shantung coat over a dusty-pink dress and a two-toned picture hat. I know because a whole lot of planning went in to that outfit!'

'She'll think I've lost it altogether if I go home and tell her that. By the way, you looked stunning.'

'A whole lot of planning went in to that, too,' she said. 'Dad did this old-fashioned thing of making me close the hall door behind us. Apparently it's symbolic – for the last time I'd leave home as a girl. Next time I'd be coming back as someone else's wife. I was so emotional I was afraid I'd cry and ruin the dress before I even got into the car.'

'I'll have to remember to do that when it's Jennifer's turn.'

'Did it upset you to see us all together like that, Kieron?'

'Yes, much more than I imagined it would. I could see the resemblance between us, and I figured Sandra had to be my birth mother, but to all of you I was, well, I was an outsider.'

'It must be awful to feel like that.'

'Well, you did ask.' He smiled. 'I actually caught up with the bridal car at the next set of lights and tailed you to the church. I was in two minds whether to go in or not. I couldn't help but wonder if your dad was my natural father too. I was so close to you all, but, to me, the woman hadn't wanted me, she'd given me away. I couldn't be sure, but I assumed you were her daughter and the young man I'd seen was her son. I didn't know about the bridesmaids, but I did know that none of them had worked nights in McDonald's and weekends in different pubs to get through college. The Mercedes and Toyota that were parked in the driveway of the house were a world away from my father's bicycle, or the furniture van he drove. Yes, I admit I was angry that day. I didn't go in. I turned the car around and drove to the Phoenix Park where I sat there for a long time. I felt my search was over, but I certainly didn't feel any 'closure'. I had all the confirmation I needed, yet it wasn't nearly enough and I knew it never would be.'

'Our wedding anniversary was two weeks ago – three years.'

'I knew that. I remembered the date.'

'You and I have a lot of catching up to do, now that you've found us.'

'Well, that's what I wanted to talk to you about … and here's Ollie. Perfect timing.'

When Ollie had sat down, Kieron began. 'Ollie, you mentioned that you'd love to try and find your mother's family and I think we three should try, if only to see if they are still alive.'

'But Mum and Dad tried to do that years ago, and they drew a blank back then, when some people would still have remembered them. No one will have any recollection of them now,' Leah said.

'Well, you didn't have me in the family then, did you?' he grinned. 'We're going to see if we can jog those memories, but don't tell Sandra or Mal. There's no point in getting their hopes up in case we get nowhere.'

'We have the internet now too – maybe that'll make a difference,' Ollie chipped in.

'We need to approach the exercise with precision, so I have a plan of action and I'll need your approval and input to start digging.' Kieron pulled some pages out of his well-worn briefcase. 'I'll contact the Department of Education, they should have records of the teachers of the time in the local school.'

'And the parish may have details of family deaths. Sometimes, people came home to be buried with their parents or in family plots even though they had moved away,' Leah said.

'We don't even have our grandmother's maiden name or whether she was a local or not. Mum mentioned a housekeeper called Dinah, but I haven't a clue what her surname was … or is, but someone might remember her,' Oliver said.

'We have Mum's date of birth, so we could get a copy of her birth cert and work backwards from that,' Leah suggested.

'I'll get a solicitor friend of mine to contact the order of nuns where Mum was sent and see if we can get them to release any information they have, and ask whatever happened to the correspondence that was never passed on to any of you,' Ollie said.

'We might find out where her parents went to, although I doubt they would still have any of the addresses.'

'Maybe not, but we might get some clues, so it's worth trying,' Kieron agreed.

Chapter Twenty-five

Sandra got home early from the courts the following Wednesday and found two letters addressed to her and Mal; one was official looking and the other obviously personal. She opened the personal one first. She heard Mal come in, deposit his briefcase in the hall and hang his jacket up. He came in to the kitchen and gave her a kiss.

'Anything interesting?' he asked, glancing at the card in her hand.

'Yes,' she smiled, 'a really lovely thank you note from Pam and Kieron, for making them so welcome and for letting them meet all of us.' Her voice caught. 'Here. Read it for yourself.' She was overcome by emotion. It was so different in tone to his original letter that had arrived just a few weeks earlier.

Mal took the card from her. 'That sounds heartfelt all right. How are you doing? It's been a bit of a roller-coaster ride, hasn't it?'

'So much has happened since then and it's all happened so quickly. I can hardly believe it.'

Mal picked the official envelope and opened that. 'I'm sorry, love, but it seems that neither of us is a suitable match for Jennifer's marrow.'

'Oh, no. I had so much wanted to be able to help them out,' she said.

'I know, Sandra, so did I, but it was always going to be a long shot. The others won't know their results until next week.'

'I know it was a long shot, but it's so disappointing.'

'At least you were willing to try – and that means a lot. And at least Jennifer seems to be doing well at the moment.'

'I'm really looking forward to meeting them. My ready-made grandchildren. Can you believe it?'

'No, you look far too young!'

'Flatterer. Well, there's no sign of Adam and Leah giving us one yet.'

She hadn't talked to Leah for a few days. They'd been playing tag since Sunday, and as she was thinking about her, her phone rang.

'We keep missing each other. I'm just going to cook some salmon fillets for your dad and me. I have plenty, if the pair of you want to come over – nothing fancy.'

'I will. Adam's not around this evening. He has a work commitment, but his old buddy Judd is in town so I suspect it could be a late one, and involve some drinking,' Leah told her.

Sandra hadn't met Judd, and only knew him from what Leah had told her about his reputation.

'Right, Mum, see you in a bit. I've loads to tell you.'

* * *

Sandra was chopping some things for the salad when Leah arrived.

'You must be very happy with how things turned out, Mum. I thought Saturday was a great success.'

'Much more than happy. It was great. I still can't believe he found us, although we never got back to getting the details,' Sandra said as they settled at the table.

'There were lots of things we didn't get back to,' Mal said, 'but I suppose that's to be expected, with a gap as wide as thirty-seven years to fill and all of us putting in our tuppence-worth.'

'I can help you there. Don't look so surprised, I met him on his own for a drink on Monday. He rang to thank me for the apples and to say how much he'd appreciated how welcoming we all were to him and to Pam.'

'They sent us a lovely thank-you note,' Sandra said. 'What did he say?'

'Stay sitting down for this,' she told them. 'You know he said he'd found out where you lived three years ago? Well, the day he decided to knock on your door was my wedding day. He stood outside and saw us all leaving for the ceremony.'

'Never. That can't be true,' Sandra said.

'Oh yes it is, but he couldn't see you properly under your big hat. He was very impressed by his glamorous mother!' She laughed.

'I can't believe he was so close and that I didn't sense it. I always felt I would know,' Sandra said.

'Like a cat recognising its kittens from their scent,' said Mal.

'Something like that,' she agreed, smiling, feeling she had unintentionally hurt him again 'but I suppose that was wishful thinking on my part. What I don't understand is why he waited so long to contact me when he knew where we lived.'

'I think I understand,' Leah said. 'There we were, a self-contained unit, leading lives he knew nothing about and we didn't know anything about his – it just made him feel more abandoned.'

'No wonder he held off,' said Mal, 'that all makes perfect sense.'

'He went for counselling for a while, I'm not sure if he'd like me to have told you that.'

Sandra agreed, more determined than ever to try to make it up to him, and to Pam too. She who must have suffered with him through all that.

'Anyway, I came around to tell you something – I've decided to go to Tassie with Adam, for more than just a holiday. He's taking leave for a year and heading off to spend some time on the farm and try out being a landowner.'

Sandra glanced at Mal. She hadn't been expecting this. For a split second, she thought Leah was going to tell them she was pregnant – not that she was moving to the other side of the world.

'Are you thinking of moving there permanently?' Mal asked. 'We'd miss you terribly if you did – it's so far away.'

'That's not on the cards in the foreseeable future, but it is a possibility. I know you haven't sorted out dates yet for your visit, but we still want you to come over whenever you're up for it.'

'And we certainly will, just not now. I can't believe what I'm hearing – I find a son and lose a daughter.'

'You're not losing me. You'll never do that, and haven't you just gained two grandchildren? I suppose this puts us into the 'blended' family category now – with half-brother and half-sister, step-sister-in-law, step granddad, the list goes on, doesn't it?' They laughed.

'I suppose it does,' Sandra said, thinking *They're all my family and always will be, no distinctions or special privileges*. But now her only daughter would be far away – too far to drop in for impromptu coffees and girly chats. She couldn't imagine what that was going to be like.

'When are you going?' Sandra asked.

'Very soon – in three weeks. Unless I turn out to be a match as a donor and no one else does, then I'll join Adam later.'

'Does Ollie know?' Mal asked.

'I hadn't made my mind up when we talked about it, but he has an inkling.'

'What a crowd of conspirators this family is turning into,' Sandra said.

Mal laughed. 'They learned from the master, didn't they!'

'Touché,' she replied.

'Mum, can I ask you something else? Before I go thousands of miles away and forget to ask.'

'Fire away.'

'Something has been puzzling me since we had that heart-to-heart. I always thought you were happy living with the Fourniers, but you said you were running away when you went to London. Was it from them?'

'I was happy there. I could have ended up slaving away in the laundries like so many other girls, but I was given a get-out-of-jail card when I was sent to live with them. I had three good years with the Fourniers and I really was part of their family. Then something happened and I left them all behind, but this time it was my choice. I was the one who walked away and never made contact again.'

'But why, Mum, what changed?'

'I suppose I grew up, and realised I had choices. I also fell in love – well, I thought it was love – with a wonderfully exotic young French pianist.'

'Tell me more,' Leah prompted.

'I've heard this one before, and I can't compete! I'm off to watch the news!' Mal said, and left the table.

'He was called André, and we all had to keep really quiet while he practised, which he did a lot in the three weeks he was with us. I was totally besotted and blushed every time he talked to me. He had the longest eyelashes I had ever seen and the darkest eyes – you couldn't tell where the pupils and irises met. He was my first crush.'

'Is he the reason you got involved in the piano competitions?'

'Probably. By the time he left, I knew every note and nuance in his extensive repertoire. I loved watching him play. He seemed to be in sync with whatever communication was happening between the notes and his soul.'

'Wow, Mum, you had it bad.'

'I did. The Fourniers had a party one night and he played the concerto he was going to perform in the National Concert Hall the following evening, It was the first time I ever saw anyone wearing tails – he looked like a film star.'

'Did he fancy you?'

'Not at all. I was just a kid, almost fifteen, but he awakened emotions I never thought I'd experience. He made me realise I was normal. I mean, I worried after what had happened, if I'd ever be capable of falling in love and having normal relationships. He awakened feelings that convinced me I had nothing to worry about.'

'Rape has to be one of the worst crimes, because of the scars and the long-term consequences,' Leah said. 'I think you're marvellous, Mum, I really do.'

'Not many people understand that. Unfortunately, I'm only one of many.'

'You're still fab, Mum, even if your first love got away on you!'

'I don't think I'd have known what to do if he'd made a move; I'd have run a mile. And although he'll never know it, it was because of him that I grew up emotionally in those three weeks and got my confidence back.'

'And then you ran away?'

'No, that was much later,' she said. 'I was sixteen when I left for good.'

Part Two

Part Ten

Chapter Twenty-six

Mayo, 1970

The summer hadn't worked out as they had planned and the girls had been really good about it. Mary was supposed to be taking Louise and Sandra to New York to visit her sister, whom she hadn't seen since she was a teenager. The much-anticipated trip Stateside didn't happen though. Con's mother slipped coming home from Mass one morning, and that put paid to that.

'I'm so sorry this hip operation scuppered your plans, Mary,' Con said.

They rearranged the furniture in the parlour to make space for the bed when she came home.

'There'll be other opportunities,' she replied, dreading the return of her mother-in-law from hospital. She'd visited every day for five weeks, with one exception. That was the day she'd taken her daughters to Dublin to get the last bits and pieces for Louise before she started boarding school. They'd shopped in Clerys and had afternoon tea in the Gresham Hotel before heading back. Mary had known it wasn't just their outing that had made everything seem brighter and more carefree somehow, it was the absence of her mother-in-law from their daily lives, her omnipresent censure of their actions and her obsession with appearances. Mary's spirits plummeted as she thought of the future. Her being away only accentuated the reality of her return.

Mary felt more trapped than ever, knowing that bad as things were before the fall, her mother-in-law would be twice as demanding now.

'Maybe when she's back walking confidently again, you could still go over to your sister. Maybe in the Christmas holidays,' Con suggested.

'It wouldn't be the right time.'

'Then maybe you could go off with the two of them next summer. I'm sure we could manage that, and it would be good for them to see a bit of the wider world.'

'I'll hold that thought, but I can't see it happening. If she weren't such a curmudgeonly old woman, she'd welcome people coming in to look after her, but as she won't ...'

'She's not going to have much choice – she'll have to keep doing the physio for the new hip if she's to get up and about again, and she's having that even if I have to threaten respite care in the county home,' he said.

'I'd love to be there when you do that,' Mary said.

* * *

'I'll miss the smell of baking when I'm gone,' Louise said to her mother. Mary Mac Giolla Tighearnaigh and her two daughters were making the most of the last Sunday of the school holidays. 'You'll just have to make crumbles and freeze them for me for when I get home at half-term.'

'I can't believe the summer's gone so quickly, and I'm sure that's not all you'll miss. It'll be a very quiet house next week and Sandra will have no one to argue with.'

A little bell sounded, then rang more insistently, followed by Gran's voice. 'Can no one hear me?' Mary wiped her floury hands on her apron and went to see what her mother-in-law wanted this time.

'You'll miss the blackberry picking this year, and Mam's tarts,' Sandra told her sister.

'But I'll have lots of adventures too.' She lowered her voice. 'But I won't miss Gran's smelly commode.' They giggled.

It was Mrs Mac Giolla Tighearnaigh's turn to host the weekly card game, so Mary was expecting the miraculous recovery from her latest ailment – it always happened like that.

Apart from such gatherings, the parlour was opened only for the occasional visitor, and on high days and holidays. Mrs Mac Giolla Tighearnaigh was fussing, leaning on her cane and straightening the antimacassars on the chairs that Dinah, who 'did' for Mrs Mac Giolla Tighearnaigh, had already straightened. The best cups and napkins were already on the serving trolley, along with the tea strainer, slop bowl and milk jugs. It had taken Mary a while, but she had gradually got used to her mother-in-law's idiosyncratic ways and her likes and dislikes. She no longer tried to gloss over them or make excuses for her behaviour.

'She's taken a spleen against the young curate,' Dinah told Mary.

'Oh! What's his crime?' she asked tossing her eyes heavenwards.

'He's been known to play a round of golf on a Sunday.'

'Eternal damnation for him!' Mary said, and they laughed.

'And as for that upstart, Jack Kelly? Blatantly washing his car on a Sunday, in broad daylight. What sort of example is that? Letting the parish down.' They laughed again. 'I think everything is done.'

'Her parlour is ready, and suitably imbued with the pungent aroma of Mansion wax polish, as befitting those in her social circle. We're expecting the parish priest and the young golf-playing priest, along with the solicitor, the doctor and their wives and—'

'I take it that Mr O'Sullivan is still on the blacklist?' Mary asked.

'No! He's earned his stripes. I believe he's also a good card player.'

Mary was Dominic O'Sullivan's niece. Mrs Mac Giolla Tighearnaigh had never really forgiven him for getting the headmaster's job above her son, despite his seniority. Mary laughed with Con at his mother's selection process – hadn't it been the parish priest's vote that had swayed Dominic's appointment, and wasn't he a distant cousin of his anyway? It was only when Con had insisted that snubbing his headmaster didn't help his situation in the same school that she had grudgingly capitulated.

'Louise,' Gran called. 'Come and help Sandra fix up the card tables, and make sure the pencils are all sharpened.'

'Can we have a game, Gran? You promised you'd teach me how to play bridge,' Sandra asked.

'I will, but not today, child, I need to keep a clear head,' Gran replied. 'Put the packs of cards out there for me too.'

'When Louise is away at school?'

'Very well.'

The girls opened the door to the guests and took their coats upstairs to their parents' bedroom. Then, they were expected to vanish from sight. During the holidays, they stayed downstairs to serve the tea and cakes when a break was called.

The solicitor always said, 'My, how you girls are growing – you'll be passing me out soon', which seemed highly unlikely as he was a gangly six foot three. His wife always asked about school.

'I'm starting as a boarder next week.'

'Of course, you got the scholarship,' she said to Con, 'With a clever Dad like yours. It cost us a fortune to put ours through secondary school and college.'

Mary was amused at this exchange. Mrs Mac Giolla Tighearnaigh thought it vulgar to talk about money, so she changed the subject, but not before Con got in, 'Well, I can't take all the credit, she has a pretty clever mother in Mary, don't forget.'

Dominic O'Sullivan added, 'And a very sharp and elegant grandmother too, if I may say.' He winked at Mary. He always wrong-footed Mrs Mac Giolla Tighearnaigh at some stage by passing a compliment, which she had to accept although it nearly choked her to do so. She acknowledged this one with a nod, before leading the way back into the parlour to commence play.

'Be good,' Mary told the girls, knowing full well the antics they'd get up to in their bedroom, mimicking the solicitor's wife's affected speech, trying to copy the accent and ending up giggling uproariously under their blankets.

She loved her girls and was going to miss Louise terribly – she knew Sandra would be lost without her too.

Chapter Twenty-seven

Sandra was already missing Louise terribly, and she was only gone a week. She was finishing her homework when her dad and gran started shouting. Her mother was visiting someone in hospital. If she'd been home, she'd have stopped them. Sandra went outside to get away from the arguing. Dad didn't get mad often, but she hated it all the same, and she wished Louise were here to talk to. Instead, Sandra did one of her favourite things and went to stroke the donkey – he had become her confidante since Louise had left. He nuzzled her and his coat was soaking wet but his breath was warm on her hand as she held clumps of damp grass for him to guzzle.

Her dad came out and joined her. 'You're not in any trouble. You did nothing wrong. It's just a tiff between Gran and me, and it will all blow over by the morning. Best just keep out of the firing line though until she cools down.' He smiled at her. 'She's just having one of her conniptions. How would you fancy running a little errand for me now that it's stopped raining? It's just up to Master O'Sullivan's. I promised I'd drop some files in to him this afternoon and I completely forgot before your mam went off with the car.'

Although he was her mother's uncle, the girls always addressed him as 'Master O'Sullivan' or 'Sir'. He was always polite, even a little aloof, and was never over-friendly with them. She grabbed her anorak and bike and set off, the brown envelope bouncing up and down in the basket. He lived less than five minutes away and she could see the curl of turf smoke rising from his chimney as she cycled up the hill, avoiding the puddles, her hair and skirt flapping in the wind.

'Well, it's Sandra, isn't it? Don't just stand there. Come in, come in, child, I'm just having a sup of tea. Will you join me?'

Sandra, afraid of being impolite, went in and sat on the edge of a chair. Without saying anything, he poured the tea, almost black in colour, and then he drowned it with milk straight from a bottle and scooped two spoons of sugar into it, without asking her if she took any. He stirred it and put it down in front of her. It was only lukewarm and far too sweet, but she concentrated on swallowing a mouthful. He'd obviously been reading the newspaper. It was folded up on the table and there was congealed fat and the evidence of fried eggs on a plate that didn't match his cups.

She noticed these things, but she didn't notice how he was looking at her.

He reached over for the envelope she'd brought and she thought he was really clumsy when he knocked her cup over and the contents spilled onto her skirt. She jumped up as the warm liquid hit her legs.

'Don't look so worried,' he said, 'we'll look after that. Your skirt will dry out in no time in front of the fire. Just slip it off and I'll dab the stain. No need to tell anyone what happened at all: sure that Gran of yours would never forgive you for being so clumsy.'

She hesitated, not knowing what to do. He'd been the clumsy one – not her. He took a rough towel from the back of a chair and handed it to her. 'Put that around you and give your skirt here.'

She wrapped the towel tightly around herself as she wriggled out of her skirt. He ran water on the stain, dried it with a none-too-clean dishcloth and hung it over the fireguard.

'That'll dry in no time there,' he said. 'Now, let's look after you.'

He reached for the towel, but she clasped it even tighter to herself. He knelt down in front of her and began rubbing it up and down her thighs. The towel was smelly, and so was he. He smelled of stale smoke and he was breathing very fast, as though he had run or cycled up a hill. She tried to move away but he held her roughly. Then he tried to kiss her. She froze, but then she turned away – for some reason she noticed the room was full of books and the surfaces were covered with stacks of papers. When she tried to break free, he stood up and he pushed her against the dresser so hard that the dishes rattled. Something toppled off and shattered as it hit the tiles. She saw a detached jug handle roll across the floor, but he didn't stop what he was doing. He grabbed her hand and put it inside his trousers, holding on to it. She tried to pull away but her tightened his grip on her. The towel fell to the floor. Then he began groaning and swaying.

He did things she had no words for, things that frightened and hurt her. She was terrified of what he was doing, but terrified to shout out. He carried on, manically. His face was covered with sweat. She thought she'd gone mad. Maybe he was having a fit. She begged him to stop, that he was hurting her, but he didn't seem to hear. Then with a moan like a wounded animal he stopped, as suddenly as he had started. Afraid to move, she stood still, trying to cover herself up again.

'Go upstairs and give yourself a little wash,' he said, handing her the towel from the floor.

He stood in the doorway and watched as she went. She wanted to bolt out the front door and run home, but she couldn't go home without her skirt. She spent a good while in the bathroom washing herself, trying to wash away what he'd done and the stale smell of him. She was afraid of what might happen when she went back down. A knock on the door made her jump. She stood there, frozen with fear.

'I'm leaving your skirt outside the door. It's nearly dry. I'm just going to get a reply for you to bring your father.' She heard him on the stairs. She had to follow him at some stage so the sooner she did, the sooner she could leave.

'We'll not say a word about this to anyone, Sandra, sure we won't? And I'll not tell the nuns or your parents, or even your gran, what you made me do, taking your skirt off like that in front of me. Sure the nuns wouldn't want you and your sister in their schools if they knew what you were like, would they? We won't mention the broken jug either, will we? Promise me now, child. We'll keep this as our secret. Promise me,' he said. His face was really close to hers. There was that sweaty odour again. She wanted to retch.

'I promise,' she whispered. 'Can I go home now?'

'Of course you can, child. Give that letter to your dad, and remember your secret is safe with me. Be careful on the road, it's raining again.'

Sandra cried so much on the way home that she could hardly see where she was going. She swerved to avoid a stray sheep and cycled straight into a pothole. The front wheel plugged and catapulted her off the bike.

The sheep scampered up the bank and disappeared. Sandra was muddy and wet and had cut one of her knees and she had to walk the rest of the way because the chain had come off the bike too. She was so happy to see the car was back in the drive and her father at the gate.

'I was coming to look for you – you've been gone a long time. What on earth happened to you?'

'I fell off my bike and your letter got all wet.'

'Don't worry about that. Are you all right, love? Did you hurt yourself?'

When she saw her mother standing at the back door, she burst out crying again and Mary put her arms around her. 'You're soaking wet, you poor little thing. Come in out of that rain, and I'll run a bath for you.'

She never told them, but every time Dominic O'Sullivan's name was mentioned something inside her tightened and her mouth went dry.

The following week, she opened the door when he called to the house. She couldn't speak.

'Ah, there's the little messenger. He put his hand on her arm as she showed him into the parlour and she froze at finding herself alone with him again. 'Don't worry, I won't tell on you, not a word,' he whispered, putting his face right up to hers, smiling his evil smile.

She panicked and shouted, 'Dad! Dad! It's Master O'Sullivan.'

Her gran checked her for that. 'That's no way to announce anyone, screeching like an urchin.'

The next time he called to the house, she pretended she was doing her homework and stayed in her room.

She often cried herself to sleep and started spending more and more time in her room. She wasn't hungry and her mam was on at her about eating properly. Her gran chimed in about it being a sin to waste food, but try as she might she just felt sick, tired and listless.

She heard her mam and dad talking – they thought it was because she was missing her sister so much. She wished she could tell them what had happened.

'She'll have her back in a few weeks for half-term,' her dad said, but Sandra didn't know if she could tell Louise what had happened anyway because of what Master O'Sullivan told her about telling the nuns what she'd done. Besides, Louise was bringing her new friend home to stay with them.

When Louise arrived home with her friend, Dymphna, Sandra felt happier than she had for weeks and they all had fun together. Going off on the bikes and down to the beach. Dymphna had a camera that developed photos instantly. She took one of Sandra and

Louise and gave it to her to keep. She actually took two and kept the one that was in sharper focus for their dormitory.

When they went back to school, Sandra felt even more miserable. She heard her parents discussing her and she could hear her gran saying, 'Listeners never hear good of themselves.'

But Sandra didn't care – she didn't care about anything any more – and she kept listening.

'I keep telling you if we'd been a big clan like the Gilhooleys no one would ever get a chance to be lonely,' her dad said. 'We should have had ten!' Her mam laughed.

'I know they are very close, but that's a bit extreme, is it not? Seriously, though, do you think she could be sickening for something?'

'I don't know. It's probably her age, but if you're really worried, take her down to see Bill Vaughan and get her a tonic.'

Sandra pretended to be surprised when Mary told her where they were going. Mary even gave her a little jar before they left so they could take a urine sample with them, so Sandra wouldn't feel embarrassed in the surgery. But the doctor still asked her for another, halfway through the consultation.

'What do you think is wrong with her, Bill?' Mary asked when Sandra had left to go to the toilet.

He leaned back in his chair and let out a deep sigh. 'Mary, there's no easy way to tell you this – I think Sandra may be pregnant.'

'My God, Bill, she can't be. She's only twelve.'

'I know that, but biologically she's a woman. Has she a boyfriend?'

'Absolutely not. Sweet Jesus, I don't believe it. Are you sure? It'll ruin her life, her education, everything. What will Con say? And her grandmother? Her grandmother will die of shame.'

'Whoever is responsible is guilty of a crime and should be reported and prosecuted. She's years under the age of consent.'

'Are you sure? What are we going to do?'

'I am, Mary. You need to find out who the father is and talk to him. He may be a minor himself, in which case you – and I mean both sets of parents – need to make plans together. Even if it's someone older, I can't report it – that would be a breach of patient confidentiality.'

Sandra came back in and handed the specimen jar to the doctor.

He continued talking as he inserted a test dip strip into it and waited. 'Sandra, you do know that you're expecting a baby, don't you?'

'What? I can't be. A baby?'

'Have you any idea who the father is?'

'There's no father. I'm not expecting.'

'You are,' he confirmed. 'I appreciate that this may be awkward to talk about in front of your mam, would you like her to leave the room? You've been feeling sick because of morning sickness, although it doesn't only happen in the mornings.'

'No. And I'm not expecting. I told you. I'm not.'

'And I'm not going anywhere,' Mary said. 'But I am going to find out who did this to her if it's the last thing I ever do.'

On the way home, Mary kept asking Sandra who had touched her, but Sandra didn't give away anything. The shock was too much.

'Have you been with any of those boys from the village? You know you can tell me.'

No response.

'Is there a particular one you like?' Mary tried. 'I'm very shocked. I didn't think you'd ever get up to anything like that behind our backs.'

But all Mary's questions remained unanswered. Sandra said nothing, the memory of Master O'Sullivan's threats; his sweaty face and grunts were far too real to tempt her to say anything.

'What will your gran say? This will be the death of her, the shame, her good name. Your dad's prospects. How could you do this to yourself? You're not to tell your sister either. The nuns won't want to keep her at that school if they find out.'

Chapter Twenty-eight

Sandra was sent to her room when she got home, so her mother could talk to her father about what the doctor had told her. When she came down, Sandra looked at her father for comfort, but he offered her none. He kept a stony face and looked away.

For days, all she heard as she lay in bed at night was the sound of her parents shouting at each other. She couldn't wait for Louise to come home for the Christmas holidays. Maybe her sister could tell her what to do, because she didn't have a clue what would happen next. She just knew that everything was going wrong – and it was all her fault. She was pregnant. Her gran wouldn't talk to her. Her mother wouldn't let her go to school. She felt sick, and everyone had been told she had a tummy bug.

About a week after her visit to the doctor, Sandra overheard her mother and gran talking about someone coming to tea. A tray was ready in the parlour, but Sandra didn't know who the visitor was or what they were going to be talking about. Then she heard Fr O'Looney being ushered in, his polished voice saying something about 'a terrible business, a terrible business altogether'. The parlour door closed behind them and she couldn't make out their muffled voices.

A while later, she was summoned. 'Fr O'Looney wants to talk to you,' her mother said. 'So we'll leave you two together for a while.'

The priest waited until the others had left, and then folded his arms. 'Now, child, you know what this is about. What you did is a sin, and I don't recall you confessing it to me, but we can talk about that in a minute. I want you to tell me who did this to you.' He spoke slowly and deliberately. 'Who have you been with?' He paused. 'Was it one of those lads who hang around Clancy's after last mass on a Sunday? You can tell me.' Sandra didn't move a muscle. 'You have to tell us. You're a child of twelve and that's far too young to get married.'

Still she didn't move. She was aware of her breathing and the clock ticking rhythmically. *Too young to get married? They couldn't make me marry Master O'Sullivan, could they? I'd die before I'd have anything to do with him.*

'Who have you been with? Who did this to you? Did you know him? Have you been seeing one of the boys from the secondary school?'

Sandra just kept shaking her head, but she snapped it up at the next question. 'Was it your father?'

'No!' She looked at him as if he were stone mad. 'Of course it wasn't my dad.' Her father would never do anything to hurt her. But she still refused to say anything about Master O'Sullivan.

'Well now, child, you have to stop thinking about yourself. You have your family's good name to consider, and your sister off in boarding school with the nuns. Not to mention the ones in your own convent school. What do you think Mother Carmel will say if she finds out what sort of a girl you are?'

'I did nothing wrong, Father. I'm telling you the truth,' she said, her voice shaking.

'Well, you and I both know that's not the truth, Sandra. Babies may be a gift from God, but they don't appear out of thin air. You have to make them happen. Are you sure you don't have anything to say for yourself?' He paused, before adding, 'You do know you'll have to go away from here for a while, until the baby is born?'

'Why would I do that?' she asked. She felt her heart race. What was he implying?

'Because, child, you can't go parading yourself around the neighbourhood, showing your sin to everyone. What kind of example would that be to the good girls in the parish? Girls who live by the rules.'

'I can stay here with Mam and Dad, and I can help with Gran. I don't have to let anyone see me.'

'And miss going to mass and the sacraments and school? I don't think that would be very wise. Away with you now, child. I need to talk with your parents and your grandmother about what's best for everyone. We have plans to make.'

She left and went back upstairs, feeling she had made a breakthrough and that he was going to intervene for her. She picked up the Polaroid snap Dymphna had given her and studied it. She wished with all her heart that she could talk to her sister. Louise would know what to do.

It was a long time before the priest left. She didn't know whether to go back downstairs or wait until they called or came up to her. They did neither, and when she woke in the middle of the night, she realised that she had fallen asleep on top of the bed, still fully dressed.

Chapter Twenty-nine

The next morning, Fr O'Looney was back again. This time there wasn't any chat. 'We're going for a little drive to take care of things,' he told her. 'Mary, have you her bag ready?'

Her mother produced a small case – Sandra didn't know when she'd packed it. She looked from one parent to another. Her mother went to move forward, but her father restrained her. 'You better go to the bathroom before you leave,' she told Sandra. Sandra went upstairs and, on her way back, she took the photo from her locker and stuffed it into her pocket. She'd put it between the pages of a book later and flatten it out again.

As she said goodbye, her mother hugged her and said, 'It's for the best, love, truly it is.'

She could have sworn that she saw tears brimming in her father's eyes, while her gran refused to come to the hall door, muttering something about the shame Sandra had brought on the family.

Fr O'Looney drove for what seemed like hours, following signposts for Dublin, but this was not going to be like her last trip there with afternoon tea in the Gresham Hotel. Instead, they drove into Navan and he parked the car outside a house in the suburbs.

'You'll stay here tonight,' he explained. 'These people are friends of mine and they'll take you to the nuns tomorrow. Mrs Dunne will tell you what to expect there.'

He stayed for a cup of coffee and a sandwich and left. Sandra felt ill at ease as she watched him drive away and just wanted to go home.

'Don't be frightened. We'll look after you. Fr Looney explained the situation. We've helped other girls like you before, although they were a lot older than you,' the woman said, showing Sandra to her bedroom.

Much later, Sandra had difficulty remembering anything about what happened after Fr Looney left. She remembered thinking that the house was perfect in an everything-for-show sort of way. But she couldn't remember discussing what was going to happen or even eating anything, although she knew she had to have her meals. She supposed the dread of what was to follow had obliterated everything else.

She did remember that the woman had a bottle-green velvet coat with a fur collar that reminded her of Scarlett O'Hara's outfit in *Gone with the Wind*. She was wearing it when they drove to Dublin the next morning. The convent was a large, imposing stone building, with a chapel alongside. There was a statue of Our Lady surrounded by a flowerbed in the middle of the lawn and large trees along the driveway. The woman took Sandra's bag and waited for her to follow her up the granite steps to the double doors. Then there was the sound of a bolt being released. A girl in a shapeless, grey tunic pulled open a door. She showed them into a room before vanishing. The furniture gleamed with a mirror-like burnish and there were artificial flowers in a bowl on the enormous circular table.

A couple of minutes later, the door opened and a nun came in. She greeted the woman effusively. 'We'll get you some tea.' She rang a little bell and, while she waited for someone to come, she nodded in Sandra's direction. 'So tell me about this one, wanting to grow up before her time, eh? No thought for her immortal soul, or her immoral one, it seems.'

'Fr O'Looney said she's from a very good home. Naturally they are shocked and disappointed. It's an impossible situation. He's a teacher in the local school. Her mother was a school teacher in the locality too, and was hoping to go back to it when this one went off to boarding school next year. Can you imagine the scandal and what the other parents would have to say about that?'

The nun shook her head and 'tch-tch-tched' in agreement.

From above the mantelpiece, the eyes in a painting of a stern-faced bishop bored into Sandra. The nun saw her looking at it. 'That's His Grace, John Charles McQuaid, Primate of Ireland, a very holy man. It's thanks to his generous benefaction that we can help girls like you.'

Another rap on the door. After permission was given, a much older woman, also dressed in a shapeless, grey tunic, came in.

'Take this girl to join the penitents,' the nun said. Sandra didn't understand. 'Penitents, child. That's what we call the fallen women in here, you are all doing penance for your sins. Take your case with you, and say thank you to the good woman for giving up her day to bring you here.'

Sandra did as she was bid and the woman said, 'Be a good girl for the sisters.'

As she left the room, Sandra heard the nun say, 'Now, with the unpleasant business out of the way, would you like a scone?'

* * *

Sandra thought that what had happened at the headmaster's house was the worst thing ever, but she soon realised it wasn't. At least that had been over quickly. This incarceration would go on for months. She went to classes of a sort, with others of mixed ability. Her gran would not have been happy with some of the people she shared with.

They were what she would have called 'common' or 'uncouth', or both. Some used really coarse language too. She hated the nuns and was always tired, hungry and despondent.

She kept her photo under the old newspaper that lined the drawer she had been allocated in the dormitory and took it out from time to time. It was the only place she could put it to flatten it. She didn't have a book to put it in. Apart from class, the only books they got to read were for 'spiritual reading', when it was their turn to take to the lectern in the refectory and they read to the others during meals. Some, a good few years older than her, faltered over words and paused in the wrong places. Because she was a fluent reader, Sandra was often given the task halfway through her meal and when she resumed her seat, her plate was invariably empty.

She whispered to one of the women who had been kind to her when she first arrived just how disappointed she was about having no news from home. The woman told her, 'They probably never got any of your letters. When you write, never say anything about being unhappy or about wanting to get out of here – the nuns just tear them up.'

Sandra was shocked that they would do such a thing. In her next letter, she wrote:

> I am settling in very well and enjoying lessons. I
> hope all is well with you and Gran,
> Your loving daughter

She waited and waited and waited through four interminable months of hell, holding on only in the knowledge that when her baby was born, she'd go back home and put everything that had happened behind her.

She thought Christmas would be a special time – celebrating the birth of the baby Jesus in a holy place, but it wasn't. Apart from a lovely Christmas tree in the main porch, which was off limits except to those whose chores brought them that way, there were no bright lights or festive food. She had never felt so alone and cold. Loneliness gnawed at her insides as she remembered what she and Louise would have been doing at this time of the year in Mayo. She missed the anticipation, the smells of home cooking, the ritual of picking and chopping the tree with her dad, and bringing it back on the roof of the car, and the laughter as they dragged it inside the hall door, and the lovely pine smell from it. She missed her family. Surely they hadn't forgotten her, but there was no card or letter, nothing at all. She wondered if Master O'Sullivan would call by on Christmas morning, as usual. She shivered and switched her mind off. 'Think of the future, not the past,' she told herself, 'when you'll go back home.'

From snatches of chat when the women and girls managed to talk as they hung the wet clothes on the lines in the yard or worked in the ironing and folding rooms, she learned that Christmas Day was just like any Sunday, and that the crib and Advent candles were the only sign of the season anywhere. She was the youngest inmate and her thirteenth birthday had come and gone unmarked. She wondered if Christmas would too.

'Don't we get presents from the sisters or from our families?' she asked the girl beside her, who was about sixteen and had flaming red hair. She had been in and out of the home once before.

'I'm dead to my family,' the girl replied. 'Since they found out about this one.' She rubbed her belly.

'That's an awful thing to say,' Sandra answered.

'God, but you're an awful innocent altogether, aren't you?' she sneered. She spoke loudly to everyone. 'Presents! She wants to know if we'll get presents.'

'Of course we will, sacks full of them,' said one of the women. 'All done up fancy-like, in crinkly wrapping paper, with big shiny bows and silvery bells. Where do you think you are – Fairyland?'

'That's not very nice,' an older woman whispered. 'She's only a kid. Leave her alone.'

'Not very nice! I'll tell you what's not very nice – them thieving sisters taking our things and giving them away to charity or keeping them for themselves. They get buckets of nice things from people for their "fallen women", but do we ever see any of it? No, we don't! I never got anything me sister sent in for me last time. There were Double Centre chocolates and Scots Clan toffees, and they all vanished – down their gullets, I bet. We did get an orange though on Christmas morning – how's that for nice? You need to grow up, young one – it's a big bad world out there.'

'No talking over there,' a voice from behind the flapping sheets shouted. 'Get on with your work.'

Once Sandra confided her dark thoughts to the chaplain in her weekly confession, a ritual that they all had to perform. The priest told her to offer up life's little annoyances for the suffering souls in purgatory. 'It'll help pay for the sins you have already committed. The sisters took you in when no one else wanted you. Remember that and be grateful to them, and to the good and merciful Lord.'

She no longer believed in anything, never mind a merciful God who supposedly loved her. He had stopped listening to her that September evening when she cycled to Dominic O'Sullivan's house. How would she ever survive the next five months in this prison?

Even the carols on Christmas Eve didn't hold their normal enchantment, and the thoughts of 'angels sweetly singing o'er the plains' did nothing to lift her spirits. She knew for certain that there were no angels hovering over her, singing in exultation at the pending arrival of her child. She didn't allow herself to cry until after the sister on duty had done the final check of her dormitory and turned the lights off. Then she let it all out.

It was only after she felt the first fluttering in her tummy that she began to feel hope again. She wasn't alone. She had a real human being growing inside her and nothing could take that from her. Together they'd survive. She was sure of that.

From then on, when the baby moved, she'd smile a secret smile. This was something that no one else could share. In bed at night, she'd put her hand on her tummy and promise her baby that no matter what it did or what happened to it, she'd never send it away.

As she grew larger she became more withdrawn. She had made no friends there. Time dragged despite the work and prayer schedule. She missed everything about her former life, her bed, reading, her mam's cakes, the donkey.

She knew that for all sorts of reasons some of the other girls and women didn't want to keep their babies, and that, when they had them, they were given away for adoption. Others never came back to classes afterwards or to work in the laundry or the kitchens. She asked where they were, but no one talked about them and Sandra assumed that they had just gone home again.

She waddled through the last few weeks of pregnancy, no leniency being shown towards her state. Her waters broke early in the morning before the morning bell had sounded. She got upset and the sister on duty told her to take control of herself. She was made to strip down the sheets, turn the mattress and make it up with fresh bedding before anyone checked on her to see if she were in labour. No one had talked to Sandra about what to expect and she was ill-prepared for the severity or the length of her labour. She called out for her mother several times. *Mam must have known it would be like this. How could she let me go through it on my own?*

'Offer it up for the suffering souls in purgatory! This is your punishment for the pleasures of the flesh,' the nun attending her said.

Sandra wanted to shout that there had been nothing pleasurable about any of it. 'Just remember these pains the next time you feel inclined to sin with a man. Now say the Hail Mary and ask the Virgin for purity.'

Sandra was totally exhausted by the time her son finally pushed his way into the world at first light the following day.

'Well, thanks be to the good Lord he made it,' the nun said. 'It's a boy and he's a healthy seven and a half-pounder. Do you have a name for him?'

'I want to call him Peter.'

'Well, that's a good strong name,' the nun said, handing him over to her to hold.

Sandra couldn't take her eyes off him.

'Heavens, that's not the way to do it. Haven't you ever held an infant before?'

'No, Sister. Never.'

'Sure you're little more than a child yourself. Well, there's no need to be so scared. He might be small, and make a lot of noise, but he won't break. Here, let me show you.'

He was the most beautiful creature Sandra had ever seen. She fell in love with him instantly. Everything would be all right now. She knew her mother and gran would fall in love with him too. Louise would be his godmother.

As she fed and changed him, cuddled him and inhaled the baby powder smell of him, marvelling at his hands and tiny fingers, his long eyelashes and the perfection of his ears and feet, she filled her head with dreams of all they would do together.

In the weeks immediately after his birth, she was put on light duties, washing up and mending, and she slept in the dormitory adjacent to the nursery with five other new mothers. She heard the Reverend Mother say that she would be ready for discharge in a few weeks. She couldn't wait.

The day they took Peter away, she was supposed to be dusting the spotless chapel – an extra duty for an earlier insolence.

'You're spending too much time hanging around the nursery,' the nun on duty said. 'You've fed your child, now put him down and stop spoiling him. The gong's gone for lunch.'

'I'm not spoiling him. I'm just loving him. He's so beautiful.'

'Molly-coddling more like. And pride is a sin. Any more insolence from you, madam, and you'll be sent to the laundry.'

'Sorry, Sister,' she said, kissing Peter's forehead when the nun's back was turned and laying him down in his cot. He seemed to hold her gaze as though he understood what a wrench it was to have to leave him until his next feed. Sandra headed for the refectory and sat at the table for those who had already given birth. They were separated from the others and got extra milk and more vegetables.

'Sandra Mac Giolla Tighearnaigh, after you finish the clearing and washing up, you're to do the chapel and the brasses. Kitty Murphy, you go too – and no talking in there, remember it's the house of God.'

She sighed with relief. It was better than being sent to the laundry or to the ironing rooms, with their heat and the steam and the overpowering smell of carbolic soap.

'You got the cushy number. You can get away with murder in there. It's never really dirty so you can skip a few benches and no one will ever know,' Nora, one of the older penitents, told her. She had been twenty-three years in the home and knew all the shortcuts.

'That's a sin,' said Kitty, who'd been there even longer.

'Kitty, you think everything is a sin. It's not,' Nora said.

'It is a sin if you do it in full knowledge and full consent,' Kitty argued. 'And God sees everything.'

'Yes, and he's going to send a flock of angels, his special dust-inspector angels, down to Ireland, to Dublin, to our chapel here, to make sure not one mote of dust has been missed. Wouldn't you think he'd have better things to be doing all the same? He must be very bored up there in heaven if that's all he can do to amuse himself,' Nora said and got a laugh from the others in the kitchen.

'But if you're going to skip every other bench, you should start at the back, that way you'll see if Sister Agnes is sitting on her perch watching you first,' Ellen, whose glasses were stuck together with pink Elastoplast, advised. 'And don't forget the prayer to St Anne, when you pass her by.'

The refectory sister came back into the kitchen and Sandra didn't have the chance to ask what she meant.

Sandra and Kitty went in to the sacristy and took the boxes of polish and dusters out from under the sink. It was eerily quiet, the smell of incense lightly lingering on the air. The walls were lined with long cupboards, some containing the pristine, starched altar cloths that had been brought back from the laundry, others held rows of snowy white albs and altar boys' surplices in various sizes. There was one with separate compartments for the coloured cinctures – red, purple, green, black and gold – all with tasselled ends. Sandra turned the key on the next one and peeped into the large wardrobe where the embroidered vestments were stored. It creaked open.

'You'll be murdered if they catch you opening that,' Kitty whispered. 'It's a mortal sin.'

'No, it's not,' Sandra hissed back, 'that's not a sin. I know what a real sin is and it's not looking into a cupboard.' She grabbed a duster from her box in case anyone came to investigate and began dusting the doors. She loved to touch the heavy brocade and trace her finger along the raised patterns and silky threads of the needlework. They reminded her of the times she and Louise used to watch their mother sewing. She couldn't wait to get home for her mother to make her some new clothes. She believed these garments and the colours of the glass in the tall windows were the only beautiful things in the convent – things that had given her pleasure in the past months. She used to sit and stare at them during mass and benediction. Like her, they needed sunshine and light to bring out their vitality. She had neither in here, but she would have soon. Then she'd fill Peter's and her world with jewel colours, cobalt blues, celandine, crimsons, ochres and emeralds. She'd never wear black or grey again – ever.

They took the brass candlesticks from another cupboard shelf and cleaned and rubbed them till they shone. Then they moved out into the chapel itself, where the smell of incense and beeswax lingered from the last benediction.

'You dust the statues,' Kitty said, handing her a long-handled feather duster. 'I always sneeze when I use that thing, and don't forget St Anne's prayer when you're doing her.'

'What prayer is that?' she asked.

'St Anne send us a man, and get us out of this damned awful place, as quick as you can.' They giggled at that. Then Kitty asked, 'Is it a sin to say "damned" in here?'

'No, Kitty, it's not. Now I'm off to tickle the statues,' Sandra said, waving the feather duster in the air. 'And that's not a sin either.' She smiled at the older woman, who was looking doubtfully at her. 'It's not, I promise!'

Kitty began systematically dusting every pew in the empty chapel. Each nun had a prie-dieu allocated to them, spaced at intervals at the ends of the pews. She carefully lifted up their prayer books and dusted each one before putting it back in exactly the same spot.

Sandra was making her way around the various larger-than-life statues of St Anne, St Anthony, St Vincent de Paul, St Joseph, St Theresa and Our Lady. She'd have to hurry to get through this lot before Peter's next feed.

The jangling of rosary beads heralded the arrival of one of the sisters, and she heard Reverend Mother's voice. A couple accompanied her. When the nun spotted Kitty, she whispered, 'Go now, you can finish in here later.'

Sandra had ducked in behind the St Anne-send-me-a-man statue. The woman was speaking then, 'We can never thank you enough.'

'Don't thank us, we're just channels for the good Lord. Let's say a little prayer before you leave.'

Then the man spoke. 'I'd like the mother to have something to help her back on her feet when she goes home.'

'That's very commendable,' the nun replied.

From her vantage point behind the pillar, Sandra saw him take an envelope from his inside jacket pocket and hand it to the Reverend Mother, who nodded and smiled, before putting on her pious face as she led them up the aisle. The woman was holding a baby, wrapped up in a blue blanket, wearing one of the little crocheted hats the penitents made at Sunday recreation. One tiny hand protruded and opened and closed as if waving at something she couldn't see.

Sandra dared not move or the Reverend Mother would know she had been there the entire time. So she pressed herself against the wall as the nun genuflected and slid into a bench; the smartly dressed couple took one at the other side. The woman bowed her head and Sandra couldn't see whether she was admiring the baby or if she had her eyes closed in respectful concentration. After a few minutes, they all rose, genuflected and left.

When she stepped back out, Sandra noticed that the nun had left the envelope behind her on the seat. Curiosity made her pick it up. It was unsealed and she slid out the contents. It was a cheque and she read the amount – one hundred pounds! They must be really rich, she thought, and kind. She heard the click, click of rosary beads that heralded the nun's return. She shoved the paper back into its envelope and ducked back out of sight again. Apart from the amount written on the cheque the only words she had been able to see were 'Bank, Baggot Street'.

Kitty returned a few minutes later. 'That's another one gone. Another happy ending.'

'How can you say that? How could—' They heard a door in the sacristy creak open and they fell silent. It was only one of the other penitents bringing back a fresh batch of altar cloths from the ironing room.

They finished their duties just as the refectory gong sounded. She knew she'd get a punishment for being late, but she had to check on Peter. She had an awful feeling something wasn't right – and after seeing a baby taken away, wanted to hold her baby tightly and tell him she'd never let him go. She ran up the stairs, another punishable misdemeanour. She didn't care. It would be worth the reprimand. When she got into the nursery, Peter's crib was empty. Was someone else feeding him? She cried out and ran to the sister in charge. 'Where's my baby? Someone's taken my baby.'

'Now, now, child, don't fret. He's gone.'

'What do you mean, "He's gone"?' Gone where?'

'He's gone to a good home where he's wanted.'

'My home is a good one and we want him,' she shouted.

'He's gone where he can grow up without any stigma. Don't you understand you couldn't take him home with you? Your mother and father would never have been able to hold their heads up again if the neighbours knew what you'd done.'

At that moment, Sandra's world disintegrated and she began to realise the enormity of what she had witnessed. That was *her* baby, *her* Peter. They had given away *her* little boy. She cried and ranted, demanding he be brought back. She became hysterical, screaming for them to bring her baby back.

The Reverend Mother summoned Sandra to her office. There were two other nuns in the room and Sandra shouted at them, 'I want my baby. You've no right to steal him from me. Just wait until my parents come, they'll get him back.'

'My dear child, you are deluding yourself. Your parents won't be coming for you. They don't want anything to do with you, after what you have done, bringing shame and scandal into their lives.'

'You're lying, all of you, you're lying,' she screamed. 'And I didn't do anything wrong. You don't know what you're talking about. You're evil, all of you.'

'Watch your tongue, young lady. You are making an unseemly exhibition of yourself,' the Mistress of Penitents chipped in. 'If you continue to act like a mad woman, we'll have to send you away too – to the asylum. Now go to the chapel and reflect on your sins of arrogance and disobedience, and pray for forgiveness, while we decide where you should go next. Stay there until we send for you.'

Sandra wanted to escape. Even the thoughts of being torn to shreds by the rolls of barbed wire crowning the orchard walls were preferable to the pain she was feeling now. She sat in the chapel, where she'd had the last glimpse of her son, but she didn't pray for forgiveness – she didn't pray for anything or to anyone. She couldn't – and never would again. And she would never forgive those evil women either.

* * *

The nuns deliberated about what they should do with Sandra.

'She's a troublemaker, and a clever one too. She'll be a divisive force if we put her in the laundry,' the Mistress of the Penitents said. 'And she'll cause problems if she goes on like that with those still waiting to give birth.'

'We can't just release her out on the streets with nowhere to go – she's too young. She'd be back in here in no time,' said the Reverend Mother.

'We could send her down to Kildare to the orphanage, until she's sixteen.'

'That *is* an option, but there could be another – what about that family Fr Prenderville told us about? I'm sure they were looking for someone older, but she'd fit in there – the child is well brought up and she's mannerly and polite, most of the time.'

They went back and forward looking for a solution before

contacting Fr Prenderville. He lived in one of the wealthier Dublin parishes and knew of a foreign family – the father was a diplomat – that needed help at home. The couple's wife had recently had a third child, but complications had meant that she needed bed rest every afternoon. They already had a housekeeper, but they needed someone to help with the other children.

'Yes, Father, I think it might be a solution to both our problems. Yes. We'll wait until we hear from you. Goodbye now and God bless.' The Reverend Mother put the phone down. 'As you'll have gathered, he'll get back to us after he has spoken to them. Meanwhile, keep her away from the other penitents. They're enough trouble as it is.'

Sandra was sent to help in the nursery and she thought it was the cruellest punishment they could have given her. There, she hid her tears when the sarcastic sister was in charge. It broke her heart to see the other new-borns tucked safely in their blankets, Peter's crib already occupied by a beautiful little girl with coffee-coloured skin and a mop of dark curly hair. Her mother had not survived her birth, and Sandra was given her to bathe, feed and change. This added to her anguish. *Who is doing these things for Peter?*

One of the young nuns was sympathetic when there was no one else around. 'It'll get easier, Sandra,' she assured her. 'And I'll pray for you both.'

But Sandra wanted to shout, 'Don't bother. I don't want your prayers. I want my baby', but instead she said, 'I don't think it ever will.'

Sandra was also banished from her dormitory. One of the sisters had taken her there to collect her nightshirts, underwear and spare tunic, and she'd managed to slip her photograph out from under the discoloured newspaper lining in the drawer in the dresser and tuck it into the folds of her clothes. She now slept in a room near the nursery, which at least gave her some privacy.

A week after Peter had been taken, Sandra was summoned again.

She was given the jumper and skirt that she had worn on the day she'd arrived, and was sent to put them on. It was liberating to be out of the shapeless, grey tunic and apron. She changed quickly and discovered that she had grown taller in the months she had been there, and that motherhood had swelled her breasts. She put her photograph under her vest, which she then tucked into her knickers.

She knocked and was permitted entry back into the office.

'Holy Mother of God, we can't send her out looking like that,' the Mistress of Penitents said. 'Sister Imelda, take her and find something that fits – and hurry, Fr Prenderville will be here any minute to collect her.'

She was given a brown skirt and patterned jumper to wear and a stone-coloured anorak that hid her curves.

'We're done all we can for you here,' Reverend Mother said to her. 'We're found a family who is willing to overlook your past and take you in to help while the mother is recovering from a difficult confinement. Please behave yourself and don't let us, or yourself, down again.'

As the Reverend Mother had predicted, there was no word from Mayo, but Sandra still hoped. 'Will you tell my family where I've gone if they come looking for me? And my baby? Please.'

'You're best putting all that behind you now and getting on with your life,' Sister Imelda said.

Sandra was given over to the priest. Was she really leaving that dark and horrid place with watching eyes everywhere? They watched from statues, holy pictures, crucifixes, not to mention the nuns. Was she really being freed from this monochrome world with its grey walls, grey tunics, grey blankets, grey stews and the all-pervasive smells of floor polish, boiled cabbage and wet laundry? The nuns didn't mention the cheque the man who now owned her baby had left for her. Somehow, she knew she'd never see that, not could she ever mention it without confessing that she had looked into the nun's private business. If they knew, they'd probably change their minds – she could still be sent to the laundry and end up like Kitty and Nora, spending the rest of her life there.

She avoided looking at any of the sisters as they watched her walk out the door, without a smile between them. Sister Imelda held a huge black umbrella over the priest until he was settled in the car.

Her family had disowned her – handed her over the way her son had been handed over – for someone else to deal with. The only difference being she hadn't known that was going to happen. They did. None of them could be bothered to write to her, to answer one of her few letters. They didn't want her to come home. Did her parents know they had a grandchild? Did they care?

Both her fate and her son's were in the hands of others, but she would spend her life looking for him, no matter what it took.

Chapter Thirty

1971, The Fourniers

Fr Prenderville's car smelled of leather and the rain made a rhythmic beating on the roof. Sandra didn't find the silence strange – she had got used to not speaking. Then he said, 'This is a new chance for you. The nuns tell me you're a bright girl and I hope you've learned your lesson. Work hard and make a good life for yourself.'

He turned off a leafy suburban road and drove into a driveway where the surface scrunched under the wheels and large drops from the overhanging trees bounced off the car. When they got out, Sandra noticed the air smelled of wet grass and damp earth. The tubs in the open porch were filled with colourful flowers, a complete contrast to the dark day. A white-haired woman showed them into the drawing room and went off to fetch the lady of the house. To Sandra, the house was huge – not in the way the convent had been, but elegant and welcoming and full of pretty things.

'Madame Fournier. It's good to see you up and about again,' the priest said, standing up and taking her hand. 'How are you and the baby doing?'

'I'm feeling good and she's thriving now, thank you.'

Sandra couldn't take her eyes off the woman who had walked into the room. She was beautiful, with brown-black eyes, dark hair and flawless, sallow skin but she had a frailty about her. She turned to Sandra next and shook her hand.

'I hope you'll be happy here with us. The older children are at a language school, so you'll have a chance to get settled in and look around before they come home. The baby's asleep, but no doubt she'll make her presence felt very soon.' She smiled, and Sandra found herself wondering if this was for the priest's benefit. No one had asked or cared about her happiness since she had left Mayo.

Fr Prenderville was talking again. 'She outgrew all her clothes while she was in the convent so Reverend Mother asked me to give you this.' He held out an envelope. 'There's fifteen pounds in it to buy her some essentials.'

'Oh, that won't be necessary. We don't need that. Put it in your St Vincent de Paul box.' She pronounced it *Sanvansen de Paul*. Sandra was embarrassed, standing there in her hand-me-down, ill-fitting clothes. As she had expected, there was no mention of the cheque the man had given the Reverend Mother in the chapel.

'That's very generous of you, Madame. Thank you and God bless you.'

The housekeeper who had let them in came back with a tray. 'I've brought the coffee.'

'Thank you, Mrs Daly. Sandra, do you like coffee or would you prefer milk?'

'Milk, if it's no trouble, thank you,' she replied.

'You go with Mrs Daly and she'll organise that for you.' She smiled again. 'You can take your case with you.' Sandra followed the older woman into the hallway and down some steps to a bright, airy kitchen with copper pots hanging on a metal rail. Something was bubbling away on the black stove. The housekeeper poured milk and put a plate with some exotic-looking biscuits in front of her. Sandra didn't touch them. Were they a trap to see if she was greedy?

'Don't look so frightened, they won't poison you. Try one, they're

Madame's recipe.' She pushed the plate towards Sandra. 'You look as though you need fattening up. Did they not feed you in that place?'

'They did, but not with things like this,' she replied, taking one of the flaky concoctions. It melted in her mouth and reminded her of the thick yellow almond paste that her gran used to put on the Christmas cake. She wanted to eat them all, but held back. She had never tasted anything as delicious in her life.

The housekeeper was busy folding clothes from a basket and putting them on the table. The ironing board was open and waiting.

'You can have another one. No one is counting.'

'Thank you.' She liked this woman. She was kind, but it was far too early to trust anyone. When she had finished she said, 'Would you like me to iron those for you?'

'Well I'll be damned. The last helper we had would do anything to get out of ironing, or anything else for that matter.' She laughed. 'Of course you can do it, but first let's show you to your room and get you familiar with the house. Madame might have other things that need doing first. She's not been too well since Monique was born. She's much better now, but she might like you to help feeding and changing the baby.'

'How old is she?'

'Six weeks tomorrow and she's a wee dote altogether and—' She stopped mid-sentence and changed the subject. 'Come on, you can put your things away.'

Sandra didn't believe people lived in houses like this. Even their neighbours, who lived in much bigger farmhouses than theirs, weren't as luxurious as this house, or as warm and cosy. To her, this was grandiose – grandiose like those she'd seen in the pictures. The rich wood of the staircase was gleaming. There was a huge dining room with folding doors leading through to another sitting room with a baby grand piano.

'They both play but Madame is much better,' Mrs Daly said. 'She has real talent.'

Sandra thought of the upright at home where she and Louise used to bang out a four-handed version of 'Chopsticks' when their gran wasn't around. It seemed to take up a whole wall in the parlour – here the piano still left tons of space for pale-turquoise sofas and armchairs with pale-grey and cream cushions. There was a conservatory off that room that overlooked the garden and even though the rain was still falling outside, the pots of coloured flowers made it seem sunny and bright inside.

There were flowers everywhere, even in Madame's bedroom. Mrs Daly put her finger to her lips as she stopped to point it out. The nursery opened on to this room and the baby was asleep in there. There was a dressing room too, and a bathroom with an enormous bath that had feet that looked like lions' paws. There were two other bedrooms – quite obviously the other children's. Both were tidy and spotless, but filled with their personal possessions. The posters told her the first one belonged to a sports-mad boy. It was decorated like those she'd seen in magazines, co-ordinated in navy, red and white. The next was a girl's. It was pretty in primrose and white, and there were rosettes and several pictures of her with a pony.

They went up another flight of stairs, and Sandra wondered how many other children they had, and how old they were. She didn't like to ask. She followed Mrs Daly into the first room, an equally lovely room that smelled lightly of flowers. It had a brass bedstead with pristine white linen, a blue and white quilted comforter folded across the end of the bed, and little matching cushions casually arranged on the pillows, but there were no personal items in here.

'It's beautiful,' she said.

'It is, isn't it? This will be your room.'

'Really? Are you serious?' Sandra asked.

'Of course I'm serious, and the toilet and bathroom are next door.

You'll have to share that with me sometimes when I stay over.'

'May I use it now?' She'd been dying to go since she arrived, but she didn't know how to ask.

'Of course you can. Away with you, there's one off the kitchen too if you're downstairs – there's no need to come all this way up.' Mrs Daly stood aside.

In the toilet, her photo fell out from under her vest and as she picked it up, she realised she didn't know how to behave anymore. Nor did she know what she was allowed do or say. In the convent, there were rules about everything – where they could walk, where they couldn't; when they could talk, when they couldn't; when they should pray – that was permitted at any time. As she came back out, quiet footsteps on the carpeted stairs announced that Madame was coming up to them.

'You shouldn't be doing all those stairs,' Mrs Daly said.

'I'll take a rest in a little while, I promise. Now that that pompous man has gone, I can get to know you, Sandra, but first let's hang up your things, *non*?' She opened the little case and said, 'Well, goodness, you don't have very much with you, do you?' Sandra felt herself flush and Madame quickly added, 'I'm sorry, that was insensitive.'

As much as she tried to stop them, tears flooded her eyes, and she looked down at the shapeless brown skirt and jumper, and at the anorak the housekeeper had over her arm.

'That's all I have,' she said quietly. 'These clothes aren't mine – I'd grown out of my clothes so the nuns gave me these this morning.' The practical underwear and nightshirts looked grey in contrast to the snowy-white bedspread.

'We'll soon sort that out. Mrs Daly, once Monique has had her feed, why don't you both go and do some shopping. I'll manage for a few hours without you.'

'But I can't afford to buy anything. I don't have any money.'

'We won't worry about that for now. And there, right on cue –'

she laughed '– that's Monique looking for attention. Come and meet her. She's *mignonette*. We'll have to teach you some French while you're with us.'

Mrs Daly went downstairs to fetch the bottle and Sandra volunteered, 'My mother used to teach French.'

'*Vraiment? C'est formidable!* Do you speak it?'

'Yes, a little bit. She used to teach us too. She taught me lots of vocabulary – a new word or two every day, when we were out walking or down by the sea or just at home. Sometimes we'd do verbs.'

'Well, we can do that too. I'm afraid I speak it with the children more than I should. They need to practise their English, so you can help each other. We can do a word exchange!'

That was the moment Sandra decided she would never mention her family again. She didn't know how long she'd be needed here, but she was determined to do everything they asked and get a good reference to help her make her own way in life, when she had to move on.

Madame cuddled her tiny daughter. 'She was in a hurry to see the big, bad world and arrived nearly two months before we expected her. We only got her home after three weeks. Would you like to hold her?'

Sandra hid her panic, smiled and took the bundle. Two beautiful dark eyes studied her with serious intent. 'She looks very like you,' she said when she averted her gaze.

'So everyone tells me. I'm not allowed to carry her up and down the stairs or hold her for too long just yet, that's why I need the extra help,' Madame told her. Mrs Daly handed the bottle to Sandra and they sat on the bed while she fed, winded and changed her.

'You're good at this,' Madame said as she took her daughter.

'There were lots of babies in the nursery. I worked in there for the past few weeks, after ... after ...' Her voice began to quiver. She saw them both exchange glances.

Mrs Daly said, 'Let's get off and do that shopping. I've Mrs Fournier's lunch ready on a tray downstairs, Sandra. Will you bring it up? I'll put this little one back in her crib. And we'll put a list together.'

As she went down the carpeted stairs, she wondered what they thought of her. Did they know everything?

* * *

Robert and Colette turned out to be just like their mother – friendly, warm and devastatingly handsome, with impeccable manners. He was eleven, she was nine.

Sandra helped with their worksheets and they were finishing this when their father arrived home in time for dinner. Mrs Daly introduced him to Sandra, and he shook her hand and bowed very slightly. He was very tall and had fair hair, not at all what Sandra had imagined a Frenchman should look like. He didn't say too much to her and when the children spoke in French, he reminded them, 'It's impolite to speak to each other in French if others can't understand.'

'But she does know lots of words, Papa,' his daughter told him.

'Already?' He looked at his wife.

'Her mother taught French.'

'Did she die?' their son asked. There was an awkward silence.

Sandra was aware that all eyes were fixed on her.

'No, she's not dead, she just doesn't teach it at the moment,' she said. 'But you can help me if you'd like.'

Later, as she helped Sandra clear away the schoolbooks, Madame apologised for Robert's question. 'He didn't mean any harm by it. He's a typical boy. He just comes out with things as he thinks of them. I know it's difficult for you coming here, but you'll get used to us. Have an early night and get settled, we'll work out your duties tomorrow.'

Was it really only that morning that I was rescued? she thought as
she took the scatter cushions from her bed and placed them on the
wicker chair. She laid her new dressing gown over them and kicked
off her slippers. She opened the wardrobe for the umpteenth time,
to check if it really had all those clothes inside. One of the drawers
was stuffed with underwear and some bras that actually fitted her
and were hers to keep. She'd put her photograph in there too. She
had her own toiletries and a new hairbrush. When they'd come back
from shopping, Mrs Daly had given her a pair of scissors to cut
all the labels and price tags off and told her to go and change into
something nice.

'Do you want me to launder your other clothes?'

'No, thank you, I never want to see them again. I don't want
anything to remind me of that awful place.'

'I don't blame you. I'll get rid of them.'

Chapter Thirty-one

The following day, Madame spelled out Sandra's duties. 'Your main tasks are to help me with Monique, although I do need extra help with Robert and Colette from time to time, when I have to do my diplomatic duties. They don't always understand that I cannot be here when they want me to be, especially when we have people in. Mrs Daly is terrific, but if she is busy preparing food, she can't keep an eye on them too. I know the nuns told us that we need only give you pocket money, but my husband and I feel you deserve a proper wage for as long as you are with us. I've asked Mrs Daly to take you to the post office tomorrow and you can open an account there to keep it safe. We all need to have something put away for the days when our umbrella doesn't open, or for when it rains or whatever you say here, don't we?' She smiled.

Sandra was speechless. Living with the Fourniers was such a wonderful change from the convent that she hadn't expected them to pay her as well.

She'd been worried that she'd have to pay back the money they had spent on clothes. She didn't know how much they had cost, but it was a lot more than she would have spent. When she'd asked Mrs Daly about it, she'd just laughed and said, 'Of course you don't. We can't have you looking like Orphan Annie in front of Madame and

Monsieur's friends and acquaintances, can we?'

It took a while for Sandra to stop comparing life with the Fourniers with her former one in Mayo. Apart from the weeks following her sister's departure to boarding school, she had never slept alone in a room. Even in the convent, when she was ostracised from the dormitory and sent to sleep near the nursery in the days before she left, the nun in charge had her bedroom partitioned off at one end.

Sandra's new room was bigger than any other room she'd slept in. It was beautiful and feminine, with its cross-stitch pictures and bookshelves painted white, the dressing table had a three-hinged mirror, and her quilted cover and cushions were made from a fabric that she later learned was called *toile de Jouy*.

But even in such a beautiful room, in a loving home, Sandra often cried when Monique demanded attention in the middle of the night. Her sadness and worry about what had happened to Peter wouldn't leave her. She seldom went out on her own, fearful of getting lost in the vastness of suburbia. Her only previous visits to Dublin had been to the zoo, to a pantomime at the Gaiety with her father while her mother went to the January sales, and that last trip, the one she had made with her mother and Louise, before everything changed. One day in the car, Madame drove down O'Connell Street and Sandra recognised Clerys and the Gresham Hotel, where they had had afternoon tea.

She didn't have too much to do with Monsieur Fournier. He was always polite and friendly, though not in an overfamiliar way, and she made herself scarce after dinner each night when the family went into the drawing room. This was their time and she respected that, even though they often told her she was welcome to join them.

When Sandra had free time, she went to her room. There, she'd sit and look out the window on to the leafy road below, the well-kept gardens and the large houses. At other times, she read or wrote in the little journal that had been left by her bed. It had a tiny lock and key. She found out that it had been left by Robert and Colette, along with a French–English dictionary, a packet of biros and a notebook for her new words. The shelf in her room had a mixture of books in both languages and she'd often amuse herself by trying to figure out the meanings, frequently jotting down a phrase or a collection of words that puzzled her.

She had never seen the level of sophistication in the people who visited the Founiers' home. But as soon as she got used to the routine and the French way of doing things, she began to relax and enjoy herself. She loved little Monique, even though she couldn't stop herself from thinking of Peter. As she bathed and powdered the little girl she told her, 'I hope he's as lucky as you and is settled in a nice home with nice people to love him. I know now that I could never have given him a proper start in life, when I see all the things you need, but then I never thought I'd be on my own doing that.'

'I love the way you talk to her,' Madame said, coming in to the room. 'This way she'll be fluent in English before her native language.'

'Do you mind?'

'*Absolument pas!* It's wonderful. I've been neglecting my duties for the past while and have to get back to entertaining a bit more, especially now that we have an extra pair of hands to help us.'

Sandra wasn't quite certain what 'entertaining' meant, and didn't know if it meant that she would have to do anything. Later, Mrs Daly explained, 'Madame is the chairwoman of the Diplomatic Spouses' Association. She takes the newcomers to Ireland under her wing, and helps them settle in.' She saw Sandra's look of puzzlement. 'Telling them where to shop, about school times and all the things they don't know before coming to live here. Tomorrow she's giving a coffee morning to introduce the latest arrivals to each other. It's her first since she had the baby. There are ten expected, so we'll need the china out from the sideboard. I'll show you where it is but be careful, it came from Madame's home in France.'

'It's beautiful,' Sandra said as Mrs Daly opened the press door and she saw the collection of almost transparent fine blue-and-gold patterned cups and saucers of different sizes, plates and serving dishes. 'And there's so much of it.'

'It's a full set – twelve of everything. It's a chore to wash, but it looks wonderful when the dining room table is extended and fully laid and the candles all lit. You'll see that next week. There's a big dinner party on Saturday.'

While the older two children were at school, Sandra often put the baby in her pram to go for a walk, going a little farther each day, familiarising herself with the roads close by, many of them tree-lined. The houses had names like Ellesmere, The Turrets, The Leys and Dovecot; the ones in Mayo hadn't been quite so exotic – St Jude's, Liseaux, St Martin's and St Teresa's abounded.

When Monique was asleep, Sandra always headed for the kitchen to watch Mrs Daly at work and help when she was allowed to.

'Cooking and baking for people who appreciate it makes the effort worthwhile. Mr Daly is a disaster. He's a meat and two vegetables man. Nothing too fancy for him. He only eats fish on a Friday – that was the way he was raised – and it has to be cod, nothing else. If you walked into my kitchen at home, you'd be able to tell what day of the week it is, just by what's cooking. He likes his routine, does Mr Daly.'

Sandra watched her make onion soup and coq au vin, chicken liver pâté, salmon and dill roulades 'and pommes gratin. She also watched Madame make custard and citron tarts, delicate choux and puff pastries, and pretty coloured petit fours. 'My grandfather had a *patisserie* and I used to spend any time I could in the back watching them bake and tasting the mixtures. Lots of these recipes are ones I got from him,' she told Sandra.

Sandra watched Madame create eye-catching flower arrangements for the tables and mantelpieces in the various rooms. She looked on like a student watching an artist, who transformed pottery jugs and crystal vases into works of art.

'Always use an odd number of the main flowers – for some reason they appear to be more pleasing to the eye than even numbers.' Sometimes she'd let her have a go at doing one herself, admiring and praising her efforts. 'And use the foliage from the garden. The colours at this time of the year are rich and warm. I love the autumn. It's my favourite season.'

Sandra realised it was a year since … since … She tried to concentrate on what Madame was telling her.

'Education is about so much more than book learning. Skills like these not only can be useful but they give you pleasure too. There's nothing like fresh flowers to lift anyone's spirits, don't you agree? That and music. I'm afraid I have neglected the children's lessons since the little one came along, but I must get them started back again now that you are here to help us.'

There was an easy atmosphere in the home as they worked and chatted together. At times like this, Sandra often wondered if she had been born into a different family would she have been treated differently when they discovered her pregnancy. Somehow, she felt she might. The Fourniers never questioned her about her life before she came to live with them, and she never volunteered anything.

'Now that the children are back at school I'm going to have some extra tuition for them two afternoons a week. I don't want them falling behind the curriculum they'd be following in France in case we are posted back there.' Sandra felt her heart miss a beat. *Are they leaving? When? Where will I go?* 'Don't look so worried – that won't be for a few years yet.'

But she did worry. With every week that passed, Madame was able to do more and more. Soon she wouldn't be needed at all.

'Their teacher is French and I thought you might like to sit in on

the classes with them. It could be beneficial for you too. You have a
good accent and you must take advantage of being here with us and
improve on those skills.'

Aware that her shortened education meant she'd never take the
Leaving Certificate, never mind go to university, Sandra jumped at
the chance and was surprised at how easy she found the translations
and comprehension.

Mrs Daly never quite got the hang of French though. 'I can't be
doing with the language,' she'd laugh. 'It's double Dutch to me.'

One day she asked Sandra to go to the Irish Yeast Company on
College Green to get some supplies. Sandra hesitated. 'You can't
miss it. It's opposite Trinity College where the buses stop. Don't tell
me you've never been on a bus in the city. Sometimes, you're awful
innocent for a young one of what, fifteen or sixteen?'

Sandra stopped herself from saying she was only thirteen. Instead,
she took the money for her fare and shopping and, with a map drawn
on the back of an envelope, headed off. When she returned, she felt
a huge sense of achievement. She suddenly felt grown up in a way
she never had before. She was trusted and hadn't let them down. It
was a great feeling and she vowed she never would. After that, Sandra
started to take the bus to town when she wasn't needed in the house,
wandering about and finding her way around the city. She loved
walking with the pram around the neighbourhood, as the leaves were
turning gold and russet and crunched beneath her feet, or danced
dizzily along the footpaths when the wind whipped them up.

One day, she answered the door and found Fr Prenderville
standing there. She showed him in and waited – for a wild second,
she thought he had come to see her, to tell her she could have Peter
back, but he made no effort to engage her in conversation, and
simply asked for Madame.

Deflated, Sandra went to tell Madame he was there. She brought
coffee through a while later and deliberately didn't close the door

properly as she left. Had he come to take her somewhere else? She heard him say, 'The girl is working out all right for you?'

'Yes, she has fitted in very well. She's like one of the family.'

'I'm so glad. The sisters said she was well bred.'

Sandra tiptoed back down to the kitchen, knowing that he would never fight her corner for her, but at least she was safe here for another while.

She fitted in to their family life. Robert and Colette had accepted her easily – she wasn't a real grown-up but wasn't a child either, and this made them less guarded with her.

However, Sandra adored Monique and, despite her overwhelming yearning for her son, found that her needs were, to some extent, filled. When she was just a few days short of her first birthday, she took her first wobbly steps, reaching out before faltering and flopping down on her bottom with a startled expression. Sandra had been willing her to let go of the coffee table for days and now she had done it – she was walking. To everyone's amazement, Sandra picked the little girl up and burst out crying. She handed her to her mother and ran upstairs, sobbing.

Mrs Daly went to follow her, but Madame stopped her. 'Let her be – she needs to cry. Can you imagine how awful it must be watching Monique and thinking about what her own baby would be doing now? I know Fr Prenderville told us not to ever talk about her child, but that seems to be an act that is very inhuman, does it not? We don't even know if she had a boy or a girl.'

'I suppose they know what they are doing. It might help her forget about it, but I often wonder about that logic. Do you honestly think a mother could ever forget? I don't – it's against our nature. The poor girl has no one but us. What sort of a family has she got to cut her off like that? And she has no friends of her own age. It's not right. Will I have a chat with her?' Mrs Daly asked.

'No, I'll do it.'

Sandra was curled up on the bed when she heard the soft knock on the door and Madame came in with a cup of tea. 'I thought you might like this,' she said, putting it on the bedside table and sitting down beside her. 'I know everything is supposed to feel better after a cup of tea, but that's not always enough, is it?'

'I'm sorry, Madame Fournier,' Sandra said as she sat up. 'I hope I didn't upset Monique.'

'There's no need to be sorry, and she's fine. I do understand though. It must be really hard watching her. How old was your baby when you came here?' Madame asked, taking her hand.

'Seven weeks, like Monique, there's only a day between them, but they took him away before that. He'll be one on Friday.

'What name did you give him?'

'Peter.'

'Peter, *Pierre*. I like that – it's manly. Is it after his father?'

'No, it's not.' She answered with such violence that Madame was taken aback.

'Forgive me, I didn't mean to intrude in your personal life or to upset you. I just wondered if you wanted to talk about it, or about anything – I am a good listener.' She sat there and offered the tea to Sandra. Neither said anything for a while.

When Madame rose to leave, Sandra said, 'Thank you, Madame. You have been very kind to me already and I really do appreciate it. I love it here.'

'And we appreciate you, Sandra,' she said, bending over to give her a hug, 'and we want you to be happy too.'

* * *

The following summer, the Fournier children were going back to France with their mother for a month. Their father was joining them for two weeks and they intended to take Sandra with them.

'Do you have a passport?' Madam asked her one morning.

'No, I've never been abroad,' she replied, remembering her mother's promise to take her and Louise to New York. Had they gone without her?

'I have to sort that out,' Madame said. A few days later she gave Sandra an application form. She filled out what she could on it, and handed it back to Madame. It was only then that they realised how young she was.

'You're still only fourteen. We thought you were sixteen when you came here,' Monsieur said.

'I didn't lie about my age. No one asked me.'

'No, we know you didn't,' said Madame, shooting a silencing glance at her husband. 'Don't worry, we'll sort it out.'

Later, Monsieur told his wife, 'I was there when you told Fr Prenderville that we wanted a responsible girl of about sixteen. But she was only thirteen when they brought her here. What were those *religeuses* thinking? She's far too young to be working – she should still be at school. He must have known that too. Can you imagine if this got into the papers – diplomat exploits underage worker? It would be the end of my career. We'll have to let her go.'

'*Mon cher*, you haven't thought this through, have you? What would that do to her? She trusts us. Can you imagine what the tabloids would say then? Exploited underage girl thrown out on the streets by diplomatic family – and an unmarried mother too. Would that be better?'

'Have you another solution?'

'Yes, we'll contact her parents and get them to sign the passport forms.'

'And if we can't?' he pushed.

'And if we can't, *mon cher*, we'll become her legal guardians and apply for her passport that way. The children don't need to know her history, but we'll have to get the address from her. And when we come back, I'll make sure she starts lessons.'

'Fine, but this is not the end of the matter. I intend to get that pompous cleric here and have a chat with him, and what I have to say to him won't be very diplomatic.'

'I want to be there when you do. I have a few things to say to him myself as well,' she replied

'He won't be welcome in this house ever again.'

* * *

Their letter to Sandra's parents containing her passport application form came back marked: 'No longer at this address – return to sender.'

'How can they do that to their child? I'd walk through fire for ours,' Madame told her husband.

'Maybe they have moved,' he said.

'I don't believe that for one moment. How am I going to tell her this?'

She picked her moment and told Sandra, who showed little emotion at the news. She explained that they'd have to apply to the courts on her behalf if they were to proceed.

'Because of your age, we'll have to vouch for you and we'll have to ask Fr Prenderville to verify your history.' Madame paused to let what she was saying sink in. 'Think about it, Sandra. If you feel this is too much of an ordeal for you, or if you'd rather not have us as your legal guardians for the next few years, then you don't have to agree. It's no problem. You can stay here while we are away – we have some friends coming over to use the house and I'm sure they wouldn't mind.'

She realised she had been through bigger ordeals than this. 'I don't need time to think about it. My family made it quite clear before now what they felt about me, but I do want to get a passport and come to France with you,' she answered.

Two days later, they drove to town to legalise the situation. Fr Prenderville was present. As Sandra had expected, the priest virtually ignored her when he had bid her the time of day, but he fawned over the Fourniers the whole time. They were back outside in less than an hour.

'That was quite painless, wasn't it, Sandra?' Monsieur said. 'Thank you, Father,' he said courteously to the priest, and then turned back to Sandra. 'You're stuck with us now so let's go and take care of the passport.'

Madame said, 'I think Fr Prenderville expected us to offer him lunch for his trouble.'

'*His* trouble. Don't get me started. He should be prosecuted for colluding in this charade. I told you, I don't ever want to see him in our home again.'

Madame steered the conversation away. 'No judge or jury, no wigs and gowns.'

'I think you've been watching too much television,' he said, and they laughed.

Sandra relaxed a little, knowing they were her guardians until she was sixteen – she didn't know what would happen to her then, but she intended to enjoy the next two years.

Chapter Thirty-two

1974

Madame Fournier's diary was always filled with social events, both personal and for her work with the Diplomatic Spouses' Association. Many of the families had young children and they included them in some of the social activities with garden parties, a sports day and other get-togethers. One long weekend, they arranged a camping expedition for those who were interested. Monique had turned three in June. She was an engaging, happy child who followed Sandra around like a shadow. Madame insisted on taking her young daughter with her other two children for their adventure.

The preparations went on for days beforehand. Mrs Daly and Sandra baked cakes and savoury treats for them to take. When they waved them off from the porch, the car was at bursting point with anything that could be needed.

Mrs Daly said, 'Hear that, Sandra, that's the sound of silence. Blissful, isn't it? And it's just us for the whole long weekend. Monsieur is working too. France doesn't have the same bank holidays as us, so we won't see too much of him. I'm going to take my book and sit out in the sunshine.' Mrs Daly loved the sun. 'I wish I had a few summery tops here. I might nip home and get them later and take advantage of the fine spell while I can.'

'I'm going to do the same.'

'Put some sun cream on, it's very hot and the forecast says it's going to stay like that for the next week.'

Before settling down on the loungers, they made tea. Sandra fell asleep after a bit and woke up to the sound of male voices. For a second, she didn't know where she was. Monsieur Fournier was standing in the doorway with a stranger. He was introduced as a former colleague who happened to be in Dublin, and he asked where Mrs Daly had gone. There was no sign of her.

'She mentioned she might nip home to get something. I don't think she was expecting you back for lunch, but I'll make it.'

'That's not a problem,' he replied. 'Everyone in this country seems to take the day off before a long weekend, so we decided to be Irish too.'

She smiled at them. 'Would you like to eat in the garden?'

'Definitely, but I'm the duty officer this weekend, so technically I'm still working until six and again tomorrow. Please make sure you answer the phone promptly if it rings, Sandra. And perhaps you'd put our guest's case in the cream bedroom when you have a moment.'

She made a quick lunch. Mrs Daly was always prepared for any eventuality so she had plenty of options. Monsieur took some chilled wine from the fridge, opened it, picked up two glasses and went back outside. She laid the table under the big umbrella and served them. She'd left her book on the ground and the visitor had picked it up. He read the title and handed it to her. 'You read French, I see.'

'Yes, I do.'

'Colette – now she was a racy woman in her time – published her first books under her husband's name I believe. They were regarded as shocking in their day.' He handed it back to her. 'Don't let us chase you away.'

The phone rang inside and Sandra rushed to answer it. She was relieved, as she felt out of place there with the two men. It was Mrs Daly.

'Sandra, I just went home to get a few things for the weekend, but my next door neighbour has had a bad fall. He turned around to say hello as I was getting out of the car and tripped over the dog's lead, a yappy little thing. I think he's broken his arm. He won't let me call an ambulance, so I'm taking him to A & E. You'll be OK on your own, won't you?'

'The poor man. Of course I will, and I'm not on my own. Monsieur is here with a guest. Don't worry, they've been fed and are out in the garden.'

'Oh, Lord, isn't that typical? I only go out for half an hour and it all goes wrong. I don't know how long I'll be. I just can't dump the poor old fellow here. His daughter is in Cork, and can't get here till later, but there's salmon and … is Monsieur's friend staying overnight? Where did you put him?'

'He's in the cream room and from what I gather, he'll be here for a few days. They want to eat early because he's just flown from New York and is jet-lagged.'

'I won't be back until this evening.'

'Stop fussing. I am quite capable of making a dinner. I've watched you and Madame do it every day. Look after your neighbour and I'll see you when you get here, whenever that is.'

'You're a treasure.'

'I know, now go,' she laughed.

'I heard the phone, was that the embassy?' Monsieur asked, taking a bottle of red from the wine cabinet and opening it to breathe.

Sandra explained and told him she'd make dinner for him and his guest. He seemed relieved to hear that and, over his shoulder, she saw the visitor topping up the glasses from the bottle already on the table. They seemed happy with their lunch. She cleared away the plates and hovered in case she were needed. Eventually, she went back to the kitchen and sat at the table to read her book. She wondered how the campers were getting on and wished she was with them.

There was no further word from Mrs Daly, so Sandra started preparing dinner. Monsieur suggested that they eat informally in the kitchen and insisted she joined them. The guest, whose name Sandra couldn't remember, praised her food and told her she cooked like a French woman. At first, she felt awkward but, as the meal progressed, she relaxed and felt very grown up at being able to hold her own in this situation.

'That was excellent. I am impressed too,' Monsieur told her. The guest looked for Sandra's glass and she told him that she didn't drink wine.

'Afraid you'll lose control and let your emotions run away with you?' he said.

Sandra felt herself blush. She didn't know how to answer that, but it was obvious she didn't need to. He had all the answers he needed in his next glass of best Margaux. He helped himself again and Sandra realised that together they had drunk several bottles since lunchtime; their voices were louder now and a little slurred at times, although they seemed capable of holding the thread of conversion with no trouble at all. She had never seen Monsieur Fournier drunk before.

Mrs Daly phoned as she cleared up. The men retired to the lounge with a bottle of cognac.

'He's been X-rayed and is about to be put in a cast. I'll get him home and settled for the night then I'll be right there with you. His daughter should be here any time now. I'm so sorry about all this.'

'Don't worry. Everything is perfect here. We never even missed you,' she teased.

'Cheeky strap!'

It was nearing nine when Sandra knocked and asked if they needed anything else.

'No, thank you, Sandra. We have everything.'

'I've put our guest's things in his room and Mrs Daly should be back in a while, so I'll say goodnight.'

It was far too early to go to bed so she took her book to her room. She seldom had this time to herself. It was usually one of the busiest times of the day – and she stretched out on the bed to enjoy every minute of it.

She heard the men on the stairs about a half an hour later as they laughed uproariously. Then there was a thud – one of them had obviously slipped. Silence and more raucous laughter. She didn't go out to investigate. She'd pretend she hadn't heard anything. More noises as Monsieur obviously helped his friend into the bathroom and into his room, which was across the hall from hers. Sandra had never felt unsafe in this house, but now she was uneasy. She wished Mrs Daly would hurry back. There was no lock on her door but she got up and quietly put a chair against it. She didn't like being the only female there. She heard the thud of shoes being dropped, one by one, on the floor. Then silence. After a few minutes, the loud rumbling of a snore punctuated the air. The visitor had obviously passed out and she sighed with relief.

The minutes ticked by and there was still no sign of Monsieur going back downstairs or of Mrs Daly coming up either. He must have passed out in the guestroom too. Then she heard the knob on her door turning and the chair being pushed out of its way. Monsieur stood in the doorway. She sat bolt upright. 'Is everything all right?' she asked, her heart thudding.

'Shh, don't make a sound,' he said, closing the door quietly behind him. He came in and sat on her bed. 'It's alright, no need to be scared. I just wanted to make sure you aren't too lonely with the children away.'

'I'm fine, thank you,' she said, thinking what she could reach for to hit him with if he came too close to her. Her senses were heightened by the awful memories that had been reawakened. This time, she'd scream and kick and bite and do whatever she had to defend herself if he laid a finger on her. But he didn't.

Instead, he just sat there looking at her in an unnerving way.

'You came to us an awkward little girl and, today, I realised you have become a woman in front of my eyes, a very alluring young woman, all grown up, and I started thinking that you must have needs and wants like all young women have and there's no one to satisfy them for you.'

'I don't know what you mean,' she said, too terrified to move.

'Don't you? I think you know very well what I mean, so don't act the innocent with me, young lady. I know your history – you know a lot more than you pretend, having sex before you were even a teenager. You must miss it. Tell me you don't,' he said, leaning his face close to hers, so close that she could smell the brandy and feel his warm breath.

'Get out of my room or I'll scream the house down.'

'No one will hear you. My friend won't waken until tomorrow and he might like to teach you a few lessons too. You know what they say about French men – we are the best lovers in the world.' He grinned an ugly grin.

'Mrs Daly will be back any minute.'

'She can't get in without ringing the bell. I put the lock on the snib.'

'I'll go to the gardaí and report you, and I'll tell Madame.'

'As if anyone would believe you, with your past. Besides, I have diplomatic immunity.'

She wasn't sure what that meant.

'Madame would believe me, so would Mrs Daly. If you touch me, I'll kill myself and Madame will come back and find me dead on the floor with my wrists cut and she'll wonder what made me do that.'

'Oh, you are so melodramatic. You should make a career on the stage.' He leaned further and kissed her fully on the lips. She raised her knees and arms and pushed him with all the strength she could muster. At that moment, they both heard the door open. Wide-eyed, he stumbled back from the bed, but there was no one there. He hadn't closed it properly when he'd come in.

He hovered for a moment. 'I've had too much to drink tonight anyway – maybe tomorrow – think about it,' he said. 'Don't look so scared, I won't force you.' And then he left.

Sandra heard him go back downstairs and close his bedroom door. As quietly as possible, she dressed and packed as much as she could fit in the bags in her room. She took the faded photograph from its hiding place, her passport and her post office book and crept downstairs and out into the night.

For a minute, she wondered whether she should wait in one of the neighbours' gardens for Mrs Daly to come back, but she decided against it quickly. She realised she needed to put as much distance as she could between her and that house. There was little passing traffic in the suburban avenue so she walked the five minutes to the main road, stopping several times to adjust her bags and redistribute their weight.

She hailed a taxi, told the driver to take her to a hostel in Harcourt Street, one she had seen often from the bus.

'You're cutting it fine. They close their doors at eleven. You'll just make it before curfew,' the taxi man told her as she paid him. She glanced at her clock in the taxi. It was 10.50 p.m.

Chapter Thirty-three

'I never contacted any of them again,' Sandra told Leah all those years later as they sat in her kitchen, scarcely a mile from where she had lived with the Fourniers in Sandymount. 'I was terrified they'd find me.'

'Oh, Mum, I don't know what to say. It's too horrible and you had to grow up so quickly. Your childhood was snatched away from you.'

'That's true. I was unfortunate in some ways until I met your dad. He completed me. He's been my rock. He restored my faith in men and stood by me when I needed him. Another man would have run and kept running when he found a stranger's baby in his house and discovered his wife had snatched it. That was a very bleak time for both of us. But Mal didn't, he believed in me and he's more than made up for those criminals. Then you were born and I was never happier. And then we had Oliver. I hope you are as lucky with Adam. You are happy, aren't you?'

'Of course I am,' Leah replied, wondering if her mother had sensed otherwise, and quickly moved off that topic. 'Did you go to the police?'

'No. I was too afraid to, because even though I was sixteen by then, the Fourniers had been appointed my guardians when they couldn't trace my family, and I wasn't sure if they might still have a hold on me and force me to return. They had been very generous to me. They bought all my clothes and they banked a wage every week as well as giving me pocket money, so I had plenty by the standard of the times.'

'They must have been frantic when you just disappeared. You never got in touch again to try to explain why you left like that?'

'I couldn't do that to Madame. She was a truly lovely and loving person. I used to feel guilty about not sending any sort of explanation for my sudden departure, but I couldn't do that without hurting others, so I ran. I did send a Christmas card from London saying I was safe.'

'Why London?'

'Because of the girls I met in the hostel. If they had been heading for Timbuktu then that's where I'd have ended up.'

'It must have been terrifying.'

'Not half as terrifying as what might have happened if I had stayed. There were lots of jobs advertised on a notice board in the hostel, and I applied for one in Selfridges, because they wanted sales assistants who had languages and I had French. I had no other qualifications but that was something I did take with me, that and confidence in all sorts of situations, thanks to Madame and her social circle. It was such a glamorous store – I had never seen the likes of it before, and the clients, as we had to call them – they weren't customers – were equally exotic. And the rest you know.'

'By comparison I've had such a charmed and easy life.'

'Everyone deserves a charmed life, but the reality is not everyone gets one,' Sandra said to her daughter. 'So it's important to recognise and cherish the good bits as they happen. Go off to Tasmania with that husband of yours and enjoy every minute of it. Your dad and I will get there some day but, right now, it's not top of the priority list.'

'Thanks, Mum. I love you.'

'And I love you, Leah.'

Part Three

Chapter Thirty-four

Mary knew that life hadn't just changed for Sandra the morning Fr O'Looney's car drove her away, it changed for the rest of her family too.

Had she failed her child? Could she have done more to protect her? She hoped no one had hurt Sandra. She was no nearer knowing when or where it had happened – or with whom. But she was determined to find out who was responsible.

When she and Con came back inside, his mother launched forth. 'She has brought shame on us all. If this gets out, we'll be the laughing stock of the neighourhood. Can you imagine the scandal? And her parents both teachers too! You're supposed to be the pillars of society. How could you have let this happen?'

'We didn't "let it happen". We're as shocked as you are, but we have to find out who is responsible and—'

'You'll do no such thing, do you hear me?' the older woman told them. 'Making any enquiries of that sort will only arouse suspicion. I told you those girls had too much freedom. Pregnant at twelve! The disgrace of it all. I'll never be able to hold my head up in society again.'

'But Sandra—'

Con was stopped by his mother. 'You'll not mention her name in this house again. Is that clear? Ever! She's gone and will get what she deserves. If she's smart enough to get herself into this situation, she's smart enough to get herself out of it. The nuns will take care of her and of the other business too.'

'Times are changing—' Mary started, but she was stopped in her tracks too.

'I'll hear not another word about it, and you better think of a plausible reason why she has gone to stay with your cousin in Dublin.'

'I don't have a cousin in Dublin,' Mary said.

'You do now! Do I make myself clear?'

'Yes, but Dominic will know that's untrue,' Mary said.

'Can he be trusted, Con? We may have to tell him the real story.'

'Yes, he can be trusted,' Con said with resignation, looking at his wife. 'He's kin anyway.'

'Then you must do it. I've discussed this with Fr O'Looney, and he thinks this is best too. The story is that your cousin is sick and needs help with the children.'

'But that's deceitful,' Mary said.

'Don't make me laugh,' the older woman said bitterly. 'I hope you're not trying to defend her. You failed in your duties and these are the consequences. What that young one did is shameful and deceitful; trying to keep it from becoming parish gossip is not. We have to try and save whatever vestige of respectability we can, knowing what sort of a girl she's turned into.'

Con was very aware that his younger daughter was not the first to suffer such a fate. He knew Dominic would understand and keep everything quiet; after all, Mary and the girls were his flesh and blood too – no matter what he thought of his mother. They had all known several families where a daughter or sister had been sent off to live with an ailing aunt or to help with a sick sibling's children in another part of the country, never to return to their homestead again. Tongues wagged for a time, but eventually they stopped.

* * *

Con told Dominic O'Sullivan that he needed to talk to him.

'Sure, Con, but can it wait until after class?'

'Why don't you drop by the house this evening?'

Mary looked gaunt and worried when she opened the door. She smiled as she welcomed her uncle and took him through to the kitchen.

Dominic looked around quickly, but there was no sign of the child. Mrs Mac Giolla Tighearnaigh sat beside the range like a queen on a throne, eyeing him up and down. *Would that auld one's face crack if she tried a smile?* he wondered.

'Sit down, Dominic. Would you take a whiskey?' Con asked.

'Aye, sure, if you're having one yourself.'

'We need to tell you something,' Mary said as she put a jug of water on the table, 'and we need it kept strictly within the family.'

He splashed some water into his glass. 'That sounds serious.'

'It's worse than that,' Mrs Mac Giolla Tighearnaigh said. 'The young one has got herself into trouble. She's in the family way.'

'What? That's shocking news altogether.' Shocked as he was, he was pleased with himself for managing to say something coherent. 'She's hardly out of nappies herself. Where is she?'

'She's been taken away to a home until it's born,' Mrs Mac Giolla Tighearnaigh replied.

'Do you know who is responsible?' he asked. 'Did someone force herself on her, or was she just unlucky? You know what youngsters are like nowadays, wanting to be grown up before their time.'

'Those thoughts have crossed our minds and whatever the

circumstances, I know what I'd like to do with him if I ever find out who it is,' Con said. 'She's years away from the age of consent. I'll see he pays for this, whoever the bastard is.'

'Has she been hanging around with those lads from the town?' Dominic asked.

'No,' Mary said, 'she hasn't been hanging around with anyone as far as we can find out. She just seemed to go in on herself when Louise went off to boarding school. We thought she was feeling lonely. We've no ideas at all, but we're going to tell everyone that she's gone to a cousin of mine in Dublin – to help out with the children while my cousin is sick.'

'I didn't know you had cousins there,' he said.

'I don't, Dominic, but no one need know that but us,' Mary said, looking meaningfully towards her mother-in-law. 'Fr O'Looney fixed everything up for us. He took her off early this morning.'

'Hopefully a few hours in a car with him might have wheedled a name out of her, and he'll have found out something by the time they get to wherever they're going. He's calling by later on,' Con said.

Dominic took up his glass and hastily emptied the remains of his drink down his throat. 'Sorry, I have to rush off but, don't worry, I'll take this matter to the grave,' he said to them and Mary hugged him.

'You've no idea how relieved I am that you know.'

'You can count on me,' he said.

'Typical of that fellow, has his sup of drink and leaves,' Mrs Mac Giolla Tighearnaigh said after Con had shown him out.

'It's great to have someone we can trust and confide in,' Mary said. Con agreed but his mother said nothing.

* * *

The house was quiet in the days after Sandra's hasty departure. It felt as though there had been a death in the family, but Mrs Mac Giolla

Tighearnaigh decided they should host the card circle the following Sunday. 'If we tell people our story first, it will stop questions being asked.'

They had the usual coterie of card players around, including the parish priest and Dominic O'Sullivan. The solicitor and his wife and possibly the doctor's wife were the only ones there who didn't know the whole story. Con's mother told them all of the cause of Sandra's absence, making direct eye contact with the doctor, almost defying him to say anything that would embarrass her. He didn't. The others nodded, praising Mary and Con for letting her go to help out with the relative's children.

'We were very lucky that Fr O'Looney had business in Dublin and he drove her there,' Con said.

The solicitor's wife asked, 'What about her schooling, won't she fall behind?'

'Sure, Mrs Fogarty,' Dominic stepped in, 'family comes first, and it's good to be able to help out when needed. And weren't you just saying the last time you were here how you had heard that she was scholarship material, like her sister? Sandra's very bright and is well ahead of her peers already. Anyway, Mary and Con can help her catch up if needed.'

There were nods of agreement and the conversation moved on. Mrs Mac Giolla Tighearnaigh looked at Dominic almost approvingly. Eventually, the visitors left and she went off to bed muttering, 'That went well.'

Mary tried to talk to Con about the situation, but he refused to be drawn. 'I think Mam is right. Let's leave it. I have to say I'm sorely disappointed in Sandra. I never expected her to let us and herself down so badly.'

'Neither did I.'

When he turned his back on her that night in bed, she wondered if he too thought she was to blame. But what could she have done differently to protect her daughters?

How was she going to tell Louise? She couldn't fob her off with a story, yet she'd have to know what they were telling everyone else. She'd have to be told the truth, but in the meantime, they had to live a lie and keep up the appearances of normality.

Chapter Thirty-five

Mayo, New Year's Eve, 1970

The doctor and his wife had laid claim to New Year's Eve. Anyone who considered themselves to be anyone didn't dare make other arrangements or issue invitations for that night in case they missed out on the Vaughans' bash. The vet's wife had made the mistake of organising a party the first winter they were in the locality, and apart from their families and a pharmaceutical rep, everyone else declined.

As befitted the standing and reputation the doctor's wife felt she held in the community, she had to do everything on a bigger scale than everyone else. They had the largest Christmas tree in the parish and, as their house was on a slope, it could be seen for miles around. So too could the sprawling fir in their front garden, which was festooned with dozens and dozens of tiny coloured lights. There was an oversized wreath on the door and the doormat played 'Jingle Bells' when anyone stepped on it.

'Tuppence ha'penny looking down on tuppence,' said Mrs Mac Giolla Tighearnaigh, when their personalised card arrived, showing a studio portrait of the family. 'Of course her first cousin is a professional photographer, so they probably struck a deal!'

'You can always give it a miss,' Con said, looking over at his wife.

'No. We can't. We have to behave normally if we're to keep our good name, and that includes socialising as usual,' Mrs Mac Giolla

Tighearnaigh said. Despite that and all the protestations at the
ostentation, Mary knew her mother-in-law wouldn't miss this event
unless she were dead. Although she was known for not being a gossip
outside her front door, nothing and no one was spared inside her
home.

'I knew if Con had married that Imelda-Rose one, she'd have him
beggared in no time. Those reindeer in the garden, the sleigh on the
roof and the icicles hanging from the gutters – did you ever see the
like?' she asked.

'I think they're fun and all the kids love looking at them.'

'They're gaudy and flashy, if you ask me.'

Well, I didn't! Mary wanted to shout, but she had long since
realised that life was easier if she said nothing. But she was tempted.

'That shopping trip to New York turned her head altogether. Still,
I suppose with the fees he charges for a visit it's no wonder they can
afford to waste money on fripperies like that … although, I suppose
it could be argued that he has to charge those exorbitant fees to fund
her tastes. And did you see this – there's a dress code. It says cocktail
wear. I ask you – she's lost the run of herself this year. I'll have to
check with my maid and make sure we don't wear the same dresses
as last year.'

Mary had to smile at that. 'That would definitely be social suicide.
We can ask the butler about taking our diamonds out of the vault
too.'

* * *

Powdered and pampered, the social circle of the small Mayo town
assembled to ring in 1971. The air was strong with the melange of
expensive perfumes and aftershaves. It seemed, thought Mary, that
the cocktail-wear diktat had been taken seriously by everyone.

'She's a bit long in the tooth and thick in the knees and ankles
for that cream lace ensemble,' Mrs Mac Giolla Tighearnaigh said as

they got out of the taxi behind the captain of the golf club and his wife, who was pulling down her skirt. It didn't make any difference. 'Shush, she'll hear you,' Mary said as they walked into the porch.

Their coats were taken by a waiter hired for the evening. Another waiter, ladling fragrant golden liquid into glasses, stood in the hall, announcing, 'It's warm cider punch', as he handed out glasses. There weren't many takers for the non-alcoholic option as Paddy McNally and his hackneys had been put on standby to drive people home whenever they wanted to leave.

Mary felt liberated. It was great to be out like this, and with Con too. She'd been avoiding people because she found it easier than fending off questions about her fictitious sick cousin in Dublin. Things were back to normal between her and Con as well, and it was great having Louise home, although that had brought a fresh set of problems – but Mary wasn't going to dwell on anything tonight. It was the last night of the year and she hoped the new one would be better. The Vaughans greeted them and Bill took Mary's hands in his and gave them a squeeze. 'I'm so glad to see you both. You're looking lovely this evening, Mary. I hope you had a nice Christmas.'

She knew what he meant and she knew she could trust him. He wouldn't have said a word to his wife about the drama that was going on in their lives. He shook Con's hand and patted his other arm affectionately.

The reception line included the Vaughans' coiffured daughters and the men in their lives. The previous year, the youngest daughter, an afterthought by nine years, had brought home a dreadlocked artist who had delighted in telling everyone he was into peace and love and was squatting in a condemned flat in Capel Street in Dublin. This year's beau was different. 'Have you met Jack? He's specialising in endocrinology,' the doctor's wife said and Mary had to cough to try and hide the 'he would be' that came from her mother-in-law's mouth.

'That was a bit uncalled for, Mam, we are guests in their home.'

Mrs Mac Giolla Tighearnaigh replied, 'She has to give everyone their position – take the unfortunate sons-in-law – Martin the pharmacist, Ernie the vet and Eoghan the rancher in Australia.'

Mary smiled at Con – as if she wouldn't have done the same if her only son had married a heart surgeon, instead of her, a humble teacher from Kerry.

'He seems a pleasant enough fellow,' said Con later, 'the wannabe endocrinologist. I had a chat with him when he managed to escape.'

'Those girls were very brave to bring their men home – I would have thought that the prospect of a mother-in-law like that would frighten any young fellow away.'

'It didn't stop you.' He smiled at her.

'Oh, Con Mac Giolla Tighearnaigh, I was young and foolish then, and didn't know what I was doing. Just think if you'd married Imelda-Rose – Mrs Vaughan would be your mother-in-law!'

'That's probably why the poor sod who did marry her whisked her off to live in Australia.'

'Come on. Food's being served and I'm starving,' she said, taking his arm.

They moved through the drawing room where a pianist played the baby grand piano to the accompaniment of a violinist. There were vases full of flowers everywhere and white and red poinsettias on every available surface.

It wasn't long before people started discussing the latest comings and goings in the town. The accountant said to Con, 'Did you see old man Doyle's fancy bit? Not a year widowed and he's found a new bird.'

'He's very wealthy and she's very well endowed,' the golf club captain said.

'A bit too obvious for my liking,' Con said, taking in her heavy make-up and scarlet lips.

The object of their speculation bent forward to reach a passing tray of canapés and her breasts rippled like an impending tsunami gathering momentum and just about managed not to spill over the neckline of her low-cut dress.

'I know it pays to advertise, but that's going a bit too far,' the very plain solicitor, who was married to an equally plain solicitor, pronounced.

'If you replace me with a model like that when I die, I'll come back and haunt you!' Mary said to Con, and they all laughed at that. 'The stroganoff looks delicious.'

'Have you ever made it?' someone asked her.

She raised her eyes to heaven – 'Mrs M would have conniptions at me destroying good beef like that. She just likes traditional rare roast and steak. She has no time for "faffing around with food", as she puts it.'

'Well, don't look now, but she seems to be enjoying it over there.'

Mary cast a sneaky look and, sure enough, her mother-in-law was tucking in to a plate of stroganoff.

'She'll probably complain of having indigestion for the next week,' laughed Mary.

'You're a saint living with that woman. I couldn't do it. How's your daughter getting on in Dublin?'

'She's loving it,' Mary lied, thinking how easily these untruths rolled off her tongue the more she pronounced them. 'I think it's good for her. She's been a bit lost since her sister went off to school – they're so close in age. It's good for her to be independent and she's enjoying the freedom too. I'm afraid her head is being turned by my cousin's tales of New York. She lived there for several years and they're hoping to move back when she's better.'

'You're lucky, mine fought like alley cats at that age and when they'd finished college, they couldn't wait to get away and "find themselves".'

'Oh, ours have their moments too. I'm all for them spreading their wings; I wish I had done it, but mine have a while to go before they take flight,' Mary told the solicitor's wife.

Dominic came over to her. 'That chicken is delicious. Do you think they'd notice if I had a second helping?'

'They've enough food here to feed the multitudes – help yourself,' Mary said. The waiters circulated with champagne. The doctor rounded up his family before he did the countdown to midnight. When the clock struck, some took it as an excuse for some opportunistic kissing and fondling. Glasses clinked and together they murdered the first verse of 'Auld Lang Syne'. No one knew the second.

'Little did we realise what the year gone by would bring, did we, Mary?' Con said quietly as they stood beside his mother.

'And what will this one bring?' she asked.

'It can't be any worse, can it?'

'Let's hope not,' Mrs Mac Giolla Tighearnaigh said. 'Now I think I'll call it a night.'

'I'll get the coats,' Mary offered.

'No, you and Con stay on. I've had enough. I'll get back to Dinah and Louise. They'll probably still be up watching the celebrations on the television.'

While Con walked his mother to the car, Dominic came over to talk to Mary. 'Any news from Dublin?' he asked pointedly.

'Not a word, but we know that's the way they do things there.'

'I've been thinking about the – the situation – could anyone we know have forced himself on her?'

'We can't talk about that here.'

'No, you're right,' he said, as the doctor's wife approached them. 'I hope you're enjoying yourselves.'

'Absolutely, we're having a grand time. You've surpassed your other gatherings tonight,' Dominic said. 'And I want to marry the cook.'

'Oh you are such a flatterer,' she twinkled at him, implying it was all her own doing. She moved on but before she was out of earshot, he added with a wink at Mary, 'I was thinking of taking a run up to Dublin to see the family before school starts. I might take the train from Westport. Do you want me to take anything up to Sandra?'

Dominic had brought Mary right back down to earth. *How was Sandra getting on? How was she celebrating New Year?* She hoped the pregnancy was going well and that she was eating properly. *The nuns will make sure she does, won't they?* She hoped she liked the cardigans and the practical nighties she'd sent her. It was annoying that she wasn't allowed write back, but Fr O'Looney had told them that was to make them all feel equal, as some of the less fortunate girls had no one to write to at all.

Con came back over to her, fresh glasses of champagne in his hands. 'Why are you looking so glum?'

'Just thinking.'

'Chin up, there's a sing-song going on in the other room and a merrily unsteady pharmacist is giving a merrily unsteady version of 'Brown-Eyed Girl'. He's priceless.'

Mary put on her happy face and went through the motions, clapping and laughing, but what Dominic had said was nagging away at her as she pretended to be engaged with what was going on.

It was almost two in the morning when they left. The sky was clear and star-studded, and the bright moon left a silvery trail out on the Atlantic. Several of the guests decided to walk home together. Dominic waited for Mary and they fell behind the others.

'You must have thought about – about what I mentioned earlier.'

'I'm trying not to. I'd rather believe that she had agreed to it than to think anybody forced her. There's not a clue to lead me anywhere. Con says I'll go mad trying to figure it out, and won't talk about it any more. I'm beginning to believe him. I can't sleep thinking about it sometimes.'

'She may not have consented. You know they often say that it can be someone the girl knows and trusts – someone who could easily manipulate and intimidate them.'

Mary felt herself go cold all over, and knew it had nothing to do with the frosting on the fields. What was Dominic implying? That Con could have forced himself on his own daughter? Surely not! She was about to tell him what she thought of this preposterous notion when Con turned around and waited for them to catch up.

'What are you two talking about?' he asked.

'Just talking about the food at the party. I was hoping I'd get a doggy bag to bring home for my dinner tomorrow,' Dominic told him.

'You should take a leaf out of old man Doyle's book and get yourself a woman, although I don't think that one would be much good in the kitchen,' Con laughed.

'Maybe I will,' he replied, chuckling.

'Well, here we are,' Con said, opening the gate for Mary. 'Happy New Year, Dominic.'

'And the same to you both,' he said as he set off up the hill from their house.

* * *

'I can't help worrying about Sandra and if she's all right. I had hoped for some word, a card or a letter over Christmas,' Mary said to her husband when they were getting ready for bed.

He agreed, but changed the subject and he asked her if she had enjoyed herself.

'Surprisingly enough I did, although I was terrified I'd put my foot in it any time anyone talked to me about the girls.'

'It didn't show and you looked lovely.'

She looked at him as though she was seeing him for the first time. She loved him and there was nothing about her husband that suggested he was anything other than the loving man she had married – and he loved their daughters. She knew he was heartbroken about sending Sandra away, but there wasn't any other way to handle the situation. *But why didn't he want to talk about Sandra at all these days?* She had wondered if that was from disappointment or shame. *Could it be from guilt?*

'What?' he said, puzzled by the scrutiny. 'Am I not allowed compliment my wife?'

'Yes, of course you are. Don't mind me, I've had too much to drink,' she lied. 'And I'll pay for it in the morning. Night, night.'

She got into bed and pretended to be asleep until Con's breathing told her that he was. She cursed Dominic O'Sullivan for planting that despicable thought in her mind, and wished she could erase it. Memories of Con and Sandra coming in together from the cowshed, or from the field after feeding the donkey in the evenings after Louise had gone away kept floating into her mind. They were very close. *Surely not!*

Con was right. She was driving herself mad, wondering and speculating, looking with suspicion at every young man she came across when she went out – and now she was adding this. Her husband? This was definitely a form of madness. How could she ever suspect him of such an unspeakable act? It was insane.

Yet the next day, when Con and Louise had gone to feed the animals, she rang Dominic.

'Do you know something you haven't told me?'

'Nothing, Mary. If I had I would have told you. I promise. Stop tormenting yourself.'

'Have you heard any talk among the lads at school?'

'Not a word, and we'll probably never know. I don't think anyone suspects anything and it's not likely anyone would own up, is it? It was probably one of the village lads sowing his wild oats. Anyway, it's all been taken care of now and no one need ever know anything about it.'

'I suppose you're right there, but it's very hard not to think about it.'

'She's very young, but she's certainly not the first young one to end up like this and she won't be the last. I know she's only a kid, but that's life. Look, it's the start of a new year – new beginnings and all that – it's a time to look to the future. You'll get through this. We all will.'

'That sounds easy but, believe me, it's not.'

Chapter Thirty-six

Mary never liked January. It was a cold, soulless month and this one seemed more so than ever. She was driving home from leaving Louise back to boarding school for a new term. She felt empty and was missing her girls and, try as she might expel the thoughts Dominic O'Sullivan had planted, she couldn't. An icy wind whipped in from the Atlantic, the sort that found gaps and cracks everywhere, whistling and groaning through window and door frames and making the eaves creak menacingly.

It had blown with this sort of ferocity every day since the beginning of January, the darkness of night barely lifting throughout the day. Tonight, it drove sheets of rain across the narrow roads, compromising visibility and making her tense at the wheel. Despite the atmosphere in her home she was relieved when she got back safely. There was no let-up as the rain ricocheted like gunfire against the windows. It made her shiver in spite of the heat from the Aga.

* * *

Dominic O'Sullivan had called and Con saw him to his car, before going to check on the handful of animals he kept, making sure the doors were secure against the raging wind. When he came back in, he hung his soppy waterproof on the hook in the back porch and pulled his wellingtons off before going through to the kitchen where Mary and his mother were sitting.

He had spent a lifetime under the watchful eyes of his mother, with her exacting notions and standards, his every action scrutinised and commented on, and lately he was getting the feeling that instead of being on his side, his wife was turning against him. She was changing before his eyes, becoming less and less like the girl he had married. It was like having two judges there to comment on what he did or to give him the silent treatment, whichever they thought the most appropriate.

Mary had never been like that – well, not before everything went wrong. She had always backed him up; now she didn't. This meant there was often no harmony in the house for days at a time. He knew it was hard having to let her youngest go, and his mother forbidding them to even mention her name, but maybe some day Sandra could come back. She was disappointed in Sandra. God knows so was he, but they had done the right thing for everyone involved. It was out of their hands now.

As he settled down with the paper, his mother remarked, 'What was that fellow doing, hanging around the house again? He never used to darken the doorstep.'

'Maybe that was because you let him know, in no uncertain terms, that he wasn't welcome to drop in,' Con replied.

'Well, from where I see it, he's taking advantage of you. It seems that he's always here on some pretext or other and, if you ask me, it's no coincidence that his visits usually coincide with mealtimes.'

'It's just school business, nothing for you to worry about.'

'Nothing to worry about? Like a pair of conspirators. Your father never brought his work home with him or bothered the other staff with it outside of school hours. Do the two of you not spend enough time in each other's company during the day to say what you have to say to each other?'

He didn't answer. Mary offered no comment; she just sat there, watching him in a way he found unnerving. She and Dominic were closer than ever to each other and even though he was her kin, if he were truly honest, it annoyed him and made him feel a bit excluded. They seemed to be ganging up on him and he hadn't a clue why.

They watched television in silence for a while and when the late news was over, his mother said her goodnights and went off to bed.

'I'm going to make some tea, Mary. Do you fancy a cup?' Con asked.

'No, I'm fine, thanks. I think I'll head on up too.'

'Are you feeling OK?'

'Yes. Why?'

'You've not been yourself for a while. I know it's lonely for you when you're used to having the girls around, but Louise will be back for Easter before you know it.'

'She's not coming home for Easter. She's going to Roscommon, to Dymphna's family. I thought it best until we've sorted everything out.'

'When did you decide this?' He turned around to face her.

'Your mother and I thought it best to keep her away, out of harm's reach.'

'You decided this without consulting me? Mary, what is going on? What harm can she come to here, with us?'

Mary just kept staring into the fire.

'Mary? Talk to me.'

'That's what we thought about Sandra and look where it got us. She should have been safe with us. Dominic said it's often someone they know. He's seen it before.'

'What is? Someone who knows what?' Con stared at his wife, trying to understand.

'Con, I have to ask you – I need to hear you tell me – I never would have thought it myself only for Dominic, but if I don't ask,

I'll go mad. I have to know, to protect my other daughter.'

'*Our* daughter – not safe ... What are you talking about, Mary?'

'Sandra.'

'What about Sandra? Oh, my God – now I get it. The cold shoulder treatment. Is that what you think? Is that why you've been pushing me away? And Mam? Jesus Christ, does she think that too? Mary, I can't honestly—'

He didn't get a chance to finish because there was a loud thump from outside the door and the sound of glass shattering on the tiles. He dropped the teapot into the sink as Mary jumped up and ran into the hall.

His mother was lying on the floor, her face contorted on one side, her arm limp. She was uttering indecipherable guttural sounds, her eyes frightened and imploring. Mary ran back into the kitchen and dialled 999, while Con held his mother and talked to her.

'Mam, don't worry. Don't try to say anything. It'll be all right. Help's on its way.'

'I'm going to call Dr Vaughan to see if he can come over – the ambulance could be ages in this weather.'

Con watched as Mary calmly got a rug and tucked it around his mother to keep her warm and comfortable before clearing the smashed jug and the spilled water from around her. Outside, the wind had become even fiercer and the letterbox rattled.

They knew she'd had a stroke, and Con wondered if she had been listening to their conversation on the other side of the door when it happened, the jug her alibi in case they came out and caught her.

'Can things get any worse?' Mary said as she opened the door to Bill Vaughan.

'Now let's not panic. Things often seem much worse than they are.' He took off his coat and knelt down beside Con and his mother, reassuring the older woman that she'd be fine. He kept talking to her as he assessed the damage and severity, testing her reflexes and mobility.

It seemed forever before the blue flashing light appeared at the bottom of their roadway.

'You wouldn't put a cat out on a night like this,' the driver said as they strapped Mrs Mac Giolla Tighearnaigh onto a stretcher. 'It's a bad one, lots of trees down and minor road accidents. It's been a busy one for everyone, but don't worry, we're going to tuck you up and keep you nice and warm,' he said, putting a tarpaulin around her before they carried her out into the elements.

'You go in the ambulance,' Mary said. 'I'll follow with the car. I'll just get a few things together for her.'

'I'll phone ahead and fill them in,' Dr Vaughan promised.

As Con sat holding his mother's hand throughout the journey to hospital, she kept trying to speak but was making no sense.

He was remembering what he and Mary had been talking about immediately before his mother fell. Mary had practically accused him of molesting his own daughter. Could she honestly suspect him? No, that was absurd. She'd never think a thing like that – yet it made sense, the way she had been treating him, the way she hadn't let him come near her for weeks. Was that what all those accusatory stares and silences had been about? Surely his mother didn't think that of him too? Maybe they had even talked about it. If they had, it was no wonder Mary had been so different or that his mother had had a stroke.

'You're mad, you're upset,' he said to himself. 'Now is not the time to think about it.' But he couldn't help himself. 'How could they imagine something so heinous?'

They were greeted by the organised chaos of the casualty department, where uniformed people were focused on doing their jobs. There was a lot of form-filling and questions, endless questions, assessments and examinations – until finally she was admitted.

Mary, her hair slicked down from the rain, arrived as Mrs Mac Giolla Tighearnaigh was being taken up to the ward. 'Is she in any immediate danger?' she asked the young doctor.

'There is always danger after a stroke. She seems to have had a pretty big one, but we'll know more as time goes on. Some people make remarkable recoveries and constantly surprise us. The longer she goes without having another, the better her chances will be. I'm afraid I can't be more specific at this stage, but the next forty-eight hours are crucial. If she remains stable in that time, we'll be able to give you a more accurate diagnosis. We'll monitor her closely and decide what treatment Mrs Mac Giolla Tighearnaigh will need then.'

They were then taken to a ward where the other beds were occupied by patients in various stages of oblivious sleep. One snored loudly with a whistling accompaniment, but his mother didn't seem to notice. She had stopped trying to talk and seemed more restful. Eventually, she closed her eyes and slept.

'It's strange to see her looking so vulnerable, as though the fight has gone out of her,' Mary said.

'She'll probably be bossing everyone around by the morning, telling them how to run a hospital properly,' Con said, trying to lighten the mood.

'Let's hope so.'

'You're very good with her,' he said. Then he added, 'Mary – what you were saying earlier?'

'Not now, Con. For God's sake, and not here.'

'But we have to talk about it.'

'Yes, we do,' Mary said. 'But let's get over this hurdle first.' Then she sat tight-lipped, as they kept a vigil by the bedside on the uncomfortable shiny chairs.

His mind was in turmoil – the fact that his mother could be dying there beside him or left disabled and dependent, unable to communicate with anyone, meant nothing in comparison with the reality that his own wife suspected him of abusing his little girl. Wasn't that what she'd meant? And that his other child needed to be protected from *him*? And it was Dominic O'Sullivan who had planted that in their minds. And he would have to carry on working with that manipulative bastard.

* * *

Mrs Mac Giolla Tighearnaigh held her own over the next two days and there were no further setbacks. Con and Mary had taken it in turns to sit with her, but even though there were no more attacks, it became clear that the stroke had had quite a devastating effect.

As promised, the doctor met with them to discuss options. 'It was a big bleed,' he told them. 'She's going to need a lot of care and rehabilitation before she can expect to walk on her own or regain the use of her arm.'

'And her speech?' asked Con.

'That will probably come back more quickly. She'll be with us for a while, but we'll work out a programme for her.'

Over the next week Mary visited every morning. She massaged her mother-in-law's hands and fixed her hair, and talked about the weather and everyday things. Mrs Mac Giolla Tighearnaigh tried to answer, but didn't make any sense, and that only frustrated them both even more. Dinah cooked tasty little morsels for her to eat and brought her a supply of ironed nighties. Con came in to sit with her as soon as school finished, when he knew Mary would be at home, and went home exhausted for his dinner.

'We can't keep this up,' he said, a week after his mother had had her stroke.

'We can cut back on visiting now that there is no imminent danger,' Mary replied.

'That's not what I mean, and you know it,' he said, barely concealing his anger. 'I want to know what you meant when you said you needed to protect *your* daughter from *me*?'

'I wasn't thinking straight, Con. I didn't mean it. I've been watching you these past few days, and how caring and gentle you are with your mam and it made me realise the absurdity of what I said.'

'It's a bit late for that now, Mary.'

'Anyway, it's not important now.'

'What do you mean it's not important? You throw an accusation like that at me and expect me to pretend I never heard it? What kind of animal do you think I am? Don't you know me at all?'

'I'm sorry, Con.'

'Sorry doesn't come anywhere near fixing this. What happened to love and trust? Did you tell my mother what was running through that warped head of yours? Is that why she's lying there in hospital?'

'Of course I didn't, and I never honestly suspected you.'

'I've heard enough. You're not the woman I thought you were. Stay away from me, and stay away from my mother too.'

He stormed out of the kitchen to the sheds and Mary put her head on the table and wept. In the shed, he wept too – for what had happened to Sandra and what it was doing to them.

When he came back in, he took the bottle of whiskey from the cabinet and poured himself a measure and went to bed – in the girls' room.

* * *

Although the first of February is celebrated as the beginning of spring, it seldom felt like it. But today the sun came out and lit the world up again. It glinted on the breakers that the weeks of gales had stirred up in the Atlantic and it illuminated Croagh Patrick's stony peak, giving it an almost snow-capped appearance.

Con hadn't spoken one word to Mary since that night, two weeks previously. He continued to sleep in Sandra's bed, making no attempt to hide the fact from Dinah. He had had enough of keeping up appearances. Where had that got them all?

Despite his instruction to the contrary, Mary still visited the hospital every day. That first day of spring, as she parked in the grounds of the hospital, she noticed a few early daffodils were getting ready to burst open and the crocus made colourful clumps against the sodden earth. But it was a false spring. It snowed and sleeted on and off over the two weeks, making driving hazardous on the country roads. She narrowly missed skidding in to a car as she parked. She made the now all-too-familiar walk towards the ward, but she was stopped before she went in.

'The doctors are with Mrs Mac Giolla Tighearnaigh. Can you go to the waiting room until we call you?'

'Has something happened? Should I contact my husband?'

'We already have, he's on his way.'

Mary didn't have to wait long before she heard his footsteps hurrying along the corridor. 'Con.'

'Leave me alone. You've done enough damage. If it hadn't been for you and your twisted mind, we wouldn't be here.'

She retreated. *Will I ever be able to put this right?* A doctor came into the room and closed the door. He looked from Con to Mary but before he could speak, Con said, 'She's gone, hasn't she?'

'Yes, I'm afraid she didn't make it this time. I'm sorry. She had a massive stroke about an hour and a half ago. She wouldn't have suffered or known anything about it.'

Mary reached to put her hand on Con's arm, but he pulled away from her.

'Take as much time as you need, then you can go in to her,' the doctor said.

Chapter Thirty-seven

Con behaved as though Mary was invisible in the days around his mother's funeral. He refused Dominic's offer of help with the arrangements. She was upset too. While her mother-in-law had driven her demented, they had been part of each other's lives for sixteen years, and Mrs Mac Giolla Tighearnaigh was still present everywhere in the house. Mary tried to tell Con how she felt but, in the end, she stopped trying. She knew he was devastated – he had no siblings and she could only guess how alone he must have felt. She wanted so badly to put her arms around him and offer some comfort, but it was as if a bit of him too had died – something that had nothing to do with the loss of his mother.

Mary turned to Dominic, who called a few times to check up on him. She had no one else she could trust. 'He's drinking a lot – too much in fact,' she told him.

'Let him be. Grief takes people in different ways, and it has all happened very quickly. What are you going to say about the young one not coming home?'

'I'm not going to make any excuses. Her gran never approved of children going to funerals or to gravesides, so Louise won't be there either. We'll just say it was her wish that they remember her as she was.'

They waked Mrs Mac Giolla Tighearnaigh in the house, and Dominic stood in as a family member, thanking neighbours for their sympathies, cakes and the odd bottle of spirits. Dinah had made enough sandwiches to feed the parish for a week. There was a huge turnout at the removal and the requiem mass and, again, Dominic walked beside Con and Mary, and did a reading in the church. The pupils from Con's school sang and formed a guard of honour outside. The group who had often gathered for cards were invited back to the house for some more tea and sandwiches, and Mary worried as the day wore on and she watched her husband become very heavy-handed with the measures of whiskey he was pouring for himself.

Eventually by early evening, people drifted away. Mary busied herself with Dinah, washing the good china and cut glasses and putting them all away.

'You'll miss her too, Dinah.'

'I will. I came to this house before Con was born. For all her airs and graces, she was a good woman – so long as I kept my place, or let her think I did, all was well.' She smiled.

'That was her all right.'

In the sitting room, things had flared out of control between Con and Dominic and their raised voices could be heard in the kitchen. Mary tried to talk over them, but Dinah heard everything. If she hadn't realised what had happened to Sandra, she would be in no doubt now.

Dinah looked at Mary, walked over and put her arms around her. 'Oh, you poor woman. I never suspected anything like that, but I won't breathe a word to anyone, I promise.' They held each other tightly.

There was the sound of a glass breaking and Con's slurred voice. 'You miserable sleeveen. Get out of my house, putting your twisted thoughts into Mary's head. You poisoned my wife against me, you sanctimonious bastard.'

'You're upset, Con, it's been a trying time, but this is no way to behave after burying your mother.'

'You leave my mother out of this. It's your fault she's gone to an early grave.'

'Right so, Con. I'll be off now. Take your time coming back to school.'

'I wouldn't hold my breath if I were you. I'll be in no hurry to do that. Now get out and don't ever come back here again.'

Mary went to go in to them, but Dinah held her back.

'Don't – it's the drink talking. Let them say what they need, and let him sleep it off. He probably won't remember half of it tomorrow.'

A few seconds later, they heard the hall door being slammed as Con continued to shout a tirade of insults. Then he stumbled in to the kitchen, looked with contempt at Mary before speaking to the housekeeper.

'I'm sorry, Dinah, there's a bit of a mess in the front room, I knocked over a vase.' He took a bottle of whiskey from the sideboard and stumbled upstairs, cursing.

Dinah offered to stay that night but Mary refused.

'He'd never harm me, you don't need to worry.'

'I'm not so sure,' Dinah said. 'I've known him since he was born and I've never seen him like this. I never knew he had such a temper. He's acting very out of sorts.'

'He blames me for his mother's stroke.'

'That's ridiculous! What gave him such a notion?'

She told Dinah about the predicament she was in and when she had finished, she said, 'You've no idea how much better I feel being able to talk to someone about it.'

Dinah nodded.

'You know it wasn't Con—'

'Of course it wasn't. I'd never have thought it was in a million years. He's a good man and a good father too. He loves those girls like his life, and he'd never let any harm come to them. And I'm staying over and that's all there is to it. Someone has to help you eat some of that food.'

'Thanks, Dinah. You're a true friend.'

Chapter Thirty-eight

Kieron phoned Leah. 'I think I've made a breakthrough. I've got an address in the States from the convent.'

'That's fantastic. How did you manage to do that?'

'Threats and persuasion. I think things have changed somewhat in recent years and the fact that I already knew so much about my maternal mother and family seemed to hold some sway over the nun in charge of the records. She didn't let me see my files though, but she extracted this address for me. It's an old one obviously, and it may go nowhere, but I wanted to tell you before you head off. I'll keep you posted, but say nothing to Sandra.'

'Of course I won't. She's had enough disappointment in her life. I don't intend adding to it – but I'll let Ollie know. Well done on getting this far.'

'It's such a shame we haven't had more time to get to know each other better before you head off to Tasmania.'

'I know, but it may not be for too long. Naturally I would have delayed it had I been a match for Jennifer. I'm in two minds about living there long-term, but I know how much Adam loves that place and what it means to him. I owe it to him to at least explore the possibilities.'

'I bet your parents aren't too happy at the prospect.'

'I know they're not, but they'd never try to influence me. We won't lose contact, Kieron, no matter how things pan out.'

* * *

A week later, Leah and Adam headed to Singapore for a two-night stopover to break their journey – just as they'd done on their honeymoon. Then, Uncle Jack's wedding present had been their first-class return tickets. This time, it was his legacy that was funding them. They stayed in the same hotel and visited some of the places they had been to the last time they'd passed through.

'We've got to go back to the orchid gardens. I loved that place,' she said. 'Remember the couple we met there who had just got married that day? And we had dinner with them that night?'

'I'd forgotten that, but I do remember your reaction when you saw black swans for the first time.'

'So do I – they're magnificent creatures.'

'I'm glad to see you looking happy again,' he said, leaning over to give her a kiss. She smiled and didn't pull away. Maybe he'd been right – this was what they needed, a complete break from work and home. A fresh start.

That evening, they walked along the waterfront promenade and took a river taxi around the bay. She snuggled up against him as they admired the skyscape and went under the Esplanade Bridge. Decorative lighting and spectacular high-rise buildings created a kaleidoscope of images and colours that dwarfed them in the panorama and reflected magically back from the water.

'It's pretty spectacular,' he said, putting his arm around her.

That night they sat on their balcony having a nightcap, reluctant to leave the awesome view. Adam took their glasses inside and when he came back out he stood behind her chair and began massaging her shoulders and upper back slowly. She felt the tensions easing away and bent her head forward. He changed his strokes deliberately, running his fingers in longer movements up under her hair and behind her ears. She groaned softly. He reached for her hand and led her inside.

They made love for the first time since he'd cheated on her just two months earlier; so much had happened since then. It was slow, sensual and satisfying, but as Leah lay there in the afterglow she knew it would never be the same again. That private space they entered when they were together like this had been invaded. It was no longer exclusively theirs. She wanted so badly to recapture it and decided she would try, not knowing if she ever would.

They made love again the next afternoon and again she kept imagining him with Helka. It would get better. It had to.

At dinner that night he talked about his plans for the estate and what they could do with it. 'I'll leave the house in your capable hands. You've an eye for that sort of thing and if you remember, it was very much a bachelor's house, crammed with Jack's possessions and he never liked to part with anything.'

'It also reeked of the smell of his pipe smoke. I could never forget that.'

* * *

They flew on to Tasmania the following day and arrived at the farm in the late afternoon to be greeted by the housekeeper, Madge, and her husband Harvey, who managed the place.

'It's great to be back, but it's bittersweet without Uncle Jack and his yarns,' Adam said.

'I know. I still keep expecting to see him come back from his daily tour of inspection,' Madge said, 'looking for a cup of strong tea. "Strong enough to trot a mouse on", he used to say.'

'The place has been well run since he died though,' Harvey said. 'The problem is he gave all the responsibility to old codgers like myself, and we're really past it now. We just want to retire and enjoy life doing nothing.'

'I'm nearly past it myself too,' Madge laughed.

'Madge, you can't desert me too. I need those lamb roasts and apple pies – it was the thoughts of them that brought me back over here,' Adam said.

'You lie like a professional,' she retorted, 'but I do remember your appetite. When you came here that first summer as a scrawny eighteen-year-old you ate everyone else under the table. You've filled out well.'

'Well, Madge, your food was definitely an enticement. That and the fact that I do need to find a new manager – you're right, Harvey, I need someone with the skills to handle both the distillery and the farm.'

'And someone who understands all the modern technology that's come in to farming,' Harvey said. 'Emails are the height of my technical expertise and even then I get confused. Anyway, it's not cost-effective to run the two ventures as separate entities. And I imagine it's not easy trying to keep an eye on things from so far away.'

'You're right, which is why I'm taking this year out to stay put and get the new systems up and running,' Adam said. 'Who knows what might happen then.'

Madge looked over at Leah, who showed no outward reaction.

The 'I' wasn't lost on Leah, but she said nothing. The last time they had discussed the trip, the plan had been to stay a month, maybe six weeks, but that wasn't the impression he was now giving and she didn't want to start rowing about it again, certainly not in front of people she'd only met a couple of times before, on her honeymoon and after Jack had died. Even then, it had been obvious to her that Adam was at home here.

Leah soon realised that Adam was in his element and enjoying his role as lord of the manor. She hardly saw him as he headed out at first light each morning to check things on the farm, appearing back to be fed in the big community kitchen at lunchtime and disappearing again until dinnertime. Life there was so completely different to Dublin and their adrenaline-fuelled careers. Though Adam was happy, she wasn't sure how she felt about her role out here at all.

They had been there a week and she was beginning to feel more comfortable going through someone else's belongings and private effects.

'I can't even begin to visualise what to do until we have sorted through all Jack's stuff. It seems wrong somehow. It's like reading someone's diary.'

'Don't be so sentimental. Just bin it all. It's no use to anyone now,' Adam said, and his attitude shocked her. Now, thrown together away from friends and family, she was starting to see something else in her husband – just how selfish he really was. Oblivious to her reaction to his suggestion, his next statement was, 'Can you imagine bringing our kids up here? Wouldn't it be idyllic and in time they could run the business with me, or for me.' He laughed.

'You have it all planned out,' she said. 'How many children do you have in mind?'

'At least five.'

'Is that all?' she said.

Adam laughed and left to ride out to the water troughs where the farm hands met every morning.

Could I settle here? she wondered as she watched him ride away. She still wasn't sure. It was beautiful and the setting was wonderful. The homestead was large and modern. It certainly lacked a feminine touch, but that could be remedied easily enough, and the other dwellings on the holding were close by, but not so close as to be intrusive. But it was still remote and on the other side of the world to her home. As for her future with Adam – that was open for debate. She was realising that she no longer had the respect and trust in him that she once had. Whether that would be a strong enough basis to start the dynasty he envisaged was anybody's guess.

She went back into the homestead and poured another cup of coffee. She'd come all this way with him and she owed it to him to at least give it a fair trial. She decided to google Tasmania again to get a better idea of what the island had to offer. A two-and-a-half-hour drive to Hobart would get her to a culture fix when she needed one and there were enough parks and hiking trails to keep her happy. She knew she'd integrate in time, but she found it difficult to imagine a life without her friends and family nearby. She weighed up her options – less than half the size of Ireland, and with a population of just over half a million, she couldn't see much use for her design talents where they'd be living – and she had no contacts to get her started. How long would it take for her to become the housewife and mother of five that Adam wanted her to be? *Is that what I really want?*

Madge had invited some of the wives to meet her that afternoon. Leah got on well with them and found it easy to talk to them all, but they all had their own lives and families. Most worked in the nearby town or did seasonal fruit picking at harvest time. She realised just how much she would have to compromise her own hopes and dreams to be a full-time farm wife. She wasn't ready to contemplate such dramatic changes yet.

Later she told Adam about her day, but he seemed preoccupied before casually remarking, 'I'm going to head to Hobart in the morning.'

'Great,' Leah answered, welcoming the thoughts of a break. She had been making a list of things she needed.

'I'll be off first thing. I've set up some meetings and a few interviews, so it'll be late when I get back.'

Clearly he wasn't intending for her to go with him – it didn't seem to have occurred to him that she might want to go. 'You're being paranoid,' she told herself, 'you have to be able to let the guy go about his business without suspecting his motives and his every move.'

The following morning, after Adam had left, she Skyped Ollie and her mum and told them that everything was great. Adam phoned her late that afternoon and said, 'I've found my man and I'm bringing him back with me tonight. I just thought I should warn you.'

'Well done. You're a fast worker,' she said, thinking if he had found someone suitable this quickly, then that could mean they would be going home sooner. 'Will you have eaten or should I prepare something for you both?'

'No, there's no need. We're going to call in to the distillery and we'll have something en route. I'll get someone to drive us back from there, so don't worry. You don't have to wait up for us if you're tired.'

She'd gone to bed at eleven when there was still no sign of them, and she never heard him come in. She woke early and Adam was still curled up in a deep sleep. He'd started to stir after she had showered and dressed.

'Come on. I'm making breakfast now, before everyone arrives.'

She went in to the kitchen. She liked this time before the housekeeper came in to start prepping food for the workforce. But the kitchen wasn't empty, and she did a double take when she saw who was sitting at the large wooden table, drinking coffee.

'What are you doing here?' she asked.

'Hello to you too, Leah,' Judd said, his eyes dropping to her breasts. 'You're looking at the new manager of Orchard Estate and Cidery. Small world, isn't it?'

Too small, she thought. *Far too small.*

Leah went back to the bedroom, where Adam was getting dressed. 'What the hell is going on?' she asked. 'What's he doing here?'

'I've taken him on as my number two.'

'Don't you think you should, or could, have told me, discussed it with me even? You know how I feel about him.'

'With all due respect, Leah, you know nothing about business and I didn't realise that I would have to run my decisions by you. You never liked the guy, I get that, but he is a wizard with finances, and that's what I need.'

'Was this all arranged when you went drinking in Dublin last month, when he was home from Melbourne?'

'Well, yes, we did discuss it then. I wanted to give Judd time to think it over.' He stopped. 'How did you know about that?'

'Not from you, obviously. You kept it very quiet, but Dublin is a small place and people talk. Of course I knew. I just wanted to see if you'd tell me yourself and you didn't. Do you honestly think this is the way to re-gain my trust?'

'Testing me again, were you?' She didn't reply to that. He continued, 'Anyway, he decided to join us and he flew down yesterday to meet me. It's all agreed in principle and I brought him back to show him around. He'll have to live with us for a bit until his bungalow is renovated.'

She was beyond anger. She had agreed to this trip because she thought he wanted a fresh start for them, which she had presumed meant he'd be away from temptations. Now it seemed as though his partner in crime would be co-habiting with them. This was a nightmare.

'What time did you get home last night?'

'We ... it was late. We had a few drinks to celebrate.'

'Is this going to be a feature of our lives from here on? If so, you can count me out of it – permanently. You brought me out here under false pretences. You knew what you were planning.'

'I didn't think you'd come if I told you.'

'Well, you got one thing right, didn't you? I don't trust him and I don't trust you when you're with him either. Does our marriage mean nothing to you at all?'

'You're the one destroying it. You have to be able to let me go out without being suspicious about what I'm doing. I like going out, I like drinking, and I like going out and drinking with my mates. I can't live with my every move being examined under a microscope. That's not what I signed up for.'

'And I didn't sign up for you to start sleeping with another woman. Don't go twisting things and making me out to be the problem.'

'From where I'm standing you *are* the problem, you and your suspicions and jealousies. I'm going out now, with Judd, and I hope you'll see sense by the time we get back. He's the man for the job.'

She sat down on the bed when he'd left, refusing to allow herself the luxury of crying. She had too much thinking to do.

* * *

Ollie picked her up from Dublin airport three days later and, after a wordless comforting bear hug, said, 'Welcome home, Sis. I'm sorry it didn't work out, but it's great to have you back.'

'Did you tell the folks?'

'I said nothing, just like you asked.'

'Thanks, I think I should be the one to do it.'

'And I think we should go there directly and get it out of the way.'

She told him what had happened, and what had finally made her walk away. 'When Adam and that odious man came back that first evening and there were just three of us in the house, he had the nerve to tell me that Adam's marriage was important to him and that I should get over the whole Denise affair and forgive him. "Denise? Who the hell is Denise?" I asked, looking from one to the other. Neither spoke and I knew from the guilty look on Judd's face that he had landed Adam in it. I told him that was it. I didn't need any more proof. Our marriage was over – I thanked Judd the Stud for saving me from future heartache, and left the two of them drinking whiskey.'

'That must have been hell for you.'

'It wasn't easy. Adam tried to tell me it meant nothing and the funny thing is, it didn't hurt – not like finding out about Helka. That had been the ultimate betrayal. After that, I think I just kept expecting it to happen and when I discovered it already had, the impact wasn't as bad.'

Sandra and Mal were just finishing a lazy Sunday breakfast when Ollie let himself in announcing, 'Look who I brought to see you, my favourite sister!'

'My God, this is the last thing I expected,' Sandra said, jumping up to embrace her daughter. Mal's face said it all and he cleared his throat, as he always did when he was emotional. As soon as Leah saw her mum, she burst into tears and Sandra hugged her until Leah was able to calm down.

'What's wrong? Is it Adam? Is he alright?' Mal asked Ollie. He nodded silently then said, 'Leah will explain.'

'I've left Adam. It's over.'

'Oh, love, that's terrible. I knew there was something up,' her mother said.

'It's no wonder he high-tailed it off to Australia,' Mal said, when Leah had finished telling them what had happened. 'You should have told us, love. Maybe I could have had a word with him.'

'It wouldn't have made any difference, Dad. Believe me, I tried that,' said Ollie.

'Why didn't you tell us sooner?' Sandra asked.

'Because it all blew up the week of my anniversary. I hoped it would go away, and I suppose a little bit of me was ashamed of Adam and how shallow he was. And I felt like a failure. I had decided to tell you and then we got your call to come over and you dropped the Kieron bombshell. The timing was all wrong. You had enough going on and I didn't want to add to it.'

'I'm sorry I didn't know, that I wasn't there for you.'

'Mum, you're always there for me, you know that. Anyway, it wouldn't have changed anything.'

'But walking away – that's a very big decision to make,' Sandra said. 'Have you really thought it through?'

'I've done nothing else for weeks now and believe me, all those hours on the flights back with nothing to do but think only made me surer of my decision. I'm not happy and I'm not prepared to sit around wondering who his next conquest will be. I want a real marriage, like you and Dad have, one where you're there for each other through thick and thin, and where real things matter. If I don't have that now after three years what are the hopes of the marriage lasting anyway? And over there away from all this made me realise that I don't want a man like Adam as the father of my children either.'

'You know we'll support you,' Mal said, 'whatever you do. Whatever you decide, you'll need a good lawyer, one who specialises in family law cases.'

'You know, Dad, it was almost as if he was expecting me to say I was leaving. Obviously we didn't discuss anything in depth, but he said I can keep Orchard Lodge. He also said he wants to ship his bloody Bentley out there.'

'He would, and he may make all the promises he wants and say what he likes, but until they're recorded legally, they mean nothing,' said Mal.

'And we all know how much store he puts on his promises,' Ollie said.

'I don't even know if I want to stay in Orchard Lodge. We bought it with such dreams and hopes. I haven't even finished unpacking everything and deciding where things should go.'

'You can make those decisions later. I'm just glad you're back here and not stranded over there. If you'd had children together, it would have made everything so much more complicated,' her father said. 'I'm glad you had Oliver to confide in.'

'So am I. My kid brother, who'd have thought?' She laughed. 'And thank you for not saying I told you so! I know he wouldn't have been your choice for me.'

Her parents exchanged a glance and Mal replied, 'You never said a truer word, love, but we're sorry it didn't work out for you.'

'I have plans to keep her busy for a while when she gets over the jet lag, and to stop her moping around,' Ollie said.

'That sounds interesting. What sort of plans?' Sandra asked.

'You'll find out soon enough. But you look exhausted, Leah. I'm going to drop you home.'

'You can stay here if you like, breakfast in bed in the morning,' Sandra said.

'That sounds great, Mum, but I'll take up Ollie's offer. I need to go home to my house. I may as well as get used to being on my own.'

'I shouldn't say it but I have to – I'm delighted you're home.'

'So am I, Mum' Leah said, and they hugged each other.

In the car Ollie told her that he and Kieron had met twice while she was away. He was still waiting for a reply from the letter he'd sent to the States.

'Let's talk about that another time. I'm wrecked.'

* * *

Kieron rang Leah a few days after she returned. She was only getting around to putting away the things she'd brought home from her trip down under. The reality of her situation was sinking in. She was sad that things hadn't worked out. For a brief period after Singapore she had believed they might. She had been so blinded by her love for Adam that she had been prepared to ignore any warning signs that had been there. Now she was beginning to see how many of those she had missed or had chosen to ignore. She needed time to come to terms with her new status as a separated woman. She had taken extended leave from work, but things were so different when that had been arranged and she intended going to talk to them about coming back sooner than agreed.

'I just wanted to say I'm sorry things haven't worked out as you had hoped,' Kieron told her.

'So am I. I never thought I'd be in this position, but now that I'm footloose I can concentrate on our mission with no deadlines to distract me.'

'There's nothing to report yet — I'm still waiting for any news of or from Louise. I don't even know if the letter has been forwarded to her from the address we had. She could have moved several times since then.'

'That's highly probable. We'll just have to be patient. Meantime I'm going to enjoy some time out for myself. Why don't you bring Pam and the kids over at the weekend? I'm dying to see them again.'

'They'd love that. I'll get her to give you a bell.'

Chapter Thirty-nine

Con didn't go back to school in the weeks after his mother's death. Mary and Dinah tried to talk to him, but he shut them out. Dr Vaughan tried talking to him, too, so did Fr O'Looney, but he refused to be drawn. All he seemed to need was more drink.

Con drank to stop himself from thinking, but the drink just made him argue with everyone, including himself. He noticed Dinah was staying over frequently. If Mary was afraid of him in this state she needn't worry – he'd never go near her again.

The priest was visiting again, trying to persuade Con that drinking wasn't going to help.

The phone rang. 'It's Dominic,' Dinah called.

'That man is evil, hang up on him. He should not be in charge of a school when he has a mind like a cess pit.'

'Now, Con, you can't go around bad-mouthing people like that, no matter how you feel. You're grieving and that takes people in different ways. It's understandable,' Fr O'Looney said. They were sitting beside the range. Mary decided to go upstairs so they could talk freely.

'Will you have a whiskey?' Con said, stretching for the half-empty bottle.

'No, thanks. What about yourself? Don't you think you've had enough?'

'What gives you the right to come into my home and meddle in my affairs? Telling me what to do.'

'Absolutely nothing, and I'm sorry if that's what you think. That's not what I'm doing. I'm concerned for you. I've talked to Dominic about the situation, and we both feel that maybe you ought to take a few months off and come back again after the summer holidays – make a fresh start again in September.'

But Con had no intention of doing any such thing. He took a slug of whiskey. 'Concerned for me, is he? Isn't it a bit late for that kind of thing? That man destroyed my marriage. He twisted my wife's mind and my mother went to her death thinking I had violated my daughter.'

'That wasn't meant to happen.'

'But it did. I cannot forgive Mary for that, ever. Our marriage is over.'

'They are strong words, Con. You made your marriage vows for better or for worse.'

'And I kept them too, but this is too much. My own wife can't look at me. And can you imagine how my mother must have felt? What she was thinking? The shame, the pain, the betrayal? Can you?' he roared. 'Between the two of them, they sentenced her to hell on earth for the last few weeks of her life. Nothing, do you hear me, nothing will ever wipe the look of horror on her face out of my mind the night she had the stroke.'

'But you still have your other child to consider, and Mary will come around, Con. Give her time. You can work on your marriage and sort things out together.'

'Did you not hear a single word I said, Father? My marriage is over.'

'She knows you're not responsible for what happened to Sandra. So do I. Sandra told me it wasn't you. She didn't say who it was, but she was adamant that it wasn't you.'

Con jumped up and made to grab the priest by his shirt, then he stopped. 'You mean to tell me you asked a child of twelve if her father had molested her? What kind of evil view of the world have you imprinted on her mind? So you thought it too, did you? Does the whole neighbourhood think it?'

'Of course not, Con. They don't know. You're upset. That's understandable. Take a few weeks – go away from here for a bit and put things into perspective again.'

But Con had made a decision. He splashed another drink into his glass, not even offering one to the priest this time. He hated his wife, his life, his work, this place. The only thing that kept him going was the thought of seeing his daughters again. Louise wouldn't be home now until the summer holidays – Mary and his mother had engineered that – *for her protection*, but he'd straighten himself out, go to Dublin and ask Sandra herself. She'd tell them.

He bid a curt goodnight to the priest and went upstairs, leaving him sitting alone at the kitchen table.

* * *

The following Saturday, Con got up and shaved off a week's growth of beard. He looked gaunt and haggard. He dressed in a suit for the first time since his mother's month's mind nearly five weeks previously. He was shocked to see how his shirt collar was loose about his neck. Mary was in the kitchen frying rashers and asked if he'd like some. He didn't answer, but helped himself to some cereal. When he'd finished, without a word he went out to his car and left. He noticed the hawthorn tree in full bloom, almost a week short of Mayday. His mother loved that tree, with all its Celtic superstitions. Planted near the house, it was supposed to offer protection to those who lived there. She'd never allow a branch of it inside before the first of the month though – that was considered unlucky. The girls used to bring in little branches of it for the May altars in their classrooms.

Next week he'd put some on his mother's grave, but before that there were things to be done. He had to clear his name. Only then would he go back to teaching, maybe even get a transfer away from this god-awful place and start afresh.

He drove to Dublin, to the convent where Sandra had been sent. He no longer cared what the neighbours would think of them when he arrived back with his daughter and her baby – she must have had the baby by now.

He sat in the car outside the austere building for a few minutes. He was never quite at ease with nuns, he tried too hard to be deferential and ended up coming across as submissive instead.

He rummaged in the glove compartment and took out a baby Powers, unscrewed the cap and took a few mouthfuls. It scalded his throat but he told himself it was fortification for the battle ahead. He knew he should not be there, but he had been left with no choice.

He was shown into the parlour and told to wait. He did, for almost fifteen minutes. There was a smell of wax polish and boiled cabbage. The silence was creepy and was only broken occasionally by the sound of a door opening and closing somewhere in the distance. As each minute ticked by on the tambour clock on the mantelpiece, he wished he had secreted the bottle into his inside pocket. The gimlet eyes of the narrow-faced Archbishop John Charles McQuaid bored into him and he could still feel them even when he turned away.

Con's hands were sweating and his heart was racing when the door opened and three nuns, headed by the Reverend Mother, walked in. She introduced the other two, who bowed in his direction and waited until she had sat down before doing the same.

'Why have you come here, Mr Mac Giolla Tighearnaigh?' the Reverend Mother asked, joining her hands together.

'I've come to see my daughter, Sandra. How is she?'

'She's no longer with us.'

Con gasped. 'She's dead?'

'Of course she's not dead. Merciful God, we would have told you if she were. She's left us, moved on with her life.'

'But she can't have. I've come to take them home—'

'That's not the way it works here. You gave her into our charge and we took care of everything, as we said we would. The infant has been adopted into a good home and your wayward daughter is with a good family too.'

'I demand to know where she is. What about her schooling?'

'Now, Mr Mac Giolla Tighearnaigh,' she said, dropping her voice, 'no one comes in here and makes demands.' She stood up, indicating the interview was over. Without a word, the other two nuns followed.

She paused at the door. 'We can't tell you anything else. Actually, I'll rephrase that – we won't tell you anything. That's the way this process works, and that way no one knows anyone else's dark secrets.' She smiled at him. 'It's for the best, you must believe me. You have to accept God's will.'

As one of the sisters pulled back the bolt and held the heavy hall door open for him to leave, the Reverend Mother said, 'Alcohol won't solve your problems, Mr Mac Giolla Tighearnaigh. We'll pray for you and your family.'

'Don't bother,' he snapped, as he went down the steps, a red mist descending over him. He got into the car and downed the rest of the whiskey.

He went to the nearest pub and drank until the barman refused to serve him. He knew no one in Dublin, but had once heard someone say there were lots of bed and breakfast places in Dún Laoghaire. He'd go there and find one. He hadn't got too far before he was pulled in by a squad car and was saved the cost of his board by being put in the cells overnight. He wasn't charged with any offence – a sympathetic garda listened to his story and took pity on his plight. He let him off with a warning.

'You may be in mourning, but that doesn't give you the right to put anyone else into the same predicament. Remember that. Now go and put the past behind you.'

'I will,' he promised, 'and thank you.'

'Go easy now. It's a filthy morning out – feels like January with that easterly wind.'

When he was released, he carried on to Dún Laoghaire, the windscreen wipers fighting to do their job in the bucketing rain. He bought a ticket for the ferry to England, went and had breakfast in a hotel where he bought a postcard and an envelope. He wrote this to Sandra, care of the convent, telling her he had come looking for her and that her gran had died. He gave it to the receptionist to post before heading off to board the vessel.

'It's going to be a rough crossing,' the barman said to him as he became his first customer once they were sea-bound. He looked around him, lost in his own thoughts. These people knew where they were going to – he was only sure of where he was coming from. He had no way of clearing his name now. He couldn't go back. What future did he have with that slur hanging over him?

Two hours later he stumbled as he got down from a bar stool to go in search of the toilets and he heard a woman with young children tell them, 'That's what drink can do. I pity his poor family.'

'You don't know what you're talking about. It's not them that needs pity,' he snarled back at her as he turned. She shrank back, putting her arms protectively around her charges.

He was shocked at her reaction. What had happened to him? He would never have spoken to a stranger like that before. He swayed out on to the deserted deck, the wind almost forcing him back inside as he pulled the heavy door open. What future did he have? He hadn't protected his daughter. His older one was being kept away

from him. His wife hated him and thought he was capable of, of ...
These demons raced around in his head. He had to stop them. He had
to stop them.

* * *

Dinah opened the door to Dr Vaughan and Sergeant Byrne two days
after Con had left. She brought them in to the kitchen – this was no
time for formality – she knew what such a visit meant.

'Mary, there's no easy way of putting this, but we have reason to
believe that Con is dead,' Bill Vaughan told her gently.

'No. No. He can't be. Did he have an accident?'

'We're not too sure. When did you see him last?'

'On Saturday. He left just after breakfast and drove off. I've no
idea where he was going. We've been having difficulties recently.'

Dinah stepped in and said, 'He took his mother's death very
badly – he hasn't been himself since.'

Sergeant Byrne explained. 'Con's car was found on the ferry
to Holyhead. When the driver failed to return to the vehicle and
couldn't be found anywhere, it became a police matter.'

'Holyhead. Why in God's name was he going there?' Mary said
to Dinah before turning to the policeman. 'And if you haven't found
him, why do you suppose he's dead? Maybe he missed it or left with
someone else, or—'

'It seems the most likely answer, Mary, but of course until they
find his body they can't confirm anything,' the doctor said.

'What am I going to tell Louise? How am I going to tell her?'

'I think you should prepare her for the worst, Mary. It mightn't
do you any harm to have her around at such a time either.'

When they left, she and Dinah made the journey to Louise's
school together to break the news and bring her back home.

* * *

Six days later, the knock she'd been expecting, yet dreading, came. Louise came running down the stairs. She refused to believe that anything else bad could happen to them.

Mary tried to prepare her. 'I know it's a lot to take in. You're scarcely fifteen and you've had so much to cope with this past what with Sandra going away and losing your gran. In some ways, you've had to grow up too quickly and I'm sorry about that, but life can be cruel sometimes.'

Dinah busied herself with the kettle. Mary took Louise's hand as she stared at Sergeant Byrne while he filled in the details.

'Some early morning walkers on a beach in Wales came across a body that had washed ashore. It's been identified as Con's. I'm so sorry. A passenger has come forward too and said he thought he had seen someone in the water for a second or two, but as the sea was heaving so much that night the more he looked, the more unsure he was, convincing himself that it had been a figment of his imagination. It was only when he read about the body being found that he came forward. And it tallies with the pathology report on how long it was in the sea.'

She had run out of emotion. She couldn't cry any more. Louise screamed and screamed. 'No, no, no, he can't be dead. I don't believe it. I want my dad. I want my dad. He can't be dead.' She cried like a small child before turning to Mary. They clung to each other, each taking what little comfort they could from each other's grief.

Later that evening, Fr O'Looney came by with Dominic.

'We've made all the necessary arrangements.'

'I want to go to the funeral, Mam. You need me and I want to say goodbye to Dad.'

'Of course, love. Now I need a few words in private. Do you mind?'

Louise went up to her room. 'What's the situation about taking your own life and a Christian burial?' she asked Fr O'Looney. 'I

know Con would have wished to be buried with his mother. I hope
you can do that for us.'

They left shortly afterwards.

* * *

Con's death came as a huge shock to the wider community, many of
whom had been brought into the world by his mother and taught by
his father or by him. It was a huge funeral. In the church, Dominic
paid tribute to Con's prowess as a teacher, and the boys from his classes
formed a guard of honour from the entrance through the graveyard,
out the end gate, and over the bridge to the seldom-used, and much
smaller, plot beyond the boundary. Dr Vaughan's short eulogy at
the graveside stopped wagging tongues and speculation about the
circumstances and about what could keep a daughter from attending
her father's burial. Mary heard him tell one busybody, 'Yes, she's taken
it very badly, poor child, and so soon after her grandmother. You can't
blame her for wanting to remember him as he was.'

Mary was very grateful to him for that. He just squeezed her arm
as he left the cemetery. 'Phone me if you need me, anytime. You
know where I am.'

They didn't invite people back to the house after the funeral,
everything was kept private this time. Mary couldn't face another
barrage of veiled enquiries and innuendoes. She just didn't have the
strength.

They got through the day somehow, and Mary felt emotionally
and physically wiped out by the end of it and overwhelmed with
remorse that she and Con had never reconciled. She craved his
forgiveness and she'd never have that now. She had spent the past
few months in turmoil and wondered if it would ever end. She had
lost her daughter, her husband, and her mother-in-law, but she felt
she had lost her integrity too. How could she ever forgive herself
for letting them all down so badly? Would Sandra ever forgive her

for sending her away? And for what? For pride and shame and convention? They hadn't stopped to think what it would do to her or how she would survive away from everyone she loved. If only she could turn back the clock, she'd be proud to walk into town, and the church too, with her pregnant daughter and to hell with what the neighbours said. *Will I ever be able to tell her that?* she wondered. *Will I ever see her again?*

'Mam, you're not listening to me,' Louise said.

'I'm sorry, love, what were you saying?'

'I said I'm not going back to school. Every time I go away, something bad happens. Look at what happened to Sandra, then she was sent away, then it was Nan and then Dad, losing his mind and drowning himself. Will it be you next time or Dinah?'

'Oh, Louise, of course it won't.'

'Well, I'm not prepared to take that chance. I hate this place. It's full of bad memories. I just want us to get Sandra and go away. We could go and live in Dublin. We could even change our names so no one would ever know who we were.'

'I understand, love, and I will think about it, but you'll have to finish school no matter where we are. I'll let you stay here for one more week, I'll be glad of your company, but not a day longer.'

Her daughter agreed reluctantly.

Later that evening, Dominic called, and Mary told him about what Louise had said. 'It mightn't be such a bad idea to get away from here.'

'I think I have to. I'm smothering. I can't live with the guilt and I keep waking up thinking that poor old woman is at the end of the bed, watching me. Chastising me. She's everywhere in the fibre of this house, everything I touch, every cupboard I open. So is Con. I drove him over the edge and I couldn't have been more wrong. And I'll prove it when I see Sandra. She'll tell me the truth now. There's nothing surer than she'll want to clear her dad's name.'

'She might never do that if she's covering up for someone,' he said, offering her a drink from her own sideboard. 'What's there to stop her accusing anyone she wants – Fr O'Looney, me, Dr Vaughan or any of the young lads at school?'

'She'd never do that.'

'She might if she thinks she and her pregnancy contributed to her father's death, directly or indirectly.'

'But they didn't – she didn't. This has all got so complicated. It's not her fault, don't you see? I have to make her understand that.'

'What about going to that sister of yours in New York? It would be a great opportunity for Louise.'

'It has crossed my mind.'

'It might be best for everyone.'

'You could be right.'

Chapter Forty

Kieron and Pam were excited. Jennifer was coming home that day following her bone marrow transplant.

'It's been a hell of a time and I can't believe the worst is over,' said Pam.

'We have to keep everything crossed that there won't be any rejection.'

Jennifer had been in and out of hospital several times in the months since her name was put on the register for a transplant, and her parents had almost despaired of anyone being a match when no one in their biological families proved to be suitable. After each infection, it had seemed to take her longer to recover to full strength. Eventually, the awaited summons had come from the hospital – a donor had been found from someone on the national registry.

What had followed was five long weeks, during which they had been instructed about the procedure, its possible pitfalls, rejection or infections and how they could expect Jennifer's body to react and recover. They had been tutored in what signs and symptoms would need medical attention and possible intervention, and those they could deal with themselves. She would have to be minded carefully, monitored continually and would need to have blood taken regularly for screening. But everyone had assured them that the prognosis and success rate were both excellent. They had clung on to these assurances.

'These past twelve months have been a bit of a roller coaster. I never thought we'd get here,' Pam said as they drove to collect Jennifer and bring her home. Ryan was in the back.

'I hate going into this place,' Ryan complained.

'I don't think anybody likes hospitals, love, but we're all glad of them when we're sick,' Pam said. 'Just think how lucky you are that you only have to visit.'

'My new nan says Jennifer will probably end up being a doctor because she's spent so much time in there,' he said, and his parents smiled at each other.

'She could be right about that,' Kieron said. 'You've been really good about all this medical stuff and when Jennifer is over this we'll do something really nice together. That's a promise.'

'Can we go to EuroDisney?'

'We'll see,' he answered. It wasn't the first time this suggestion had been made and Kieron had already checked prices and flights for a few months' time. He wouldn't book anything at this stage, not until they were sure Jennifer would be able for it. Even if she wasn't, he was going to take his son there. Ryan deserved a reward for standing in the wings for so long.

They'd all taken turns sitting with her, reading, doing jigsaws and puzzles and playing word games. The crisis had enmeshed the two families in a way that none of them would have envisaged, and Kieron had been proved wrong again about them not wanting to know him. They tried not to talk too much in front of the children, but they were the ones who had the hang-ups, not the younger ones. They had accepted the changed family structure as totally normal.

Ryan had called Sandra his 'new nan' from the beginning. They loved Uncle Oliver, who had assumed that role with gusto, and he had taken Ryan to the cinema a few times when Jennifer was under the weather. They found their Auntie Leah's big house and garden a magical place to explore. Pam and Leah had an affinity that had blossomed through emails and Skype when Leah went to Tasmania. Since her return, they often met for chats.

Kieron pulled into a parking spot at the hospital.

'Don't forget those chocolates for the nurses,' Pam told Ryan as they got out of the car. He grabbed them and ran on ahead.

* * *

There had still been no response from New York and so Leah, Ollie and Kieron decided it was time to make a visit to Mayo and scout around Sandra's hometown and surroundings to see if they could find out any more information. They stayed in a B&B and got up early on Saturday so they could start asking questions in the village shops and at the presbytery.

The sun was glinting on the sea beyond and Croagh Patrick was radiant the morning they headed for the cemetery to look at all the headstones.

People were arriving for a funeral. Curiosity made Leah suggest they poke their heads inside to see if they'd get any clues. Two dark-suited men carried wreaths up to the altar rails where three celebrants were waiting to start mass. A diminutive woman with a floral headscarf bustled in late and loudly greeted some of the congregation as she shuffled into a seat near the back. Leah was sure she heard someone say 'will you whist there, Dinah' before the oldest priest began in a suitably pious tone.

'We are gathered here to welcome the body of Master Dominic O'Sullivan on its last journey and to commend his soul to God on high. He would be very pleased with this great turnout of past and present pupils from his old school who have come back to honour this inspiring teacher and pay tribute to the way he influenced and shaped their young lives.'

* * *

Three months after that weekend Leah summoned the family to Orchard Villa. Adam had pushed through their separation agreement with, according to Sandra, undignified haste but he had signed over the house to her. In return, she had waived any hold on his Tasmanian properties. In the interim, she had grown to love the house and watching the garden change from its stark bare trees and empty flowerbeds to drifts of cheerful spring bulbs and cherry blossom trees that snowed pale pink petals on her car and the driveway as they fell.

A friend of hers had moved in after her landlord had been forced to sell the rental property she had considered her home. It was only a temporary arrangement, but it had taken the empty feeling from the place and now Leah was getting used to living there as a single woman.

Everyone was arriving at noon, except for her parents. They thought they were going to Leah's for Sunday lunch and Oliver had agreed to collect them at 12.30. Kieron's car was parked down the road and out of sight.

Ollie ushered Sandra and Mal into the sitting room; the folding doors to the dining room were firmly shut.

'We have a surprise for you, Mum,' Leah said.

'A surprise, but what's the occasion?' she asked, looking quizzically at Mal, who shrugged his shoulders, denying he knew anything about it.

'Wait and see,' she grinned as the doors opened from the other side to reveal Kieron and Pam. Mal looked about for Jennifer and Ryan but they were nowhere to be seen. Instead, an elegant woman stepped out from behind them. They waited for an introduction, but none was forthcoming. Then the stranger moved forward. 'Don't you recognise me, Sandra?'

There was something familiar about her, she couldn't tell what, But the American accent threw her.

'I'd know you anywhere with that hair.'

'Mum, it's Louise – your sister,' Leah said.

'Louise, I don't believe it. My God, Louise. Is that really you? You're beautiful.'

'So are you.'

They all laughed as the two women rushed towards each other and hugged, never wanting to let go, neither able to talk with the emotion of what was happening.

'I don't believe it,' Sandra said again, scanning every feature of her sister's face. 'How did …'

'Neither do I,' said Louise. 'I was so sure I'd never see you again. I'd given up trying. We have so much catching up to do.'

'That's why we didn't bring the children,' Pam said.

'Were you all in on this?' Sandra asked.

'All of us, except Dad.'

'Oh my God – I'm sorry – this is my husband, Mal.'

He gave Louise a bear hug. 'I knew you'd turn up some day and I'm really thrilled to finally meet you. How did you find Sandra?'

Louise said, 'You have Dinah to thank and these three wonderful children of yours.' She smiled.

'Dinah, is she still alive?'

'Very much so,' Leah said. 'She told us what it was like after you left and how it affected everyone, but let's sit down to lunch and we'll talk then.'

'You spoke to Dinah?'

'Lunch, Mum!' Leah insisted.

* * *

No one would remember, what, if anything, they ate that day. There were thirty-odd years to unravel from several perspectives.

'When did you arrive? Where are you staying and for how long? You have to stay here with us.'

'Why did you never write?' Louise asked. 'I came home for

Christmas and you were gone – vanished completely from my life.'

'But I did write, lots of times. Why didn't you?'

'I did, every week, but I was never told where you were. Mam sent my cards and my letters with hers. I know she did. I only discovered where you'd been when we went to tell you about Dad. We wanted to get you and take you to the States with us. The Reverend Mother didn't even remember if you'd had a boy or a girl when we went to get you. Mam asked her. Sorry, Kieron. I didn't mean that to be insensitive.'

'I've heard worse.' He smiled at her.

'They never told me you came for me,' Sandra said.

'It was that visit that was the final straw for Mam. I don't know how you survived that prison. Did they put you to work in the laundry? I was afraid they'd send you to one of their orphanages when the baby was born.'

'Fortunately, they didn't.'

'Two days after Dad's funeral, Mam and I drove to the convent. The Reverend Mother looked at me and said, "Another one for us to take care of?" Mam told her we'd come to take you home with us. The nun smiled at another nun and said to Mam with measured words, "I told your husband when he came here a few weeks ago that your daughter and her infant are no longer with us. And we have not changed our minds, nor will we, about divulging their whereabouts. You knew the conditions when you entrusted her to us."

Mam said, "What did you just say?"

"You knew the rules."

"No, about my husband – did he phone you?"

"No, he arrived on our doorstep, unannounced. Three or four Saturdays ago. He had drink taken."

'Mam told her that he had since died, tragically, that you didn't know yet and that she needed to tell you herself. She was crying and all the nun said was, "That won't be possible. We're not at liberty to give you any information. Rules are rules and must be obeyed. But may the good Lord have mercy on his soul." She refused to get word of his death to you, saying, "Once a penitent leaves us, that's the end of our association with her unless she gets into trouble again, as many of them do."

'I remember taking Mam's hand when she asked if you'd had a boy or a girl. The Reverend Mother said, "I don't actually remember, do you, Sister Patricia?" The other nun did remember and said you'd had a boy. Mam asked more questions – what had your labour been like, were you still with your baby, but the Reverend Mother just said, "It's called labour for a reason." Then she told us that your baby had gone to a "good Catholic home" and she got up to leave. But Mam wasn't finished and asked about your education and where you were going to school – but the nun wouldn't tell us anything. She just said that you weren't our worry any more.'

'How did they ever become so powerful?' Kieron asked. 'They seem to have made their own rules and everyone kowtowed to them.'

'Maybe if they'd ever had children themselves they might have been more humane,' Pam said.

'But looking after your young is such a basic instinct. How could they expect any mother to just walk away and forget you ever existed just because you became pregnant?' Leah asked.

'They did though, and Mam was devastated,' Louise continued. 'While the news that Dad had gone to the convent the day he'd driven away and had gone looking for you didn't explain everything, it helped me to understand why.'

'What happened him?' Mal asked.

'He drowned: it was suicide. When you wouldn't tell them who the father was, someone had suggested you might have been raped by someone you know, someone in the family, and Mam told Dad this. He never forgave her. He thought she was accusing him. They hardly spoke to each other during their last few months together but he started to drink seriously.'

'I never realised I had caused such trouble,' said Kieron.

'Don't ever say that,' Mal said. 'It was not your fault and it was certainly not your mother's either.'

'Mam never blamed you,' Louise continued to Sandra. 'She blamed herself and she always maintained that probably in his drink-fogged logic he thought that if his daughter couldn't be found, there was no one else who could clear his name. She told me so often that he wouldn't listen to her when she tried to tell him she was wrong to have said anything and that she never really believed he was capable of doing anything to hurt you or anyone. But Mam just heaped more guilt on herself, saying she was the reason he'd felt the need to clear his name and when he couldn't find you, he took the ferry to England. What a lonely, hopeless, desperate journey that must have been for him.'

'Poor woman,' Mal said.

'She was. She had nightmares all through her life and struggled to push images of how he must have been feeling as he hurtled towards the water – the pain, the panic, the desolation. It was hard. Before we went to the convent, I thought you just never bothered to write. You never even told me I was an auntie, I never thought you could be so selfish. We didn't talk very much on the journey back to Mayo, we were both trying to come to terms with what the nuns had told us.

'Mam told Dinah what had happened, every detail, and then announced that she was taking me to the States to live with her sister. She said she never wanted to see Mayo again. I was shocked hearing this, and I remember vividly her saying, "The only people I'll be sorry to leave behind are Dinah and Dominic". I never really liked that man, did you, Sandra?' – she asked but didn't wait for a reply – 'but he was really good to Mam through everything, and he urged her to go. I loved Dinah though and I kept in touch with her over the years.

'How could I never have thought about that?' Sandra said. She was close to tears too. 'I honestly thought nobody cared. I never knew they did.'

'Of course we cared but Mam was never the same after Dad died. The fight seemed to go out of her. It was a very sad and bleak time.'

'But where is Dad buried? Mal and I visited the cemetery and saw Gran and Granddad's grave, but his name wasn't on it. Maybe no one got around to doing that for him; if so, we must do it.'

'Mam did it – she organised that before we went to the States, but he's not with Gran and Granddad. Because it was a suicide, he wasn't allowed to have a Christian burial – he's across the bridge in the other bit, the un-consecrated bit.'

'We saw his grave when we visited,' Kieron said. 'Dinah took us there and told us what happened.'

'The hypocrisy of that,' Mal said.

'You met Dinah? When did you go to Mayo?' Sandra asked incredulously.

Kieron replied, 'The three of us went – Leah, Ollie and me – when we were searching for clues. We put flowers on the graves too.'

'That was very thoughtful and kind of you,' Sandra said, and Louise agreed.

'We didn't say anything in case we couldn't get any answers for you. We didn't want to get your hopes up,' said Ollie.

'What happened to Mam?' Sandra asked her sister.

'She never got over losing Dad – and that was compounded by the fact that they hadn't reconciled when he died. It ate away at her. She ran away from here, but she couldn't run away from herself. She talked about you and him incessantly all her life. You never knew where you were with her – she swung between depression, despair and drink, and it was a combination of all three that got her in the end. She didn't look after herself and she died five years ago from liver failure.'

'I can't take it all in.'

'She wrote to you as well, sent you cards and presents and our forwarding addresses.'

'I never knew that.'

'There's a lot you don't know. I never wanted to go to the States because it meant you wouldn't be able to find us if you wanted to. Dinah was the only contact I had with home.'

'I still can't believe Dinah's still alive. She must be well into her nineties now.'

'She's a sprightly ninety-six-year-old who goes to mass every day.'

Leah said, 'She told us she doesn't go to pray. She doesn't believe in all that any more. She said, "That fella up there, if he exists at all, has a quare warped sense of humour and he'll get more than the sharp edge of my tongue if I ever get to meet him, messing with people's lives and sending misery to them." She goes to mass to meet people and keep up to speed with the gossip.'

Sandra laughed. 'That sounds like her all right. She always had strong opinions.'

'I always sent her Christmas and birthday cards and scribbled a little note,' Louise said. 'I suppose I hoped that if you ever came looking for us, she could tell you where we were.'

'So how did she come to make the connection with you, Leah, Oliver and Kieron?' Mal asked.

'That was by fluke,' said Kieron. 'When we went to Mayo we went to the cemetery. There was a funeral taking place and afterwards when we went looking for Con's grave this old lady whom we'd seen in the church – Dinah – came up to Leah and said she reminded her of someone she used to know. She asked if she had relatives buried in the churchyard there. Leah told her and she pointed us to her great-grandparents' grave. Then out of the blue she asked if we were Sandra or Louise's children? And bingo, it all fell into place.'

'That's incredible,' Sandra said. 'I never asked – have you children, a husband too?' she asked Louise.

'Yes, three – children that is, and just one husband, back in Brooklyn.'

'Did you have the five bridesmaids in purple satin?'

They laughed. 'I did not. Fancy you remembering that,' Louise said as the others looked on, wondering what that was all about.

'You'd be surprised at what I do remember. I just locked it all away when I thought you had all rejected me.'

'We never did that, Sandra. My family know all about you and you'll have to meet them now, and Mam's sister and her boys too. I brought some photos.'

'The Christmas card list is growing by the minute in this family,' Ollie laughed.

'Apart from my memories, do you know the only thing I have from my childhood is a Polaroid snap of the two of us. You probably don't even remember it but—'

'It was taken down on the beach at half-term. I have the other one here with me. Mam kept it with her all these years and I took it from her handbag when she died. I brought it with me. I wonder where Dymphna is now.'

'I can't believe this. I'd given up hope of ever seeing you. I was convinced you'd never want to see me anyway after the shame I'd brought on you all.'

'I was never ashamed of you, and I always told everyone, including my own children, about you. I'm so glad Kieron found you, and then me too.'

The questions continued, as did the revelations and discoveries.

'And Dinah – I'd love to see her,' Sandra said. 'Do you think she'd welcome a visit?'

'Whether she does or not, we're going there next weekend, just the two of us. We've a lot to talk about.'

'I know I keep saying it, but I just don't believe this is happening. How did you manage to keep it a secret from your dad and me?' Sandra asked her children.

'It wasn't easy,' Ollie said.

'Are there any more surprises?' Mal asked.

'There is one more, for Sandra and Kieron,' Oliver said. 'I know I hid it from you, but I didn't want to spoil the surprise either. A legal mate of mine managed to procure some of the letters that were sent and received for you both from the convent; there are some addressed to you too, Kieron, but we think you should have privacy to read those. We don't know what's there as we haven't looked at any of them, so you can sort through them together.'

'That's amazing – these really are the final pieces in the puzzle,' Kieron said.

'You've never said a truer word,' Sandra agreed, tears coursing freely now. Louise handed her a tissue and they both laughed and, linking arms, they took the large brown envelope into the sitting room and Kieron handed it to her to open as she sank into a chair.

'What a day. Are you sorry you ever found us?' she laughed as she spread them on the coffee table.

'I'm sorry I ever felt I was the one who was hard done by,' Kieron said. 'It seems you all paid a huge price because of me, but finding the truth is the best thing I ever did. You're great, all of you, and I feel very lucky to be part of your family, and of knowing where I come from and where I belong.'

'We're the lucky ones, Kieron, to have found you.'

'It almost didn't happen, you know, finding out what happened to your parents and then tracking Louise down. Any other day, even an hour later and the opportunity would have been gone forever,' he said.

'How do you mean?' Sandra asked.

'The funeral that was taking place the day the three of us went to the cemetery in Mayo was that of a former headmaster of the local boys' secondary school, where I believe your father had taught.'

Sandra stiffened. 'Do you remember his name?'

'It was something or other O'Sullivan. I don't really recall,' he answered.

'Was it Dominic O'Sullivan?' She felt the blood drain from her face and was glad she was sitting in an armchair or she might have keeled over. She fiddled with the envelope.

'Do you remember him?'

'Yes, of course we do. He was Mam's uncle,' said Louise. 'He's the one I was talking about earlier. He persuaded Mam to go to the States.'

'Enough talking,' said Sandra, 'let's open these envelopes and see what's inside them.'

She welled up again when she saw her mother's handwriting and Louise's flowery cards. The sisters both cried when they read the postcard that their father had sent on his last day on earth. He had loved her and the last words he had ever written to her said that – then he'd added 'forgive me'. Was he asking forgiveness for sending her away or for what he was about to do? She let out a sob before glancing at Kieron. She saw tears glistening in his eyes as he went through the birthday cards she had sent over the years on the off-chance that they would make their way to him. She went and sat beside him and he put his arm around her. Louise joined them on the squashy couch.

'These faded notes say so much, don't they?' he said, his voice thick. He took her hand. The final barriers had crumbled.

She smiled at him. All but one, and that would go to the grave with her. Dominic O'Sullivan no longer had the power to hurt her or anyone she cared about. Could the long shadow he had cast over her life and the lives of all her family really finally be gone?

She looked at her sister and at her son's hand holding hers and she placed her other one over it. Kieron Peter need never know who his father was, or that he'd unknowingly been present in the parish church at his funeral.

Acknowledgments

Once again I have to say I'm delighted to be part of the dynamic team Hachette Ireland. And it is just that, from copy editors to cover designers, administrators and publicists. They're like a house of cards, all supporting each other and relying on that support in return.

Out of Focus was a difficult book to write, spanning three generations and trying to weave their stories together, so I have particular reason to be grateful to Alison Walsh and Claire Rourke for checking and managing those timelines and for Claire's astute comments.

As always a big hug and thanks to the best editorial director anyone could have, Ciara Doorley.

Thank you all.